Luck of the Irish

Liz Gavin

Happy Reading!! :)

Liz Gavin

Luck of the Irish

Luck of the Irish

Copyright 2014 by Liz Gavin

Published by Elessar Books

ACKNOWLEDGMENTS

Thank you, my dearest alpha readers: Allison, Alyssa, Erin, Genna, Kimber, Leigh-Ann, Loralea, Miake, Maureen, Niki, Sam, and Tonya. This book wouldn't have been half as good without your unrelenting commitment and impressive hard work. You've taken time out of your busy lives to read, comment and send me feedback, which is priceless nowadays. Also, you've nudged me on when I got stuck.

Not to mention the fact that through your eyes, I was able to see interesting and different aspects of Keira, Declan, and the other characters, which enriched the story and took it to whole new levels.

I'm very proud of what we have accomplished as a team.

Luck of the Irish

CHAPTER 1

Rick merged into the heavy traffic heading towards Boston, his wife sobbed softly, and he glanced her way. He recognized the onset of a potential meltdown and decided to do something, right then, in order to prevent further problems.

"Claire, please, stop crying, sweetheart. Keira'll be fine."

"How can you be so sure? Call it a mother's intuition or whatever you want to call it. I feel something bad is going to happen to her."

"Nonsense. You used to say the same thing when she started going to school. Then, again, when she'd go to her friends' houses for sleepovers. I don't want to start on your reaction when she went to college. Remember?"

She sniffed and looked away before answering, "I know it sounds crazy, honey. I can't explain it to you. I just feel it."

"Nothing will happen to Keira. She's a lot tougher than you give her credit for. In fact, I think she's so insecure because *you* overprotect her. This trip will be a great opportunity for Keira to find out how strong she is. She'll be on her own for the first time."

"That's exactly why I'm so worried. She won't have anybody there to take care of her. Here, she's always had Megan or me to look after her."

"Come on, Claire. She's twenty-two years old and hardly in need of a nanny." He laughed when his wife scowled at him. "Don't give me the dirty look. It's true. And it's not only you. Megan's a great older sister. She's always encouraged Keira, but I feel her strong personality sometimes overshadows her younger sister."

When it became obvious that his wife wouldn't reply to him any time soon, Rick rubbed his palm on her left thigh gently, trying to calm her down. "I know you mean well, baby. It's just that Keira needs to find out, by herself, that she's a strong young woman."

4

Claire nodded before intertwining her fingers through her husband's. Feeling confident he had restored peace to his marriage, Rick begged her, "Promise me you won't call Keira every ten minutes."

"Oh, you're unbelievable!"

Claire let go of his hand with a shove and turned to the window, leaving her husband to wonder what he had said to offend her.

I grew up with four sisters. I've got a wife and two daughters. But I've never been able to understand what women want.

* * * *

A few hours later, Keira got off the Aer Lingus plane at Dublin Airport, still feeling like she was walking on air. Her heart beat fast and she had a lump in her throat. She felt stupid for having an anxiety attack instead of being happy she was finally in Ireland!

Breathe, Keira, she told herself as she took deep breaths.

She looked around the hall, taking in the beautiful building. Made of glass and tubular structures meant it was amazingly modern. Not exactly what she had expected to see in "the old country," as her grandfather used to call Ireland.

It was also surprisingly bright, at least, as bright as any Irish day could be. The sky was overcast, but the large glass windows captured the little light able to pass through the massive clouds.

The sight of those heavy clouds didn't calm her down much, but she was going through a good kind of anxiety attack. Understandable, too. She had been so excited about the trip that, for the past couple of weeks, she hadn't been able to sleep or eat. This trip was a dream come true.

Since she had been a toddler, her grandfather—almost eighty at the time—used to sit her on his lap and tell the most fantastic stories about the Emerald Isle. Padraic had never set foot in Ireland, but his parents had immigrated to Salem with little more than a bag full of hopes, dreams, and loving memories. As she grew older, Keira would sit by his wheelchair and listen to him talk about the Old Country for hours. He used that expression with pride, even though he had been born on American soil. She never got tired or bored. Her grandfather had passed away over ten years ago. Yet, he seemed more alive than ever in her mind and heart. The trip was also a tribute of sorts to Padraic.

As a little girl, when she played with her friends, they all talked about fairy tales or Harry Potter, pretending to be one of those characters. Keira would rather be a Celtic princess or a Druid priestess. She grew up feeling a strong connection to Ireland and the Irish people. She would read every book she could find about the island. And, although aged only twenty-two, her favorite authors were Wilde, Shaw, Yeats, Beckett and Joyce.

Keira loved music, too. She listened to Maroon 5 and Linkin Park, like any normal person, but she was really into Irish music, both traditional and modern. She listened to many Irish singers and bands, but her first and biggest love was U2. Since she had turned sixteen, Keira had been to all the concerts U2 had played in the Boston area—and then some. However, it didn't seem enough. Her most cherished dream was to watch the band perform in Dublin. Every U2 fan knew the concerts in their hometown were magical. That was why, during college, Keira worked and saved all the money she could in order to pay her trip to Ireland.

She wanted to get to know her family's country, experience the places that had inspired all those many awesome stories her grandfather had told her, as well as watch U2 perform for their most loyal and most demanding crowd—the Dubliners.

That explained part of her anxiety. Lately, she had been feeling a strange sense of doom. She had just finished college and had reached that point in life when a person has to face the future. She had to decide what she wanted

6

to do with her life. Her parents owned a trendy and very successful restaurant in South Boston. They wanted her to take part in the family business, but she wasn't so sure about it. She had done her share of waiting tables to save money for the trip, but now they expected her to take a more active role in running the restaurant. Keira didn't know if she wanted that for her life.

In fact, she didn't know what she wanted to do at all. At seventeen, she used to tell people she was going to be a famous singer. She took some guitar lessons but quit them after a month or two. Then, when she turned nineteen, she decided to be a fashion designer. After all, her friends told her she had an excellent sense of fashion. She had never gotten to study fashion, though. Later on, Keira considered becoming an actress. She looked up some acting classes in her neighborhood but never worked up the courage to enroll in any. One day, feeling particularly lost and disappointed in herself, for being so indecisive, she asked her older sister for advice.

"Be true to yourself, sis, and you'll be fine. That's what I've always done. But you must *try* something. If you don't try it you'll never know how you feel about it, right?"

Megan, her only sibling, was a lawyer. Ten years Keira's senior, she had established herself as an independent woman and a successful professional. When Megan was younger, their parents had asked her to join them in the restaurant business. She had never liked it and had declined the offer. Keira was their last hope for keeping the business in the family. Although they had never pressed her with that kind of argument, Keira had an acute sense of loyalty to her close-knit family. If, on the one hand, she didn't want to let them down, on the other hand, she didn't want to choose a career she didn't like out of duty to her loved ones.

Her sister Megan was right: she needed to be more assertive. But knowing you must do something doesn't make it any easier. At that moment, the only decision she cared about was choosing between a taxi and a shuttle bus to

7

take her to downtown Dublin. As Keira wanted to arrive in style at the Clarence Hotel, she decided to take a taxi.

"Good morning, sir," she greeted the taxi driver as she stooped down to talk to him through the window. "Can you take me to the Clarence Hotel?"

"Oh, a U2 fan, are you?" He laughed and opened the door to get out of the car. "Here, let me help you with that bag."

He sounded friendly and didn't wait for her reply before he grabbed the bag from her hands and stored it in the trunk of the car.

"There you go. Climb in and I'll take you there. I'm Seamus, by the way," he told her, still smiling and holding the door open.

As soon as Keira settled in the back, the driver pulled away. In no time, they were moving sluggishly through the traffic.

"Nice to meet you. I'm Keira. How can you tell I'm a U2 fan?"

"Young people like yourself don't stay at that kind of hotel—unless they're fans."

She laughed at his reasoning. "I guess you're right. I found it too fancy when I looked it up online. But, I wanted to know their hotel. I think I'll feel a little uncomfortable there."

"Don't you worry your pretty head about that. I'm sure you'll feel just fine. Everyone is very nice there."

The driver's talkativeness surprised her. She'd heard about that particular Irish trait, but felt surprised, nonetheless. She also delighted in their beautiful accent, and could listen to them talking for hours.

Even though she didn't answer him, Seamus kept talking and driving, "You got lucky, too. The weather is nice today."

"Really? It's so cloudy."

"But the rain's stopped. It rained for more than a week. Bloody weather, if you ask me. You wouldn't be able to see much of our beautiful city in that kind of rain. Now, you can go around and be fascinated by our many wonderful attractions."

There it was. The famous Irish modesty. "I'm sure I will," she said without concealing her amusement.

"Did you come for the concert? U2's, that is."

"Yep."

"I hope you bought tickets, because they're sold out, you know."

"I did, actually. I've got to pick them up at the stadium. Is it too far from the hotel?"

"There's no such thing as 'too far' in Dublin," he said with a chuckle. "At least, not for American standards. Where are you from?"

"South Boston," she replied.

"That figures."

"What do you mean?"

"You look like a beautiful Irish rose but sound American. I figured you must have Irish blood running in your American veins. Where else would that combination be more popular than in Boston? Hence, a beautiful, Irish-looking girl like you should only come from Boston, right?"

She laughed wholeheartedly at his assessment and the way he expressed himself, "Oh, my! Do all Irish people speak like that?"

"We speak just like any other person—except we're more eloquent than the others. Blame it on Blarney Stone."

Keira wasn't as embarrassed by his compliments as she would normally be. Maybe the legends around that stone held some truth.

"You sound like my grandfather. His parents were Irish."

"Where in Ireland were they from?"

"Cork."

"See? Blarney Stone, again. It must be fate." He winked at her through the rearview mirror, and she actually blushed. "My family's also from Cork. I moved to Dublin a few years ago."

She studied his profile. Seamus looked young and handsome. Her cheeks burned a stronger shade of red as she realized he was very attractive. She wasn't very adept at dealing with attractive guys.

"Hey, have I said something wrong? I'm sorry."

"No, it's fine. It's just that I'm not used to compliments, that's all."

"Why is that? Are American guys blind?"

She felt like telling him her American friends were just more private but, not wanting to offend him, weighed her words carefully before answering, "I guess I look like any other cute American girl. You know—blonde hair, blue eyes, and all. Plus, I'm too short and slender."

"If you say so." He grinned and winked again at her reflection in the mirror.

Keira didn't have time to say anything else because he pulled over in front of a gorgeous building. While he got her bag from the trunk, she stood on the sidewalk admiring the river, which divided the city in two and flowed serenely by the hotel.

"That's the Liffey, right?"

"Indeed, it is. You should take a walk along it whenever you can."

"I'll do that. Thank you, sir." She paid the fare and added a five-Euro tip.

"Thank you, miss. I hope you have a pleasant stay and come back many times."

She waited for Seamus to drive away before turning and looking up at the white-and-red brick, six-story building. It reminded her of those beautiful buildings on Beacon Hill. It wasn't tall or impressive, but rather welcoming and friendly. Just like Dublin city had been, so far.

"Good morning, miss," the front desk clerk greeted her when she opened the heavy double door made of golden metal and glass. "Welcome to Clarence."

Keira overcame her initial shyness and gave the lady a quick smile, "Hello, I have a reservation. I've asked for early check-in. The name's Keira Ashe."

"Just give me a moment, Ms. Ashe. I'll search for your reservation and check you in."

Less than fifteen minutes later, Keira stood in the elevator, along with a nice bellhop named Peter, going up to her room. She loved the wood-paneled walls and the sophisticated yet subtle décor. She'd never stayed in such a luxurious hotel. Her great-grandparents hadn't had any of that legendary "Luck of the Irish" when they got to America.

Neither had her grandfather. He had an almost-fatal car accident when her father was a baby. Because of that, Padraic had spent most of his life in a wheelchair. He had managed to raise his little family quite well, but money had been tight for a long time for the Ashes.

Nowadays, with the successful restaurant, her parents had a more comfortable lifestyle, but she could never compare her home to that hotel. She tried to shake off the feeling of inadequacy as Peter opened the door and showed Keira into her room.

"Where do you want me to put your bag, miss?"

She looked around and pointed to the space between the bed and the window.

"You can leave it over there, by the bed, please."

Opening the closet, Peter got a foldable stand and arranged her suitcase on it. Then he opened the dark blue curtains. Light coming through the large windows flooded the room. Another brick building stood across the street, behind the hotel.

"That's Temple Bar, miss," Peter told her as he pointed out of the window. "At night, it gets quite busy and noisy, but I guess you'll like it there. The pubs are full of young people."

"Thanks."

Keira didn't bother to explain to him that she'd never cared much for clubbing with her friends. She had always been the quiet, nerdy one in the gang. She pushed her glasses up her nose and gave him a tip.

"Thank you, miss. Call me if you need anything."

As the door clicked closed, Keira plopped herself down on the center of the bed and looked at the ceiling. "Grandpa Paddy, I'm home!" she said sotto voice.

Once she'd rolled onto her stomach, Keira buried her head in the soft pillows. She felt like crying yet couldn't understand why, so she fought against it. An ominous feeling had haunted her in the previous weeks but Keira wouldn't let it ruin her vacation.

I miss Grandpa. Besides, it's the first time I'm alone and away from home. That's why I want to cry.

Her rationalization didn't stop a few tears from falling silently until she fell asleep.

* * * *

After a warm shower, Keira felt like herself again and asked the concierge for directions to Croke Park stadium. The concert wouldn't be for another couple of days but she wanted to grab the ticket in her hands to make sure it was real. She decided to take a bus to be able to see more of the town as she went to pick up the ticket.

On the bus, she sat near three people who spoke in Portuguese. Her neighborhood had many Portuguese speakers, which made it easier for her to recognize it, although Keira didn't speak it. She just sat there and listened to them, feeling more at home than before. Dublin had turned out to be quite a surprise. She'd never expected to find another city so far from Boston and yet so similar to it.

When she stood up to get off the bus, the three Portuguese-speaking friends got off as well. They were probably U2 fans too, and she felt an impulse to strike up conversation but didn't have it in her to do that. She walked a couple of steps behind the small group, which consisted of a woman and two men. They seemed older than her—probably in their late thirties. The woman walked between the two men and spoke excitedly about something, and the three of them laughed a lot, obviously enjoying themselves.

After a short walk, the four of them got to the Will Call counter and stood in line waiting to get their tickets. The redheaded woman had glanced at Keira on the way but hadn't said anything. Now that Keira was standing behind them, she introduced herself.

"Hi, there. My name's Carla. You look too young to be a U2 fan," she said with a smile and a gentle tone. Except for a very light accent, her English sounded excellent. "Are you from around here?"

"No, I'm from Boston. I'm Keira," she replied as they shook hands. "I guess I've been a fan since before I was born. My mom is a fan and she used to listen to U2 all the time when she was pregnant with me."

"These are my two best friends—Fábio and Doni. We're from Brazil."

"How do you do?" Fábio shook her hand.

"How are you?" asked Doni, blushing and looking more uncomfortable than Keira when she held his hand.

"Don't mind him. He's shy and hates me for talking to strangers. He'll get over it," Carla said and winked at Doni, then gave him a tight hug. "Won't you, dear?"

"I'll try," he said and laughed, but his face grew redder.

"How long have you been in Dublin?" Fábio asked.

13

"I arrived today."

"Is it your first visit?" Carla added.

"Yes, it is. I'll stay for three weeks and travel around the country, after the concert, you know?"

"Oh, I'm, sure you'll love it here. This is our second visit. First time, we stayed only in Dublin, which is a wonderful city, in my humble opinion!"

Fabio and Doni laughed at her comment, most likely because it didn't sound humble at all, while Keira tried to figure out the three Brazilians.

"This time we got to drive around for almost three weeks before coming to Dublin. You have to visit the little villages by the coast, and the castles, and the parks. There's just too much to see."

Keira just nodded at Carla's enthusiastic descriptions of the places they'd visited recently. Her friends contributed to the narrative as well. The four of them were so enthralled by the lively conversation that it took them some time to notice a certain commotion going on at the head of the line. When people started shouting, others complaining, they stopped talking and tried to understand what was going on.

"How come it's canceled?" a man shouted at the person behind the glass window.

They couldn't hear the answer because they were too far away. The line disappeared as people got closer to the Will Call booth, as did Keira and her new friends. When she heard the woman's answer, her brain refused to process the information.

"The concert was canceled due to a minor accident Bono suffered earlier today. He's fine but it'll take a couple of weeks for him to be able to perform again. I'm sorry, I don't have much more information at this moment. We just got the news. All I can say is that you can choose to file for a refund or use your tickets for the re-scheduled concert."

"When is it going to be?" the same man asked.

"We don't know yet."

The ground disappeared from beneath Keira. She'd dreamed about that concert for so long, had planned her trip so carefully around it, and now there would be no concert. Fábio squeezed her shoulder in a sympathetic gesture.

"I guess I know what you are going through," he said as the four of them sat down on the curb. "A couple of years ago, I went to Vegas just for a Cher concert. When I went to the theater to pick up my tickets, I found out she had gotten sick and canceled the concert. I had only the weekend off and went back to Brazil feeling very disappointed."

On the curb, Carla sat on Keira's right, Fábio on her left, and Doni sat beside Carla, trying to comfort her, but sounding as sad as she was. Nothing they could say would make her feel better. Eventually, they stopped talking and sat in silence for a long while, feeling disheartened.

When Keira stood up, the other three kept looking at their feet. "Guys, I've got to go. I'll ask for a refund because I won't be around long enough to watch the rescheduled concert. What about you?"

"Same here. We're heading back home in three days. No way we can stay longer," Fábio answered.

Carla looked up at Keira, opened her mouth to say something, but nothing came out. She hid her face in Doni's shoulder and Keira guessed she was crying. She wanted to get back to the hotel before breaking down like that. Already, she had a lump in her throat and had to make an effort to say goodbye to her newfound friends.

She walked fast to the bus stop, and managed to hold back her tears until she got to the hotel. Once safe behind a closed door, she threw herself on the bed and cried. The trip had fast turned into a disaster.

* * * *

Keira spent that day, and the following one, in her hotel room, sulking. It was childish but she didn't really care. She felt entitled to a little of that. After

15

all, she had worked so hard to pay for the trip, had fantasized about that concert for so long, that she felt empty. She didn't feel like going out to eat, so she ordered a little snack from Room Service and went to sleep earlier than usual.

On her third day in Dublin, she woke up early, got out of bed, showered, and went downstairs for breakfast. Back home, when Keira had planned each detail of the trip, she had filled her third day in Dublin with a lot of sightseeing. She had figured it would help her keep the anxiety down because the concert was scheduled for that night. Now, she would use those plans to keep herself busy and forget the concert had been canceled.

Although breakfast looked delicious, it tasted like cardboard to her numb palate. While munching on her meal, it dawned on Keira that her trip shouldn't only be about U2. Granted, she was a big fan, but she had wished to visit Ireland ever since she could remember. She owed it to herself to make a harder effort to have fun while she was in the Emerald Isle.

These thoughts cheered her up. She left the hotel and walked the short distance to Trinity College, where she took a tour guided by one of the students. He was a cute, funny Irishman and she finally started enjoying herself. She got to see most of the beautiful halls. They brimmed with history and tradition. The old library took her breath away and she spent a long time there gawking at the priceless rare editions—mainly the Book of Kells.

After the tour, she took a double-decker sightseeing bus and got off at Dublin Castle. She walked around the stone buildings and beautiful gardens and took a lot of pictures. The Dubh Linn Garden, with its large Celtic designs made on the grass, gave her a much-needed pause. She sat on one of the wooden benches and stayed there for a long time admiring the intricate patterns, the amazing sculptures, and colorful flowerbeds. The peace and quiet of that place restored her usual sunny disposition.

16

Later, she went through Temple Bar to her hotel, where she left the two bags full of souvenirs she had bought at Trinity College, Dublin Castle, and in the little shops along the narrow streets in between. Then, because it was a warm, beautiful day, she left the hotel and took a stroll along the Liffey River. She admired the centuries-old buildings lining the riverbanks as well as the beautiful bridges. The map of the city she had downloaded to her smartphone showed her where to leave the riverside, and she walked up Winetavern Street to Christ Church Cathedral.

The stone building was impressive enough, but the bells—which started pealing as she approached—made her heart beat faster. They sounded so melancholy and welcoming at the same time, in other words—so Irish. She walked around the church building, admiring the smooth green grass and tall trees, and the amazing architecture of the cathedral, before leaving and heading towards Saint Patrick's Cathedral.

She entered the church to see the Gothic arches and stained glass windows. Again, the peaceful atmosphere soothed her and she left the building feeling much better. While she stood and waited for the hop-on-hop-off red bus, Keira thought about the wonderful emotions she had experienced so far, and concluded that maybe the trip could still surprise her.

She got off the bus at Guinness Storehouse. Following advice she'd received from a friend, Keira had bought the ticket online to skip the long lines at that highly popular tourist destination. She wasn't very fond of alcoholic drinks in general, and she particularly disliked beer—except Guinness, of course. Although she didn't drink often, it proved quite an experience to visit the Brewery. The round restaurant at the top offered a breathtaking view of the city through its floor-to-ceiling glass windows. She got her pint of Guinness, found a table near one of the windows, and sat there to admire the city. Due to the clear weather, she could see far, even the distant mountains around Dublin. Their round summits covered in green grass shone in the early afternoon sun. The

17

strong beer traveled through her veins and took away whatever tension still remained in her muscles. She relaxed on the chair, feeling surprisingly well. Only when she felt drunk did Keira remember she hadn't eaten since breakfast. With a shrug, she drained the last drops of the black beer, and then sat the glass on the table with a satisfied, yet dopey, smile.

Life is good! I'm in Ireland, alone, and single. It's about time I learned to have some fun.

At least, her older sister had kept telling her that. Megan also nagged Keira non-stop about her insecurities and shyness. She used to tell Keira she underestimated herself. It was very easy for Megan to see life as a big adventure and to think everybody was as confident as she was. She was the badass daughter—Keira, the geeky one.

At that moment, though, Keira felt much more confident, thanks to the generous dose of liquid courage she had just taken. She stood up, intending to return to the hotel, and the restaurant swayed around her. She grabbed the back of the chair until the room stopped moving.

As she took the metal stairs to the ground floor, she had a comprehensive view of the brewery. Halfway down, she regretted her choice— the steps seemed to either rise to meet her or sink away from her feet. She grabbed the railing and took a long time to finish those few last steps, before heading back to her hotel.

It was past three in the afternoon when she took the elevator down to the lobby and went to the Octagon Bar. There wasn't a hostess at the door to assign her a table, so Keira sat at the nearest one. In fact, there wasn't anybody in the pub except for the bartender. He was on the phone and signaled her that he just needed a minute. She nodded back but the room swirled around her again and she had to close her eyes and grab her head in both hands to make it stop spinning.

I need to eat. Now! she thought as a buzzing ring pierced her ears.

"Are you all right, miss?" a deep voice sounded above her.

Keira made an effort to lift her head and look up at the bartender. When she did, she found herself drowning in a pair of unbelievably green eyes. They were the most beautiful eyes she'd ever seen—a dark, lush shade of green—set in a breathtakingly gorgeous face. The young man standing by her table could easily be on the cover of a fashion or entertainment magazine. When Keira wasn't able to form a coherent sentence to answer his question, the crease between his perfect eyebrows grew deeper.

Damn Guinness!

"I beg your pardon, miss?" The crease deepened.

Her face got redder and hotter. *Just my luck*, she thought, and this time she really kept it inside her head. She cleared her throat and forced herself to say something, "I'm sorry, Declan." She read his name on the tag on his black vest. "I haven't eaten anything since breakfast. I think I'm a little dizzy. That's all."

He handed her a small menu and smiled. Her knees went weak and she was happy to be sitting. She wouldn't have remained standing otherwise. His electrifying grin lit his handsome face up and made his eyes sparkle. The effect would be hypnotic and devastating to any sober woman, and so Keira was easy prey.

"Miss?" He waved the menu and she grabbed it.

She mumbled some excuse to justify her behaving like a stupid schoolgirl, and buried her impossibly-red face inside the menu.

"I'll give you a minute to decide. Call me when you're ready ..." He winked at her and made a brief pause, before adding, "... to order."

His attitude appalled her. Regardless of his good looks, the man was a cocky little bastard. He ought to be ashamed of himself for going around embarrassing other people like that.

You embarrassed yourself! Drooling over a cute face, said that pesky voice inside her head that always told her to tread carefully whenever she felt a little adventurous.

Keira squared her shoulders and told her inner self to shut up because she was merely drunk, not drooling. She studied the menu and found that there weren't many food options. The decision made to ignore the available drinks, she waved at Declan.

He couldn't hide the shadow of his smile or disguise a mischievous glint in his eyes.

"Are you feeling better, miss?"

She nodded and cursed her voice for disappearing every time he got near her.

"Are you ready to order or would you like a suggestion?"

"I—ahm—I'll have the fish and—ahm—the salad, please," she stuttered and had to avoid his eyes to be able to finish the sentence.

"Very well. Anything to drink?"

"Just water, please."

He nodded. "I'll take this order to the kitchen. I'll be right back."

When he went out of the room, Keira took a deep breath and looked up. The bar had a beautiful octagonal dome in the middle, and she tried to use it to distract herself and calm her pulse. It didn't work. She had bought a pocket guide of the city, so she opened it on the table and discovered a map filled with suggestions for sightseeing. She forced her hazy, drunken mind to concentrate on which places she'd like to visit next. The next day would be her last in

Dublin. After that, she would take a rental car and drive around the countryside. Keira got distracted by her plans and didn't hear Declan return.

* * * *

He stood by the table for a while, studying her. She had a lovely, heart-shaped face framed by golden, wavy, shoulder-length hair. The locks caressed her rosy cheeks as she moved her head to better study the map on the table. Her mouth and eyes seemed to be her strongest features. Her eyes were as blue as a cloudless winter sky. Her lips looked full and naturally red. She didn't wear make-up, but her natural coloring didn't require any. The reading glasses gave her a serious look.

She looks too serious for such a young beauty.

Declan had been fighting his primal instincts since she had walked into the bar. There was something about the girl that moved him in ways he hadn't been moved in a long time. He didn't have time to look into those feelings; he needed to work. He put the lustful thoughts aside, pushed the X-rated images of steamed eyeglasses knocked askew by knee-melting kisses to the back of this mind, and cleared his throat to call her attention. When she looked up at him, a dreamy expression in those gorgeous eyes, he almost forgot himself and did something stupid like bending down and kissing her senseless. He felt the familiar tug of desire, the heat traveling down his body, and did his best to ignore it.

"Food won't take long, miss." He nodded to the map. "Do you need any help getting around town? Can I give you any suggestions?"

"Please, call me Keira," she said. "I've visited some places. I'm planning my day tomorrow." She seemed to have difficulty answering him, but continued, "Last day in Dublin, so I want to make the most of it."

"What have you seen so far?"

"Trinity College, Dublin Castle, Christ Church, and St. Patrick's Cathedral, and Guinness Storehouse," was her slurred answer. He smiled.

21

Declan felt amused and he could see he had an effect on this pretty girl. She looked down at the map and fidgeted.

* * * *

Keira hadn't had much experience with men in her young life, and almost zero interaction with gorgeous men like Declan. She didn't know what to do with herself and her shyness got worse when she was embarrassed. Add a dizzy, drunken head to the equation and the result was that pile of raw nerves sitting on the cushioned seat and trying to act as a normal person.

Get a grip on yourself, girl, that little voice made a comeback inside her head. Only, this time, Keira agreed with it.

She took a deep breath and looked up at him. Big mistake. Her ears rang and her mouth got dry. She ran the tip of her tongue over her parched lips to soothe them but the movement drew his eyes to her mouth and she felt faint at the intensity she saw in his stare. She heard a soft moan but wasn't sure whose it was—hers or his. Time stood still as their eyes locked.

Declan moved and broke the spell. He stretched his hand towards the map, "Do you mind if I take it?"

She handed him the paper instead of answering him.

"I can suggest some places tourists don't know about," he said as he grabbed his pen and scribbled the names of some restaurants, pubs, museums, and even some stores.

"I'll have a busy day tomorrow," she said with a laugh when he gave the map back to her.

"But you'll have fun." His voice sounded thick. "I'll check if the food is ready. I'll be right back."

* * * *

Declan almost ran out of the bar, headed away from the kitchen, and into the employee restroom, because he needed a breather.

22

He splashed some cold water on his burning face. Another part of his anatomy also burned like hell, and there was nothing he could do about it. He liked the young American, but he would never take advantage of a drunken woman, no matter how attractive she was.

Studying his reflection in the mirror, Declan couldn't understand what was wrong with him. He wasn't a simpleton or a naïve country boy. He had dated gorgeous women before, so he couldn't figure out why Keira had spurred such powerful, instantaneous reactions in him.

Get a grip on yourself, man! Don't go falling head over heels for a pretty face who's leaving town tomorrow!

He shook his head, ran his fingers through his short dark hair, and regained control over his treacherous body before going to the kitchen to fetch Keira's order. He knew what he had to do even if it hurt him. Declan could only hope it wouldn't hurt Keira too much.

"Here you go, miss. Enjoy," he said in a most professional tone.

"Thank you."

Declan felt like a fist had connected to his midriff at the bewildered, hurt look in Keira's eyes. He made a huge effort to ignore his own pang—an equal mix of pain and guilt.

Just my luck to finally meet a woman who makes me feel alive again one day before she leaves town, he pondered as he took his place behind the bar counter again.

* * * *

Keira finished her meal in a confused state of mind, made worse by the alcohol she had drunk earlier. The food tasted excellent but she paid little attention to it, as she tried to understand what she had done wrong. The conversation replayed in her mind, and she concluded she hadn't done anything wrong.

Luck of the Irish

You must have read the signs wrong. He was just being nice and friendly, like most Irish people are, her annoying inner self pointed out to her. *Did you seriously think a guy like Declan was interested in a girl like you? Get over yourself, Keira!*

She forced the last mouthful down her throat with a sip of water. The drunken fog had lifted, allowing her to think straight. As depressing as it sounded, her inner self was right. What could he possibly see in her? She wasn't stunning like Megan. She was the smart one, not the pretty one in the family. At least, that was how she had felt her entire life.

* * * *

Declan remained safely behind the counter, where he felt more in control of his reactions, and watched Keira closely. She had leaned forward, hunching her shoulders, ate slowly, and had some difficulty swallowing the last couple of mouthfuls. His conscience scolded him as he observed her posture. He was responsible for her withdrawal, and it made him feel like a big asshole. He shouldn't have gone bi-polar on her. He should have managed his emotions better in the first place. It wasn't her fault if he'd had a shitty love life. She hadn't ripped his heart to pieces, had she? And it was absolutely not her fault if he couldn't keep his damn lustful body in check, right?

That train of thought didn't help Declan calm down, but caused a new rush of graphic scenes to invade his mind. For a while, he let himself indulge in the possibilities. If Keira were to stay, he would find a way to know her better.

I'd love to spend hours getting to know her—every little inch of her.

He closed his eyes and imagined her small, perfect body under his—felt her silken skin under his fingertips. He wanted to kiss her until they were both breathless, and try all his moves to discover her secret spots: what made her tick, and moan, and shout his name.

"Hey, Declan!" her clear voice yanked him from the daydream. He looked at her, still in a daze, and she smiled. "Can you bring me the check, please?"

He was mortified at the huge bulge in his pants, which prevented him from going to the table without making a bigger fool of himself than he had already made. So, he pretended to study some papers on the counter.

"What's your room number, miss?"

"It's 305."

"I'll add the check to your room bill."

"Don't I have to sign it?"

"That's not necessary," he said, then added to himself, *I'll have to sign it myself because there's no way in hell I can stand up right now, you little bewitching thing.*

Keira glared at the cold treatment he'd given her, and stood up to leave. At the doorway, she stopped and looked over her shoulder.

"Goodbye, Declan," she said in a thin voice.

"Goodbye, Keira," he replied, using her name for the first time. She seemed to hesitate a moment or two, but then turned around and left.

* * * *

To sit and watch television turned out to be impossible for Keira, because the news programs focused mainly on Bono's accident and the canceled concerts. Besides, the lively sounds coming in through the windows from the Temple Bar pubs made it hard to concentrate on the small screen. She gave up pretending to pay attention to it, changed into a pair of jeans and a clean T-shirt, and went out, bound to enjoy her last night in Dublin.

She left the hotel through the backdoor and found herself smack-dab in the middle of the bustling Temple Bar scene. Hundreds of people crowded all around, and the street offered countless pubs to choose from, so she decided to walk around and find the one most appealing to her.

She walked further down the road until she saw a crowd gathered around a bright red building on a corner, which called her attention. Through a large window, she could see a band performing on a small stage. She stood across the street, watching the people singing along with the band, until she noticed someone inside the pub waving at her. She recognized the redheaded Brazilian she had met at the ticket line. Her two friends were with her and they seemed to be inviting Keira to join them.

Oh, what the heck? I'll go in and get drunk. Maybe then I'll forget about stupid concerts and even dumber but drop-dead-gorgeous bartenders, she decided, as she tried to find a way through the crowd.

Carla met her at the door, "Hey, Keira, right? Are you by yourself? No U2 fan should be alone tonight. It's not safe." She slurred a little but Keira got her point.

"Damn right! I want to get as drunk as I possibly can without passing out on the street." Keira followed Carla to the table.

"Hey, you've made it!" Doni, obviously very drunk, didn't seem to know whom his friend Carla was anymore.

"I've been here the whole night, sweetie. Come on! You can't be that drunk." She laughed and looked at her other friend. "Can he?"

"Yes, he can and he is," Fábio said. He turned to Keira and smiled. "Sorry."

"No worries. You seem sober," she stated the obvious with a playful smile.

"I'm driving." He shrugged. "Can I get you anything? I'm going to the bar."

"Another pint?" Carla asked, showing her empty glass of Guinness.

"Me, too," Doni joined her.

"Yes and no," Fábio pointed at each friend as he answered. "Would you like one, too, Keira?"

26

She hesitated for a fleeting second then nodded in agreement as he pulled a chair for her.

"Sit down. I'll be right back," he said and disappeared into the middle of the crowd surrounding the bar counter.

"This place is awesome, isn't it?" Carla asked her.

"Yes, it is. How long have you guys been here tonight?"

"Oh, we've just got here," Doni offered.

She looked at him in surprise but turned around when she heard Carla's laugh.

"Don't mind him. He's lost track of time. We've been here a while. Enough for him to get that wasted, anyway."

They all laughed and told Fábio the joke when he joined them with a fresh round of pints for Carla and Keira. He brought water for Doni.

"Wow, that was fast. I thought it would take you forever, with all those thirsty people hanging around the bar," Keira said.

"A little Brazilian charm does wonders." He winked then nodded towards the counter.

She got his meaning when she saw a beautiful barmaid stretching her neck to look at their table over the customers' heads.

"I see." She laughed and raised her glass to her new friends. "Sláinte mhaith!"

"Sláinte!" they answered before drinking their smooth and strong black beer.

Keira was surprised at how at ease she felt around them. Ordinarily, she wouldn't be comfortable in that kind of situation, but they were friendly. The pints of beer that kept coming to the table certainly helped her relax. After a couple of hours, she was laughing at their jokes and funny stories until her jaw hurt. They had many stories to tell. They had traveled around the world, met the strangest people, and seen the most amazing places. She had a great time with them, which definitely took her mind off the depressing thoughts that had plagued her earlier. But, eventually, the night came to an end.

"Sorry, Keira, but we've got to go. We need to get back to our hotel, near Croke Park, of all places." Carla rolled her eyes and made a funny face. "We have a long day tomorrow."

"That's fine, guys. I've got to go, too," she replied, and they left the pub.

Fábio was the only one who could walk straight. They made a hilarious picture and laughed hard at that.

"Are you sure you can get these two to their hotel rooms?" Keira asked.

"Don't worry. I've done it before," he said.

"As have I, mister!" Carla slurred, in feigned annoyance, pointing a shaky finger at him, which he grabbed and kissed.

"Yeah, right! Whatever." He laughed.

"Bye, friend." Doni waved in Keira's general direction and she waved back.

"Goodbye, Keira. Remember to have fun," Carla said, blowing a kiss.

"Goodbye, Carla." Keira laughed and blew her another.

Fábio shook his head at his two drunken friends and stretched his hand out. "Goodbye, Keira. Are you sure you can walk back to the hotel? We can drop you off there."

"Thank you, I am fine. Walking will help clear my head. You drive safely now." She waved and turned towards the Clarence, which wasn't far, but her legs didn't want to obey her and her feet seemed to drag.

After what felt like an eternity, the yellow backdoor of the hotel appeared in front of her and she climbed the few steps to the glass doors. She did so a bit too fast and felt dizzy. When she entered the hotel, Keira leaned against the wall while the room spun around her, and she promised herself never to get drunk like that again.

28

CHAPTER 2

Declan came out of the bar and stopped dead when he saw Keira, looking pale and about to faint, leaning against the wall. In two long strides, he was beside her, and gathered her in his arms to avoid her collapsing to the floor, but she startled.

"What are you doing?"

He smelled alcohol on her breath—she was as drunk as she could be. She might fall if he let go of her, but her indignant expression left him no other choice.

"I'm sorry. I thought you were going to faint." He released her.

Her body swayed, but she looked at him over her glasses and stuck her nose in the air.

"I am perfectly fine, sir. Thank you very much." She straightened as if trying not to look too drunk, but she needed to put a hand on the wall to steady herself. That gesture dampened her remark a bit but she pretended it didn't happen and just stared back at him with a stern look.

He wanted to laugh at her expression, kiss her pouting lips, and scoop her up in his arms, and never let her go. All at once. But he did none of those things. He just nodded at her.

"Are you sure? You look a tad tipsy," he offered her the understatement of the year, because he knew that, in her drunken state, she wouldn't get his sarcasm.

"I told you I'm fine. In fact, I'll just go inside and have a drink." She let go of the wall and stepped towards the bar.

"Maybe that's not a good idea. The pub is full. You'd have to stand up at the counter," he told her as he discreetly held her arm when she stumbled.

"I don't mind it. That's how most people drink, isn't it?" she replied and managed to enter the bar.

In fact, it wasn't that crowded and there were two or three empty stools. She chose one and frowned at him as she plopped herself down on it.

"I'd say somebody doesn't want to work tonight, huh?" She raised an eyebrow at him.

Declan rolled his eyes and went back behind the counter. His two colleagues looked at him but he just shrugged and muttered under his breath. "It's a long story."

They smiled and gladly put him in charge of the drunken American.

"We'll take care of everything. You take care of her. I think you'll have your hands full, anyway," the tall red-haired woman said, laughing.

"You got that right, Màire. He already seems to be in trouble. She doesn't look too happy with him, does she?" the dark-haired older man replied.

"Oh, fuck off, Harry. You're jealous, that's all." Declan laughed and pushed the man playfully.

Keira watched their exchange but got so caught up in their Irish accents that she lost half of their meaning. She laughed because everything seemed amusing.

"A pint of Guinness," she ordered when Declan turned to her.

"Maybe you should drink some water, first."

"You should mind your own business and pour the ale, sir," she answered, smacking her hand on the counter for emphasis.

"It's actually a stout," he replied as he filled a glass with the black beer.

"What's the difference?" she asked.

"If you have to ask, you shouldn't be drinking it." He had lost his good mood and his temper. Declan took a deep breath to calm himself down. "I'm sorry, miss. I didn't mean to be rude. You are right. It's none of my business what you do with yourself. I apologize."

30

Keira looked sad—had she picked up on the hurt in his voice? Maybe she was too drunk.

"Please, Declan, don't apologize. I'm the spoiled brat here. I should have noticed you were just looking out for me. I'm sorry." She reached over the counter and grabbed his hand.

He looked at her in surprise. He had felt a sudden charge of electricity run from his hand and into hers. She jumped back and let go, so she'd felt it too. He was astonished by their reactions to such a simple touch. He told himself not to think too hard about it. He shouldn't think of what might happen if he touched her more intimately. He needed to remember what had happened earlier that day.

But it was too late. He had already imagined it as he leaned over the counter and trapped her cool hand between his warm ones. He looked her in the eyes and saw conflicting emotions in their blue depths—desire, surprise, curiosity, and insecurity. The last one was the strongest and the one he couldn't understand—why a beautiful, intelligent young woman such as Keira was, would harbor so much self-doubt.

****

Keira stared back into his eyes and went speechless. His already dark green gaze seemed darker and more dangerous. She felt like she had walked into an enchanted forest. His eyes were alluring and frightening at the same time. She wanted to get lost in them but was terrified of the possibility. His stare seemed to connect to something buried deep inside her, some basic instinct, or primal feeling, she didn't know she had. She felt her body tingle in the strangest places as that feeling raised its head and threatened to smother any rational thoughts the beer had left intact. There weren't many.

She was alone in a foreign country, holding a stranger's hand, looking into his eyes, and dreaming of all the dirty things she'd like to do to him, with him, or let him do to her. She must be out of her mind. Those thoughts made the butterflies somersault in her stomach and she felt sick.

31

Declan let go of her hand—had he noticed her discomfort?

"Tell me why you wanted to get drunk tonight, Keira. I'm a bartender, remember. It's my job to listen to the customers." He winked.

"Is that right?" She laughed and felt thankful to him for breaking that dangerous spell she had been under since he had taken her hand in his. "Well, let me see. Where should I start telling you about my tribulations?"

Later, Keira would blame the beer for having opened up her heart so completely to Declan that night. The truth was, though, she felt comfortable talking to him like she had never felt with another man. She told him about her grandfather and her childhood dream of visiting Ireland. She talked about her hardworking days and how she had saved money for the trip. She found it hard to convey her expectations about the concert and the disappointment at its cancelation. That kind of feeling could only be understood by another fan. Preferably, one who had gone through something similar. Normal people didn't get it.

"But your trip is only beginning, isn't it? You still have a couple of weeks ahead of you to enjoy yourself," Declan said. He was definitely a normal person.

"You don't understand it," she was feeling sorry for herself, like any other drunkard. Her eyes filled with tears. "I've always wanted to watch a U2 concert in Dublin. Now, I can't do that. I won't watch a U2 concert in their hometown," she whined and sniffed.

"Please, don't cry. I don't know what to do around crying women," Declan begged her.

It was useless. Once the floodgates had opened there was no turning back. She crossed her arms on the counter, rested her forehead on them, and cried like a little girl.

****

He looked at Màire and Harry in panic. They shrugged back at him.

"What do I do?" he mouthed.

A few customers looked at them as her sobs grew louder.

"Take her upstairs," Màire mouthed and gestured in reply.

He rolled his eyes and took a deep breath.

"Come, come, Keira. I know you like the guys, but missing one little concert doesn't seem that bad," he whispered, softly in her ear.

That seemed to be the wrong thing to say, though.

"Ooh! That's my favorite song," she wailed and he looked at the ceiling as if in prayer. The woman was too drunk to make any sense. Then, she started singing out of key and he understood what she meant. "See you break away! La-la-la—to fade away! La-la-la—I'm not sleeping!"

"All right, missy, time to go up to your room. This isn't a karaoke bar," he said as he walked around the counter, snaked an arm around her narrow waist, and grabbed her arm, draping it over his own shoulders. "Up you go. That's a good girl."

He looked at his colleagues and they shooed him away.

"Go, go! We've got it covered," Harry said, trying without success not to burst out laughing.

Màire shook her head at him and teased, "It's amazing what that Declan guy has to do to get a date, huh, Harry?"

He gave her the finger as he stumbled out the door and heard their roaring laughter behind him. Although Keira was a small thing, it was difficult to stir a drunken person. She could barely put one foot in front of the other, so their legs got intertwined. Declan feared they would stumble to the ground, and decided to scoop her up, and carried her to the room.

"Yay! That's nice," she said as she let her head fall on his shoulder and laced her hands behind his neck, closing her eyes.

She snuggled closer to his body. His heart beat like crazy inside his chest. He could hardly breathe, and closed his eyes for a second to wait for the

33

surge of blood in his veins to flow back upwards. It had gone straight down to his groin and he moaned at his body's reaction to her proximity. He told himself he was a grown man—one perfectly capable of taking a helpless woman to her room, putting her on the bed, and going back to work. It was as simple as that.

He pretended not to know his shift was about to finish as he carried her inside the elevator. He had a master keycard for when he needed to deliver drinks to the guests, so he used it to open her door since he was in no condition to go through her pockets to find her card. She wasn't carrying a purse.

What kind of woman doesn't carry a purse?

Obviously, one who didn't fit the stereotype. He felt in his bones that the situation was bound to end in disaster. After all, that was his luck, anyway.

He stooped over the bed to put her down, but, when he tried to straighten up again, Keira laced her hands behind his neck, holding him in place. She was surprisingly strong for a woman, especially a drunken one.

"Don't go, please. I don't want to be alone, Declan," she said.

At least she knew who he was. He took her hands in his and sat beside her.

"I'll stay until you fall sleep," he told her, hoping it would be soon.

Keira's eyes looked out of focus. She put her hands on his cheeks.

"You are so dreamy. Are you for real?"

He laughed, because he felt sure she wasn't aware she had said it aloud.

"Why are you laughing, silly? You don't know what I'm thinking."

He hid his smile behind a stern expression.

"It's late, Keira. Close your eyes and try to sleep."

She did so, but after a short while, she sat on the bed and looked around, startled.

"What's wrong, sweetie?" he talked to her as if she were six years old. "Go back to sleep."

She shook her head and looked ashen, "My head is spinning," she said before turning a deeper shade of green.

Declan rushed to the bathroom to get the wastebasket, but wasn't fast enough. She threw up over the bed before he returned. There wasn't much he could do other than wait for the heaving to stop. He held her hair and soothed her with gentle words, but she looked mortified. She made incoherent apologies.

"Shush, Keira, don't speak. Everything will be all right," he told her.

When it was over, he helped her stand up. Her legs were a little shaky.

"I need a shower."

When he saw her legs get firmer, he knew she could handle the shower on her own. That was a relief, because he wouldn't be able to help her there.

"Go ahead. I'll call housekeeping and tell them to clean up this mess. Don't worry."

****

She took her time under the showerhead trying to relax and recover. The hot water helped her accomplish that. She didn't expect Declan to stick around and wait for her. After all, she had already put him in enough awkward situations for one night with her drunken stupidity and horrible behavior.

When she left the bathroom, she was surprised to find him sitting on the blue armchair by the window. The bed had been cleaned. Her embarrassment prevented her from looking him in the eyes.

"Thank you, Declan, for everything. I'm so–," she started speaking but stopped when he raised a hand to interrupt her.

"No apologies necessary, Keira. I'd never leave you alone in this kind of situation. It's something we'd better leave behind us, don't you think?"

"You're absolutely right."

"I guess you'd rather stay alone now you're feeling better, right?"

She hesitated briefly before nodding.

"Well, this is goodbye, then." He stood up to leave.

35

Luck of the Irish

As he walked towards her on his way to the door, Keira felt like grabbing his hand and asking him to stay. When he passed by her she did nothing. He stopped beside her and stared into her eyes. It seemed he wanted to read her mind, know her soul.

He stood there, looking into her beautiful blue eyes.

Declan's hesitation to leave surprised Keira. Unable to think straight after all that she had gone through, Keira acted on impulse and stepped closer.

He stepped backward.

She licked her dry lips and looked at his, hypnotized.

He stared into her eyes and looked starving.

She cupped his cheeks in her hands.

He put his big hands behind her fragile neck and ran his thumbs over her cheeks and lower lip.

As they faced each other, their bodies almost touched. The warmth of their bodies enveloped them as a blanket. She had to lift her head high to be able to look into his eyes.

He held her stare as he bent his head down. He stopped his mouth a fraction of an inch from her lips to give her time to change her mind. When she didn't push him away, he eliminated the distance and covered her mouth with his. With his fingers buried in her hair, he pulled her closer, pressing a hand down on the small of her back.

When their bodies touched intimately, Keira moaned, his mouth trapped the sound, and she opened hers wide in surprise. She stood on tiptoes, holding his shoulders, and pressing herself against him. When she felt his manhood brush against her soft belly, she was amazed at how fast her insides melted. She had kissed a few boys in high school and in college. She had even fooled around a bit with a steady boyfriend or two, but she had never gone all the way with a man. The thought of doing it with a stranger, no matter how

36

gorgeous he was, should terrify her. Yet, it didn't. She wanted to enjoy the moment.

She ran her hands over his broad shoulders and down his chest, as Declan deepened the kisses, invading her mouth with his tongue.

He held her face and played with her lips, kissing and nibbling them, running his tongue over her swollen lips to soothe and tease, at the same time.

She sighed and opened her eyes, seeing in his the same fire that consumed her. She threw her head back and offered him her neck.

He showered steaming kisses along an imaginary line from her chin, down her neck, and stopped at the first button of her blouse. He looked up at her.

"Are you sure?"

She nodded and opened the first button of his vest.

He lowered his head and opened her button with his teeth, kissed the patch of skin it revealed, and looked up at her again. He smiled and waited.

She got his intention and, with a sinful smile, yanked free the last two buttons of his vest. She did the same to his shirt.

He would need to buy a new uniform, but didn't seem to care right now. He opened the rest of the buttons on her shirt, pushed it off her shoulders, and slid it down her arms. He held his breath then let it out in a low whistle. She wasn't wearing a bra and he cupped her small breasts in his big hands, rubbing their hardening peaks.

"You are perfect," he whispered against her mouth before taking it again in a passionate kiss.

Keira fought to get rid of his shirt, and marveled at the feel of his smooth chest against her taut breasts when she finally managed to push the clothes off of him. She sighed and pressed closer against his hard body.

He grabbed her hips and molded her soft body to his hardness. He let go of her lips with reluctance and gasped for air against her soft neck.

"Christ, you'll be the death of me. But I'll die a happy man." He smiled and pushed her away a little to look at her. He ran his eyes over her flushed face, disheveled hair, and half-clad body. "You are so beautiful."

"You're not bad yourself," she replied as she pulled him by the hand and sat on the bed. She patted the spot beside her, an innocent smile playing on her lips. "Come. Sit down. I'll strain my neck looking up at you like this."

He didn't need a second invitation. They resumed kissing and exploring each other's skins.

She ran her fingers shyly over his strong shoulders and smooth chest but never went too far down.

He fondled her breasts and teased her nipples with his fingers. He kissed her shoulders and neck, before his hands traveled south. He kissed her mouth and whispered to her, "You are driving me crazy. I want to feel your hands on me, Keira."

She scraped his back and held his shoulders again.

"Like that?"

"No, sweetie, like this." He kissed her mouth again, and her reaction to his searing lips and tongue distracted her. She didn't notice his intentions until it was too late. He found the waistband of her sweatpants and managed to thrust his hand between the pants and her fevered body. She jumped and grabbed his hand when his fingers found her entrance.

"Do you want me to stop? You just have to say it and I'll stop."

She opened her mouth but couldn't say anything. She shook her head and let go of his hand. She closed her eyes to better feel it as he pushed her down on the mattress and moved up to hover above her.

"Look at me. Are you sure?"

She nodded but he didn't move.

"Are you sure you want me to go on, Keira?"

38

"Yes, Declan, I'm sure," she said. He kissed her as he yanked the sweatpants off her body in one swift movement.

She wore only a flimsy, lacy pair of panties.

"You have no idea what you do to me, woman. Your skin is creamy." He ran his hands over her body. "I could look at you for hours. Your breasts fit perfectly inside my hands." He cupped one, then the other, to prove his point. "Your mouth was made for sinning. It's so delicious." He ran a thumb over her lower lip. She gasped and closed her eyes. "Please, look at me. Your eyes turn darker when you're excited. I want to drown in them."

He bent down and kissed each eyelid as his hand moved south again. She held her breath when his finger played with the elastic band of her panties. He stretched it then released it. It snapped against her soft skin and she jumped.

"Ouch! That was mean."

"You have no idea, sweet thing. I want to do a lot of mean things to you." His smile melted her bones. "Let me start by soothing that pain."

He moved too fast for her slow mind to follow. Although she wasn't drunk anymore, the sensations he provoked in her were almost as intoxicating. Before she knew it, he'd knelt on the bed, bent his head down, and kissed her navel where the elastic band had left a thin red mark.

"Feeling better?"

She nodded and the melting smile returned to his lips. His eyes had a strange glint she only understood when it was too late.

"Good. Because I plan to make you feel very uncomfortable."

Declan slid her panties down her legs slowly as he held her stare. He bent down again over her body, never letting go of her eyes. She frowned at him but he only smiled, scattering a few innocent kisses around her belly button. When he stuck his tongue inside it, she jumped and giggled. He held her hips down and rubbed his cheek against the soft skin of her navel.

"Relax, Keira. I'm just starting."

She was still trying to figure out what he meant by that when he kissed the top of her thighs, where they met her hips, and it dawned on her. How could she have been so stupid? She felt her legs turn to jelly when he looked at her while he kissed the inside of her thigh before moving his body between her legs, spreading them apart. She couldn't breathe or speak. She only stared back at him in expectation.

****

Declan saw when understanding reached her and was surprised at how long it had taken her to read his intentions. He blamed it on her recent drunken state but decided to give her a little bit more time to adjust to the idea. Instead of kissing her where he was dying to kiss, he returned his attention to her luscious mouth. He covered her body with his and kissed her lips. His pants still clad his lower body, but his painfully hard erection rubbed against her soft skin when he moved over her and pinned her down to the mattress. His lungs were burning up. He felt his bones melting in the heat she stoked with her tentative movements beneath him, with her eager mouth opening for him, and her hesitant fingers digging into the flesh of his back. That wasn't enough. He wanted more from her. He wanted to see her come undone in his arms, to lose control completely.

"Don't hold back, Keira. Let it go," he whispered in her ear.

He kissed her again and his blood boiled when she hissed inside his mouth.

"That's it, give it to me," he said as he pushed himself up on one arm to see her expression as his fingers found her curls.

She gasped and opened her eyes wide. "What are you doing?"

"Worshipping you, my golden goddess," he said, holding her stare and tapping her innermost part with his index finger.

"Oh, that feels good!" She threw her head back, exposing her neck to him.

40

He bent down, kissed and nibbled the white span of skin, and added a second finger. She sank her fingers in his shoulders for support as the world spun around them. Her hips moved up, on their own, to meet his hand and she moaned when his fingers went further inside her body.

He chuckled against her soft breasts and covered a nipple with his hungry mouth. Her reactions were innocent—almost too innocent. She was young but he had expected her to be more experienced. He forced himself to slow down a little. He withdrew his fingers and she grabbed his hand.

"Don't stop."

"No worries, gorgeous." He smiled. "As much as I'd love to tear my pants off and bury myself inside you, I think you need me to go slowly. Am I wrong?"

"You're right. But, I want you so much." She moved her hands tentatively over his chest, lower than she had done before.

She found the button at his waistband and played with it before inserting a finger and running it along the elastic band. He moaned and grabbed her hand.

"You don't play with fire, little missy, until you're ready to burn," he said as he gently took her hand away from his erection and held it against his chest. "Leave my pants on until it's time. I don't trust myself otherwise when I'm near you." He returned his attention to her pebbled nipples, kissing and sucking them until Keira was breathless, smiling when the telltale goose-bumps creased her sensitive skin.

"Please, Declan, stop torturing me."

He moved between her legs again. His fingers found her and she fisted the covers in her hands as he kissed her mouth, invading her deeply with his thick tongue at the same time and in the same rhythm as his fingers reached inside her drenched body.

41

Luck of the Irish

Declan felt the barrier but it took him a few seconds to understand what it meant. His mind was lost in the haze of desire, and his body was ready to explode, taking both of them to oblivion. He tried again to reach further but the thin slice of skin barred his advances again. Keira moved her head from side to side and seemed lost to her own pleasure. Her body trembled under his fingertips and her release wasn't far way. He couldn't stop it now and leave her hanging. He wouldn't take her innocence, either. He couldn't make love to a virgin who was about to leave town in a day. It wasn't in his nature. He wasn't that kind of man.

He braced himself, concentrating only in her satisfaction. He didn't move his fingers further inside her body but rubbed her entrance and clitoris instead. She gasped and held his shoulders tighter before she opened her eyes wide and looked at him in awe.

He told himself that her surprised expression was reward enough for him, as he rubbed her faster and the first waves of pleasure hit her hard.

****

Keira didn't grasp the intensity of her emotions until that first wave hit her. She had climaxed before when she played with herself. The sensations Declan brought to her nerve endings were a million times stronger, more fulfilling. She wanted to keep staring into his gorgeous eyes, but the pleasure was too intense. She closed her eyes and her body rocked in rhythm with his movements.

She didn't see him move down her body and almost jumped out of her skin when he kissed her there. She tried to sit up but he held her in place with a big hand splayed on her navel.

"Declan! What are you doing?" she screeched. "You can't—you shouldn't do that."

"I can and I will. You relax and enjoy the ride."

He smiled at her before disappearing from her sight. She was too weak to resist and the sensations were too damn good. She decided not to argue with him. Instead, she let her head fall back on the pillows and enjoyed the pleasure he brought her. Each time the sensations ebbed away, Declan sucked harder or pushed his tongue further inside her and the waves came crashing down on her again. She moaned and thrust and heaved and he kept going.

****

Declan rejoiced in her ecstasy. Every time she sobbed and sighed in wonder, each time she whispered his name, he felt a correspondent rush of pleasure coursing through his veins. His problem was all that blood was rushing down his body, as it naturally would, and concentrating in his groin, but he wouldn't allow his body to find release under those circumstances.

He slowed down his rhythm, letting Keira's body come down from the heights he had taken her to, as he pressed a hand against himself, over his pants, calming his body. He plopped himself on the bed beside her, out of breath, watching Keira as her moans turned to soft sighs. She opened her eyes to stare into his, a deep crease formed between her eyebrows.

"What happened? Why did you stop?"

"You know why I stopped. I couldn't take you. Not like this."

He kissed the tip of her nose to take away the sting of his words. He knew he was hurting her, but the alternative would have been much worse, much more painful.

"Your first time shouldn't be in a hotel room, with a stranger, one day before you leave town. It wouldn't be fair to you. You deserve much more than this, bright eyes."

She closed her eyes and seemed to swallow hard.

"How can I argue with your logic or be mad at you when you're so sweet? Why did you have to be so sweet and noble? I wanted you. No, I *want* you. Doesn't that count?"

43

"Tonight, that doesn't count at all. You are vulnerable and lonely. You were drunk as a skunk up to a couple of hours ago. I can't trust your judgment," he said and laughed, then rubbed his nose against hers before kissing her swollen lips.

"You were willing to go all the way when you didn't know I was a virgin."

"If you weren't a virgin, and you were to regret our little adventure tomorrow, that would be the only thing you would regret."

"Meaning?"

"You would regret a drunken one-night stand with a stranger, not losing your virginity to an asshole you don't really know. I can be quite an ass—don't get me wrong—but I try to keep some boundaries. Taking advantage of a naïve tourist is one I never cross."

Her face clouded and he saw her eyes brimmed with held-back tears, which she disguised with an angry look.

"If that's how you feel, why don't you just leave already? I'm a stranger, right? A crazy, dumb American, huh? Go away! Leave!"

She sat on the bed, grabbed the sheets in front of her naked body, and pointed to the door. She was visibly holding her emotions in check by a very thin thread judging by the way her nostrils flared and her voice sounded. He decided to call her bluff and only stared back at her.

"Go!"

"I won't leave you like that. I'm not the bad guy, here. I won't leave you feeling miserable like this."

"I'm not feeling miserable. I'm pissed off, that's what I am, you asshole."

She punched him weakly in the chest and tried to free herself of his arms when he embraced her, but he was much stronger.

"Get your hands off of me! Haven't you done enough?"

44

"You don't fool me with this little act. I know you're hurt. Your eyes tell me so. I refuse to leave you alone like this, Keira. I need you to understand I did what was best for both of us."

His voice remained gentle, and the concern in his eyes deep. She caved in, buried her face in his smooth chest, crying and sobbing until she couldn't cry anymore. He held her close, running a soothing hand up and down her back. When she stopped crying, he pushed her away and lifted her chin until their eyes met.

"I didn't want to stop. I forced myself to stop because it was the right thing to do, hon. You have no idea how hard it was for me. I don't want you to leave Dublin, either. But, I think you should. Too much has happened, too fast. I'm not in the habit of picking up customers at the bar. Believe me!" he said. A shadow crossed her eyes, and he continued with more force, "I haven't felt attracted to a woman so fast in a long time. Hell, I think I've never felt anything so strong so fast. You obviously haven't, either."

He paused and waited for her reply.

"I haven't."

He held her chin when she tried to look down.

"Then, you must agree with me this is all too new and confusing for both of us, eh?" She nodded. "I suggest you take your vacation through Ireland as you had planned it. Go visit your great-grandparents' hometown. See as much of the country as you can, meet as many new people as you can. But leave off the last week to me, to us."

"How so?"

"Come back to Dublin for a whole week. We'll go out together, as a proper couple should do. I'll show you the town and you'll have a chance to know me better. I'll have a chance to know you, too. Then, we'll see where it takes us. How does that sound?"

Keira considered it for a while but kept staring into his eyes.

"I don't think a week will be enough for us to know each other. Maybe I should stay here for the whole vacation."

"That is absolutely out of the question, missy. Family always comes first. You owe this trip to your grandfather and to yourself."

She looked at him, her pupils dilated, her face flushed and he could almost hear the conflicting thoughts running around inside her head.

"You're right. But, I'll come back as soon as I can."

"Don't rush anything. If we're meant to be, we'll find our way back to each other. You'll see."

"Do you trust the luck of the Irish that much?"

"On the contrary, my sweet thing. I never had much luck. I hope you might be my lucky charm," he kissed her gently and stood up.

He felt her gaze following him around the room as he grabbed his torn shirt and put it on.

"I'm not so sure about that. Look at what I've done to your clothes."

"It was worth every button and then some."

He leaned to kiss her and things got very hot very fast again, so he reined his desire in and broke their hungry kiss, sighed, and rested his forehead against hers.

"I've got to go now or I'll never leave you. See you in two weeks."

"See you," she replied in a thin voice.

****

Keira's eyes followed Declan until he closed the door behind his broad shoulders. She buried her head under the pillows and tried to sleep but it eluded her. She replayed the last couple of hours in her head, trying to understand what had happened.

How could she trust a man she barely knew? She had been reckless. Her mother had always told her she should be more careful and Keira had always snapped back at her saying she knew what she was doing. Now, in her

46

first time away from home on her own she had gone and invited a stranger to her bed and begged him to make love to her.

Oh, but it felt so right!

Her body still tingled and new waves of pleasure surged inside her as she remembered Declan's tender kisses, his silken touch, and his strong arms around her trembling body. He had been so gentle and considerate. He hadn't forced her. In fact, he had been the one who stopped and came to his senses when she would have been only too happy going all the way. He had respected her and her feelings.

Declan was such a sweetheart, and Keira wondered if she could be falling in love with him so soon.

Only if you had fallen on your head as a baby! He's a total stranger. He could be a crook or a murderer, for all you know. Besides, he lives thousands of miles away from you. What are you thinking? the annoying voice in her head returned.

For once, Keira ignored her inner self and that was when she managed to fall asleep, with a sweet smile on her lips, and the memory of Declan's warmth to keep her company.

****

The next day, Declan got up earlier than usual, before six, feeling more energetic than he had in a long time. With his running gear on, he headed towards nearby St. Anne's Park. He loved jogging and the park gave him an excellent opportunity to relax and enjoy another rare, beautiful day in Dublin.

He had a lot to sort out and running had always given him a chance for thinking more clearly. Classic rock songs blasted from the earphones as the early morning cold air beat against his face. He picked up speed when he entered the park and let his mind and feelings run wild as well. Thoughts collided inside his head as the trees flew by him. He was falling fast for Keira—something very foolish to do. She had her life established across the ocean. She had a family who supported and encouraged her. She was young, naïve, and innocent.

While he was a struggling working-class young man with a horrible family history. Declan's personal history had left him with invisible, yet deep, scars. Life had made him cynical and distrustful. As a result, the strong attraction he felt for her innocence had caught him off-guard. Usually, he fell for more experienced, hardened women. Women who knew exactly what they should expect from a man like him. Keira was too sweet and wide-eyed.

Why the heck couldn't he keep his wits about him when she was around? His past relationships had ended badly, most of the times, which just added to his cynical views on women, relationships, and marriage. He didn't believe Keira could change that in the short run. Besides, he was probably on the rebound from his recent breakup with Jennifer. That should account for these strange feelings.

Declan checked his watch and found out he had exercised for more than an hour. Time to go back. He turned towards the park exit but his inner self decided to make a guest appearance. It bothered him more and more since he had met Keira.

Jennifer split up with you over a year ago. That is no excuse.

He ignored the warning and sped up the street. He was having second thoughts about the whole thing. He'd better keep his distance from Keira. There would be no future for them together, only more pain for him and bitter memories for her—not fair for either of them.

He got home, took a quick shower, and sat on his sofa. All that reminiscing left him with a bad taste in his mouth. He felt weak for wanting to talk to her again, but he couldn't avoid it. It was complicated.

It's screwed-up but I can't help it. It's going to be bad for me, I know, he told himself as he got his cell phone from his pocket and dialed her number.

She picked up fast, but sounded sleepy, "Hello?"

"Hey, Jen. It's me. Can I buy you breakfast?"

"Do you really think we should, Declan?"

"No, but I need my friend right now, not my ex. Can you be there for me?"

He heard muffled voices. She wasn't alone. He braced himself for the usual painful stab in his chest but nothing happened.

"Give me an hour. I'll meet you downtown," she said, then sighed. "Text me the address."

Jennifer was totally over him. Not only did she have a new boyfriend, but also she didn't remember their usual place. Declan refused to be hurt by that. He had told her he needed a friend. He had suffered enough over her. It was about time he set things straight, for his own peace of mind.

He took the train downtown and was halfway there when he remembered something. He just needed to do one more thing before he met with Jen. He picked up his cell phone and scrolled the address book for Keira's number.

* * * *

Declan got to the coffee shop a little before Jennifer and chose a table for them and they ordered as soon as she arrived. When the waiter left them alone and an awkward silence fell between them, Jen broke it first.

"Long time no see, Declan. What have you been up to?"

He looked at her for a moment and studied her face. She was as beautiful as always, but he didn't feel anything at all when he looked into her brown eyes. That was good. He smiled and took her hand in his.

"It's funny. I thought I'd be sad, or even regretful, when I saw you again. I feel neither. In fact, I don't feel anything."

"That's good. I don't want to see you suffer. I like you too much for that," she replied, smiling, as she pulled her hand away gently. "Now, you said you needed a friend. What's going on with you?"

49

Luck of the Irish

The waiter returned with their order and while Declan waited for him to finish serving, he told himself that since Jen was his oldest friend, she would understand his hesitations better than anyone. He hoped it wouldn't be too uncomfortable talking about his love life with her. Before they became lovers, Jen and Declan had been friends for a long time, since they were children, in fact. She had left Cork and moved to Dublin first and had welcomed him when he had decided to live in the capital. Jennifer had offered a haven to the frightened seventeen-year-old country boy he was then. He'd been a runaway trying to leave his past behind and hide away from his demons. He had crashed on her couch for almost six months until he found a decent place to live and a job to pay the rent.

During all those years of friendship, Jen had witnessed him at his worst and had never judged or condemned him. She could be tough with him whenever she thought he was wrong and she would tell him so without hesitation. That was why he'd thought she would be the perfect girlfriend. That was also why he had been devastated when it hadn't worked out, because he valued her friendship too much. Since it had taken them more than a year to have a normal conversation again, he had been right to fear the consequences of their breakup.

When the waiter left them alone, he asked, "Is it weird, Jen, that now I feel like we have never gone through that painful breakup? Is it only me, or do you feel that way too?"

"I feel it, too. When we split up, there was much more at stake than our romantic relationship—there was our friendship. Neither of us wanted to lose that, yet neither of us knew how to keep it."

"You're right. I guess we needed time apart to sort it out."

"Anyway, I love having my best friend back." She smiled and squeezed his hand. "So, why do you need your old buddy?"

50

"I met this gorgeous American the other day ..." Jen rolled her eyes. "Don't do that. I'm serious!"

"You're always serious when you meet a beautiful woman. Then you're excited, and finally, you get depressed when she takes your heart and tears it to pieces. I've seen it so many times, sweetie."

"This time it's different. I mean it. It feels different. But, your assessment is right—I've been down this road many times. That's why I wanted your input."

"Fair enough. I won't say another word until you finish telling me your story."

"Refrain from making faces as I tell it, too."

"That I can't promise you." She winked and he had to laugh.

It felt great having his best friend back. Declan told Jen about how he had met Keira, about the sudden and strong feelings he felt for her, and about his doubts and fears since any long-distance relationship could become quite complicated.

"She's leaving town today and will return in two weeks. I don't know what to do. I haven't felt this way in a long time."

After a long pause, when Jennifer played with her cup and didn't look at him, Declan felt uncomfortable.

"I'm not sure how I can help you with this Keira situation, Declan. It sounds pretty serious to me. I know you've just met her, but I don't remember you talking so enthusiastically about a woman you had just met. Granted, I said you do that often but, the truth is, it seems different this time."

"I know! I think so, too. But, don't you think I'm heading for disaster? I mean, we are literally an ocean apart."

"Well, that's something you'll have to work on together, when the time comes. It's too soon to say anything now. You need to know each other better.

She's travelling for the next two weeks, you say. So, why the rush? Why did you want to talk to me today?"

Declan blushed and looked down at his hands on the table, not knowing how to explain himself.

"Hey. What's the matter?" She put her hand on his arm. "What happened? I can't believe you're blushing. You're so adorable sometimes." She laughed.

His color got deeper and he made an effort to lift his eyes to hers. "I'm sorry. I'm an ass! I went jogging this morning, wanting to think this whole situation over. Naturally, when I did, I started having second thoughts. You know me."

She nodded and he continued, "Then, I convinced myself I was still on the rebound from our breakup, and that I shouldn't start a new relationship under these circumstances."

"Oh, come on! We broke up more than a year ago. That's just an excuse, you coward." She laughed louder, and slapped his arm playfully.

"That's what my conscience told me. That's why I decided it was about time we had a little chat, you and I. I wanted to be certain if I was over you or not."

When he stopped talking, she looked at him and raised an eyebrow. "Well, when you got here you said you didn't feel anything. That's a good thing, right?"

"Yes, it is. I'm relieved and I'm happy we had this conversation." He sighed and winked. "I just hope I can talk to Keira as easily as I talk to you."

"I doubt that. You've always had communication issues."

Although Declan knew she was right, he didn't want to go into that particular subject. "I noticed you weren't alone when I called this morning. Is it serious?"

She sighed and a dreamy expression came over her face. "We met at work and have been going out for a little over six months."

"You seem happy, Jen. I'm glad for you."

Their conversation turned to other subjects and, when they finished breakfast, they had patched up their friendship. Declan felt grateful that Jen had accepted his invitation. When they stepped outside to say their goodbyes, it felt natural for both of them to hug.

"I really want you to be happy, Declan. You deserve that." She squeezed his arm "You do, sweetie! Don't ever doubt that you deserve happiness." She gave him a chaste kiss on the lips as if trying to make him feel better.

She turned around to go to her office and he ran to cross the street when the pedestrian light flashed red. He needed to take the bus to work and he didn't want to be late. He felt excited and hopeful for the first time in a long while. All of a sudden, life seemed to offer him lots of good opportunities.

* * * *

Keira woke up feeling horrible. She had the worst hangover, which she wasn't used to having. She opened one eye with difficulty to check the time—almost eight in the morning. She had to get up, pack, and hit the road. Once out of bed, she stumbled towards the bathroom, washed her face, and looked in the mirror. She barely recognized herself—puffy and red eyes, dirty and messy hair, and swollen lips. As Keira took a shower, she relived the events of the night before. Her life-long insecurities kicked in and she concluded she was out of her mind for thinking she had a real shot at a guy like Declan. She certainly hadn't gotten it right. He wasn't into her. He wouldn't be interested in an ordinary-looking American virgin if he could have any Irish beauty he wanted.

Although she wasn't hungry, she went down for breakfast and forced herself to eat, because she needed her strength for her road trip. Everything tasted like cardboard. Besides, she had a lump in her throat, which she fought to control because she wouldn't let anything ruin her vacation. Not even a pair of gorgeous green eyes. Every time she remembered Declan's eyes, the lump felt bigger.

When she returned to the bedroom, her phone was beeping, telling her she had received a new text message. Her heart skipped a few beats when she saw Declan's name on the screen. She hesitated to open it because she didn't want to confirm her suspicions. He was probably apologizing for the previous night, and saying he couldn't keep their appointment in two weeks. She couldn't read it. Like a coward, she locked the screen again and stowed the phone away in her back pocket.

Keira headed downstairs again, then checked-out and asked the clerk to call a taxi. At the nearest car rental, she got a car and was on her way in no time. She stopped at a traffic light and looked around, admiring the beautiful old buildings that surrounded her. Her thoughts went back to her career choices as she analyzed a quaint little coffee shop at the corner. She should take up architecture. As she stared, a couple left the building and hugged for a while. The woman kissed the man before they went their separate ways. The traffic light was about to change so the man sprinted towards the other side of the road, passing right in front of Keira's car. Her heart sank inside her chest like an anchor when she recognized Declan.

"Son of bitch! He never told me he had a girlfriend!"

* * * *

CHAPTER 3

You never asked, that annoying voice inside her head reminded her, but Keira ignored it, as she tried to shift into first gear, when the driver behind her honked because the light had turned green and she hadn't moved. She didn't know how to drive a stick shift and the bitter tears of anger welling up in her eyes didn't help, either. She wiped them away and focused her attention on mastering the damn car and GPS system. However, when she got to the road, there was no escaping her accusing conscience. *I told you that you were a fool to believe he meant what he said. Did you see the woman? She's gorgeous.*

Keira hated to admit that she was jealous. She was and there was nothing she could do about it. Although she drove through beautiful countryside, she saw none of it—her thoughts and feelings were chaotic. Her insecurities got the best of her and she convinced herself it was better to find out who he was from the beginning. After all, nothing serious had happened between them, which meant she could get over Declan easily and quickly. At twenty-two, she had her life ahead of her. So, why did a painful pang in her chest make it so hard to breathe? Maybe getting over him wouldn't be that easy. On the other hand, Keira was a resolute woman. "Stubborn as a mule" would be her mom's definition for her. She would manage.

After around forty minutes, Keira got to her first destination, Wicklow, where she had planned to stay for three nights in order to go hiking and sightseeing. The beautiful area was perfect for those kinds of activities. Guided by her driving app, she found the little B&B without any incident. The house was a masterpiece in stone dating from the early eighteenth century, and the surrounding countryside looked peaceful and lush.

Luck of the Irish

The owners greeted Keira when she entered the front hall—a lovely elderly couple who made her feel at home right away.

"Hello, my dear. I'm Sylvia, and this is my husband, John. Welcome to Burtonderry House," said the silver-haired lady. She wore a spotless white apron. "I'm in charge of the kitchen, as you can see from my outfit," she added with a self-mocking expression. "While John, here, takes care of the rooms and leisure activities."

"Nice to meet you both. I'm Keira. I've made a reservation for three nights."

"Yes, yes, my dear. We were expecting you." John bent and took her bags. "Come this way. I'll show you to your room."

"See you in a bit, Keira. Lunch will be served in half an hour," Sylvia shouted as they walked away and up a beautiful wooden staircase that led to the guest rooms. When John opened the door to her room, she felt like a little girl again.

"Oh, my gosh! I've always wanted a bedroom like this." She giggled. "It's like a fairytale bedroom." She ran a hand over the soft fabric of the curtains that hung around the canopy bed.

John smiled at her childish enthusiasm before putting her bags beside the armchair on the corner. "Glad you like it. There's a phone over there. Dial zero if you need anything."

She held out her hand to give him a tip, but he smiled and closed his calloused hand over hers.

"There's no need for tipping us, Keira. We love sharing our home with our guests. Your money is good here only for the room and fare, nothing more."

"Thank you, sir. It's very kind of you and your wife."

"Please, call me John. I'm old enough to be your grandfather, but I don't like formalities, especially where beautiful lasses are concerned." He gave her a playful wink, then left her alone.

56

She smiled for the first time that day, while she put her bag on the bed and got fresh clothes. It would be nice to take a walk around the place after lunch. When she took off her jeans and tossed them on the bed, her cell phone fell from the pocket, bounced off the mattress, and landed on the floor with a thud. The thick carpet prevented any damage and she stared at her phone as if it were a reptile, remembering she hadn't opened Declan's text message.

Don't be a wuss. Read it already! Postponing the inevitable will only make it worse.

She summoned her courage, took the cell phone, and opened his short message, "Miss you already, gorgeous. See you in fifteen days."

Keira's face got red with rage. How could he be so cynical? The lying, cheating bastard sent her a message while having breakfast with another woman. She threw the phone back on the bed and left the room, fuming. She stomped her feet as she climbed down the wooden stairs, and as soon as she noticed, made an effort to control her temper.

When she got to the dining room, which was a small room with eight square tables, six guests were already enjoying their lunch. She chose an empty table and, as she sat down, Sylvia came towards her with a plate full of salad and a small basket of freshly baked bread on a large tray. She settled the food in front of Keira with a smile.

"Enjoy, dear. I'll bring the rest as soon as you finish."

"It smells so good," she replied, taking a slice of bread from the basket and spreading butter on it. "Thank you."

"My pleasure."

Keira thought she wouldn't eat anything, because her throat was so tight, but she ended up devouring the meal. Everything tasted delicious. She hadn't had such good food since she had left her parents' home for college. When she had eaten the last crumbs from the generous slice of chocolate cake that Sylvia had served as dessert, Keira smiled and pushed the plate away.

"Thank you, Sylvia. That was the best meal I've had in a very long time. I need to watch my weight around here."

"Thank you, dear," Sylvia replied, as she took the dirty tableware away. "Don't worry about getting fat, though, you're so skinny."

"Nevertheless, I'd like to take a walk around to burn some calories."

"Walking around is a good idea. This area is very beautiful. Enjoy."

Keira explored the extensive property with its gardens, hills, beautiful orchard, and some small farm animals scattered on the fields and over the hills. She thought the one-hour walk would help take her mind off Declan. It didn't.

She went back to her room to search online for a local travel agency. That area had many options, and acting on an impulse, Keira chose a more adventurous agency that offered a rock climbing and rappelling package.

I hope the adrenalin gets my good mood back so I can enjoy my vacation better.

She spent the following day, alongside a small group of people who had booked the same tours, hanging from ropes and conquering steep climbs. When she got back to the inn, she was exhausted, but proud of herself. She took a long bath to relax her sore muscles before going down to have dinner.

"Did you have a nice time today, my dear?" Sylvia asked.

"Oh, it was the best. I went rock climbing and rappelling. I met a bunch of interesting people, too."

"Any particular lad worth mentioning?"

Keira blushed before lowering her eyes to her plate.

"I don't know about that."

"Oh, so you have a boyfriend. What happened? Did he get cold feet at the last minute? He shouldn't have left a beautiful woman traveling alone through a foreign country."

"I don't have a boyfriend."

"Then, that's a shame. I hope the Irish men can change that for you," Sylvia winked. "They are very talented, you know."

Keira's face turned a deeper shade of red and she offered the other woman a shy smile before Sylvia turned away and went back to the kitchen, laughing.

She is so nice that I can't be angry at her. Besides, why do I have to be so shy?

Keira finished the meal in record time and returned to her room before the other guests showed up for dinner.

Her cell phone rang as she entered her room, and she answered it without checking the number—which was a mistake, she realized, when she heard Declan's voice.

"Hey, gorgeous. I haven't heard from you since you left Dublin. Are you all right?"

She hesitated and considered hanging up but her natural good manners didn't allow her to be rude. She took a deep breath, "I'm fine, thanks." She sounded cold even to her ears.

"Ouch! What happened, Keira? You didn't answer my text or return my calls. You sound colder than the Arctic. Why is that? Are you having second thoughts about us?"

She considered his question for a brief while and decided it gave her the perfect opportunity to avoid future heartache, "To be honest, Declan, I'm not having second thoughts. I'm not in doubt at all." She paused when she heard his sigh of relief and a sly smile played on her lips as she continued. "Actually, I'm sure this is not going to work. It was a huge mistake. I'm sure you can understand why and I guess you'll be relieved I'm letting you off the hook. Goodbye."

"Keira, wait! Don't hang ..."

She ignored his pleas and hung up the phone, shut it off, then sat in the armchair by the window feeling proud of herself, which lasted for less than a few minutes. The time it took for her treacherous heart to flip inside her chest and the damn butterflies to return to her stomach. She ignored those symptoms and looked outside the window.

It was such a gorgeous place. She loved that kind of rural landscape. Why the heck couldn't she appreciate it? With her eyes closed, she leant her head back against the headrest and lost sense of time. Two nagging questions went round and round inside her head—what if he was the one? Was she giving up on Declan too soon, and without a fight?

* * * *

Miles away, Declan stared at the phone in his hand, unable to believe Keira had hung up on him. He had a deep crease between his eyebrows, but the dead phone wouldn't give him the answers he wanted, the answers he needed. He tried her number again but wasn't surprised when his calls went straight to voicemail. He sent her another text message.

"I don't know what's happened to make you change your mind. I'd love a chance to hear your reasons and explain myself. You're upset and I feel responsible, even though I have no earthly idea of what I might have done to you since we last saw each other. Please, don't shut me out."

After pressing the send button, he could only wait and pray she would give him a chance. He hated feeling helpless.

* * * *

Early next morning, Keira woke up with a gasp and sat on the bed, startled. Her hazy mind took some time to remember where she was. Her face got hot with embarrassment when snippets of a very vivid dream came to mind. She looked down and noticed the bed sheets, and her clothes, were drenched. They clung to her body because her skin was covered in sweat.

In the steamy dream, Declan had made love to her—thoroughly and without haste. Granted, she was a virgin, but the sensations he had showed her in Dublin had given her creative imagination a lot of material to work with. Her body had responded promptly. Her muscles still tingled from the recent, very intense orgasm she'd experienced in the dream.

Oh, my! I'm doomed. She plopped back on the pillows and covered her face with her hands. *I can't control my dreams. I can't control my body. What do I do?*

Her body relaxed gradually as the last waves of pleasure ebbed away, taking with them the tension she had accumulated in the last couple of days. She couldn't deny she felt wonderfully calmer, but that didn't change the fact that Declan had kissed another woman and then pretended nothing had happened.

I can't trust him.

After a much needed shower, she went downstairs to have breakfast. Because she was the only guest, Sylvia had a chance to chat as she served Keira's food.

"You're an early bird, dear. What are you up to today?"

"I'll go hiking and won't be back until late in the afternoon."

"Sounds fun. Thank you for letting me know you'll be out. I worry about my guests."

Keira smiled at the woman's sincere concern, "I know you do. But you shouldn't. I mean, what could happen to me in such a quiet and peaceful place?"

"You never know. There're crazy people everywhere. You're a sweet girl who reminds me of my daughter. I want to be sure you're having a good time, but that you're safe, too."

Keira reached out and squeezed the old lady's hand.

"That's very sweet, but don't worry. I've booked a tour with a local agency. They'll send a van to pick me up and there'll be guides, and other people. I'll be fine."

She went upstairs to get ready, and heard the van parking while she laced up her sneakers. Not wanting to make people wait for her, Keira rushed down the stairs, leaving her phone in the room. She realized it as she sat down on her seat but didn't feel she could go back for it.

The day went by quickly and Keira had a great time with the small group guided by a young Scottish woman, who knew everything there was to know about the Wicklow Mountains. By the end of the day, when the van dropped her off at the B&B, Keira's head was still spinning with everything she had learned, while her body was deliciously sore from the intense hiking. She went straight to her room to rest before dinner.

After dinner, she read before sleeping, which was an old habit of hers. Keira loved reading all kinds of books but had recently discovered erotica. In the past, she used to think these books weren't worth her time because they didn't have literary value. She was surprised to learn there were actually good authors writing hot, kinky stories and that there were well-known writers, who published erotica under pen names, to avoid public criticism or in order not to antagonize their regular readers, despite their books being good.

She finished the steamy short-story and went to sleep hoping Declan would stay out of her thoughts. She wasn't that lucky. He haunted her dreams again and once more she woke up with a start, out of breath, and trembling with yet another powerful sexual release.

"Seriously?!" she said aloud, as she got out of bed and stumbled across the room to the bathroom. Her legs felt wobbly, her throat dry, and her head faint as erotic images popped up in her mind.

She splashed her face with cold water, returned to the room, and sat on the bed. The alarm clock showed six in the morning. Still too early to get up, but she didn't want to go back to sleep and risk having more disturbing dreams. Besides, she had a long day ahead of her because she was going to drive to Waterford, stopping at Wexford.

She went downstairs for breakfast, and was the only guest in the dining room. She invited Sylvia to sit down with her to keep her company.

"I'll miss you and John, you know? I had a wonderful time here."

"You're very kind, my child, but if I can be honest with you, you don't seem like you had a good time at all. You've got a shadow darkening your face. It's so sad to see that."

"Don't worry. I'll be just fine."

They talked about trivial stuff as Keira finished her meal.

Only when she returned to her room, did Keira remember she hadn't turned her phone back on since Declan called two nights ago. She hurriedly turned it on again, only to find many missed calls. Two from her parents, one from her sister, and seven from Declan. She rolled her eyes and played the voice messages.

"Hey, honey. How are you doing? We haven't heard from you since you told us the concert had been canceled. Are you feeling any better? How is the road trip going? Call us when you have a chance. Your father and I worry about you. Drive safely! Bye, sweetie."

She smiled as she listened to her mother's voice. She considered calling home, but remembered it was too early to call her family in Boston. Ireland was five hours ahead, so she decided she would call them when she got to Waterford.

The next message was from her sister, "Hey. I called just to check up on you, but I guess you must be sleeping. It's late in Ireland. You should be out having fun and getting hammered with a couple of new friends. That was the plan, remember? Having a blast?" Her sister laughed before adding, "Anyway, call me! Tell me you've met a handsome Irishman who's swept you off your feet. Or just call me because I miss you, little brat. Bye."

She smiled at her sister's good mood. She had always wished she were more like her in that aspect. *Who am I kidding? I've always wanted to be more like her—end of story.*

Keira loved her sister deeply, but she felt a little intimidated by Megan's beauty and independence. Now, she wished Megan were there to help her, listen to her, and give some advice.

There were no more voice messages. She frowned, then realized Declan had sent her a text message instead of leaving voice mail. When she read it, Keira felt that familiar feeling as her stomach summersaulted. She could be stubborn, but she had always taken great pride in her ability to be fair, *I have to agree with him I didn't give him a chance to explain himself.*

Her inner self returned with a vengeance. *You didn't let him explain anything because you were afraid he'd convince you to change your mind. Judging from your recent dreams, you can't trust yourself where Declan is concerned. If you let him talk you into forgiving him, you'll open up yourself to more pain.*

Keira hesitated and almost gave in to that annoying version of Jiminy Cricket. When she checked her watch, she saw it was around two in the morning in Boston. She decided to call Megan, because her sister rarely went to sleep early. She picked up before the third ring.

64

"Hey, little sis. What's up?"

"Not much, big sis. I just wanted to hear your voice."

"At two in the morning? Yeah, right! What's wrong?"

"Oh, there's nothing wrong."

Her sister sighed loudly. "Keira, you know I hate it when you do that. It's obvious there's something bothering you, otherwise you wouldn't call me at this time. Spill it!"

She took a deep breath and told her older sister all about Declan—how they had met, how they had hooked up in her room in Dublin, what she had seen the next morning, their last phone call, his text messages, and the sensual dreams—everything.

"How do you feel about him?" Megan asked.

"I don't know."

"Bullshit. Listen, you've got be honest with yourself, at least. Think about it. If he were just another guy, would you be that annoyed? Would you feel so sad because of a potential betrayal? Would you have let him under your skin like that?"

"Potential betrayal? How do you mean?"

"Honey, you saw what you saw, but you have no idea who the woman is or what kind of relationship they have—if they have any."

"Oh, so people go kissing and hugging total strangers in public. Is that what you're saying?"

"Don't twist my words, little brat. And don't lash out at me. You've asked my opinion, I've given you that. I'm sorry if you don't like what you hear. You can't be sure of anything until he tells you what happened that morning."

"You're right. I'm sorry. How can I be sure he's telling me the truth?"

"You can't. Until you know him better, you can't be sure of anything. That's true for any new relationship—friends or lovers. You're not that naïve, are you?"

"I hate to admit it, but you know me better than myself."

"Don't whine and pout, little one. I've known you longer than you've known yourself, that's all." Megan laughed before adding in a serious tone, "Keira, I do know you and that's why I trust your instincts and good sense. But, when the heart is in charge, things can get complicated. We can make stupid decisions. Promise me you'll be safe."

"I will, Megan, don't worry."

"Call me if you need anything, all right?"

"Will do. Go to sleep, now. It's late. Talk to you soon."

"Bye."

Keira checked the time and considered calling Declan before she left Wicklow, but decided she'd better get going if she wanted to spend some time driving around Wexford and seeing the sights, before continuing to Waterford. She'd call Declan when she got there. That would give her time to mull things over, including her sister's advice.

* * * *

The trip from Wicklow to Wexford was quite an easy one. She did a little sightseeing around town before finding a nice pub to have lunch at. Her grandfather used to talk about Wexford all the time because her great-grandmother was born nearby, in a small village called Kilmore. Keira found the little town and drove around its narrow streets, trying to picture what it would have looked like over a hundred years ago.

After leaving Kilmore, she headed towards Waterford. The trip shouldn't have taken much more than an hour but the car broke down. She'd been barely able to pull over by the side of the road before the car stopped moving. The area had no cell phone service, so calling a breakdown company or the rental car service wasn't possible.

She got out of the car, trying to see further up or down the road, to find out there wasn't much around her for miles. She worried when she couldn't

66

remember when she had last seen any sign of civilization along the way. She didn't know if she would find help walking back and she had no idea what lay ahead. A couple of cars passed by, but she was afraid of hailing one. She had watched too many scary films to trust strangers driving on semi-remote roads.

For lack of a better alternative, she decided to walk up the road, try to find a spot where her phone would have service, and call the rental car company's emergency number. After walking for over ten minutes, her phone remained dead and the sun hid behind heavy clouds. Afternoon turned slowly into evening. In no time, thin tendrils of fog appeared around her, enveloping her and hiding the landscape behind white curtains. The first signs of panic kicked in as a car pulled over behind her.

When the driver turned the engine off, she glanced over her shoulder and saw a couple inside a dark pickup truck. She stopped walking and turned around when the door opened. The woman, in her mid-fifties, climbed out from the passenger seat and stopped beside the car, as if she were afraid of Keira, as well.

That should be a good sign. If they meant to hurt me, she would be more forward. Right?

"Is the white car back there yours, child? Do you need a lift somewhere?"

"It broke down, but it's a rental. I meant to call the company's emergency number." She pointed to her cell phone. "But I can't get service. I was walking up the road trying to find a better spot to make the call."

The woman smiled and her features relaxed.

"I'm afraid you won't get cell service for the next ten miles or so. I'm Mary Wilkinson, by the way. That's Ted, my husband. We can give you a ride to our farm. It isn't far. You can use the landline there to call the rental company."

Keira hesitated, thinking that it might not be a good idea to get inside a stranger's car in the middle of nowhere when evening was coming down fast. On the other hand, walking aimlessly in the dark seemed a much worse option.

"Thank you, Mrs. Wilkinson."

She walked towards the truck and climbed inside it after the woman. After a less-than-five-minute drive, they arrived at the farm. The big stone building impressed her, and it seemed to have endured centuries of bad weather. The house looked beautiful and she finally relaxed when she saw the place was in good shape and that other people were busy at work there.

They entered the house through the backdoor, which opened to the kitchen, and Mary took her to a small den. A roaring fire blazed in the fireplace and an old-fashioned telephone sat on a side table, by a large window, overlooking a beautifully designed rose garden.

"You have a wonderful home."

"Thank you. There's the phone, Keira. I'll give you some privacy." She turned away and went out, but left the door ajar.

Not wanting to abuse the Wilkinsons' hospitality, Keira phoned the rental company, told them what had happened, and gave them the address to the farm.

"We'll send a tow truck to pick up you and the car as soon as possible. The driver will take you to your final destination, miss. Where were you heading?"

"Waterford."

"Where are you staying there?"

"At St. Joseph's B&B."

"Very well, miss. Tomorrow morning you can get a new car at our office in Waterford."

"Thank you. Good night."

"Good night."

Actually, the truck arrived at the farm in a little over forty minutes, but already had her car in tow. The driver pulled over in front of the Wilkinsons' house and climbed out to greet her. He looked young, not much older than Keira, and all of a sudden she felt uncomfortable.

"You must be the damsel in distress. I'm your knight in shining armor, milady, but you can call me Paul O'Hallon." He walked towards her with a big smile on his face, and his hand out to shake hers.

Keira didn't know why she felt an impulse to ignore it but she wouldn't be rude.

"Hello, Paul. I'm Keira Ashe." She gave his hand a brief shake and stepped back when he came to stand too close to her. "Can you drop me off at St. Joseph's B&B in Waterford?"

Even though Keira had already arranged that with the car rental company, for some reason, she wanted the Wilkinsons to know where he was taking her.

"My pleasure, milady," he answered, bowing and winking at her.

He opened the passenger door for her, and Keira turned to the Wilkinsons. "Thank you again for helping me."

"Don't mention it."

"Have a safe trip," Mrs. Wilkinson said.

"Goodbye."

Keira walked to the tow truck and tried to climb in even though the cabin was a little high for her. With a foot on the running board, she moved to boost herself up when a pair of strong hands seized her tiny waist from behind, lifting her in the air and settling her down on the passenger seat. Paul let his hands linger on her a second or two more than necessary. Keira frowned at him but he gave her a wide, apologetic grin and bowed his head.

"A lady shouldn't have to do this by herself. I'm here to help you."

He closed the door, with yet another wink, and climbed behind the wheel. In no time, they returned to the road, heading for Waterford.

"So, first time in Ireland?"

"Yes, it is."

"Are you traveling alone?"

"Actually, I'm meeting up with friends in Waterford."

Inexplicably, she felt an impulse to lie. Paul was friendly and polite yet it didn't seem wise telling a stranger that she was traveling around the country by herself. He nodded and kept his attention on the dark, deserted road. Keira took the opportunity to study his profile. He was a good-looking young man whose job consisted of helping people out. She was the one at fault. She should be more grateful and stop acting like a frightened little mouse. Her mother had told her so many times to be careful during her adventure in Ireland that she felt over cautious. Maybe Paul was just another nice, helpful Irishman trying to get her out of a bad situation. She sighed and shook her head to get rid of her gloomy fears.

"What about you? Are you from around here?"

"From Limerick, actually. I moved here a few years ago."

He gripped the wheel tighter without looking at her. The winding road, made slippery by the light-falling rain, required his full attention and it relieved Keira that he kept his eyes on the road while talking to her.

"Is there anything interesting for me to see in Limerick?"

That was the right question to ask, because Paul's face lit up, "Oh, yeah! There's plenty to see, milady. Limerick is the best city in the world."

Ask any Irish about their hometown, and they'll fill your ears with stories about it, Keira thought as she observed his enthusiasm.

Paul spent the rest of their ride describing the sights, the cultural events, and the places she should visit in Limerick. He also told her stories about his

70

childhood and his huge family. When he pulled over in front of the B&B, she felt like she had known him for most of her life. She got out of the truck before he reached her side and he got her baggage from the trunk, taking it to the B&B's lobby.

"Here you are. What time should I pick you up tomorrow?"

"Pick me up? What for?"

"To take you to our office."

"Oh, don't worry about that. I'll take a taxi. Thanks, though."

"Nonsense. It's no big deal. I live nearby and I'll have to take the car there tomorrow, anyway."

He made a reasonable point, and she had gotten more comfortable around him, but she didn't want to be a burden. "Thank you so much, Paul, but there's no need for that."

He looked disappointed but didn't insist. "I think it's goodbye, then." He grabbed one of her hands in both of his. "I don't suppose you'd give me your phone number, either, would you?"

"I don't think it's a good idea." She blushed, looked down at her feet, and added, "My boyfriend is a very jealous guy."

He laughed and pretended to be scared. "Whoa! We don't want him smashing my face up, do we? I'd better be going. Take care."

"You, too."

By the time she got to her room, she felt so exhausted that she forgot about calling her parents or Declan. She took a shower, to wash away the weariness, and slept until eight in the morning.

After a delicious breakfast, she took a taxi to the car rental office. While she signed the papers, Paul pulled the tow truck over, with the broken car still on top of it. He waved at her but didn't approach, and she nodded back in reply.

Luck of the Irish

When the clerk gave her the keys to the new rental car, Keira looked around to say goodbye to Paul, but he wasn't there. She shrugged, got inside the car, and drove away. She had booked a tour with a local agency, so she drove there, and spent the rest of the day visiting interesting places, including Admore and St. Declan's stone. Keira did her best not to let the stone's name remind her of the man.

* * * *

Declan checked his phone for the thousandth time that day. He wasn't surprised to find there were no missed calls or messages from Keira. It had been three days since they'd last spoken. In fact, three whole days, and three miserable nights, since she had hung up on him. He had called and sent messages but hadn't gotten any replies. He was worried sick, and couldn't sleep or concentrate on anything.

Irish roads could be quite dangerous. Besides, she was a young woman traveling alone. All sorts of things could go wrong in a situation like that. She could have gotten involved in an accident. After all, they drove on the wrong side of the road in America. The car could have broken down, in the middle of nowhere. Maybe she had a flat tire, and didn't know how to change it. She could have been mugged or worse. He ran his fingers through his already messed up hair, as the gloomy thoughts went round in his head, and he added up the bill for table ten for the third time. He got yet another number and smashed the paper in frustration.

She may have found another man. Someone better than you, his conscience poked fun at him and the blood drained from his face. His hand trembled slightly as he stared at the numbers on the new slip of paper without seeing anything.

"Earth to Declan," called Harry behind him, tapping on his shoulder.

"What's up?" he asked, pretending he was busy with the bill.

72

"How difficult can it be to add up two pints of Guinness and an order of chips?"

Declan's face flushed violently and Harry just laughed louder as he yanked the paper from his coworker's dead fingers.

"Oh, give me that, will you? You've been pretty useless for the last couple of days or so, you know? I mean, more useless than you normally are." Harry's playful tone turned to sincere concern before he asked, "What's going on, mate?"

Declan felt tempted to tell Harry about his worries but changed his mind.

"There's nothing wrong. I'm just tired. I haven't been sleeping well, that's all."

"Well, I don't buy it but I won't push you. If you need to talk, you know where to find me—right here behind the bar." He laughed and handed the bill back to Declan. "There you go. Now, take it to table ten and get the hell out of here. It's almost eight and your shift is about to finish, anyway. Go home earlier and get some rest, if that's what you need."

"Do you mean it?"

"Yeah, it'll be fine. It's a slow night and Màire will be here soon. Shoo. Go."

Declan smiled and followed his friend's suggestion. Just as he arrived home, his phone rang—in the ringtone he'd set for Keira, so he picked up quickly. He smiled when he saw she had started a video call. He'd missed her and it would be great to see her face again, even if only on video. She looked worried, though.

"Hey. Are you all right?"

"We need to talk," was her curt reply and his heart skipped more than a couple of beats.

"I know that. Which is why I've been calling you for the past three days. I'm worried sick. What happened?"

She looked thoughtful for a moment or two, "I'm fine. I'll tell you everything later. We need to talk about something else, first."

"I'm relieved just to hear your voice and see your face again. Are you going to tell me what that was all about? I mean, last time we talked? Why did you hang up on me?"

She closed her eyes. When she spoke, her words came out all in a rush, as though she wanted to get the words said as fast as possible. "On my last day in Dublin, I went to the car rental to get a car. While I drove out of town, I had to stop at a traffic light in front of this quaint little coffee shop. It was so lovely that it distracted me from the GPS I was trying to figure out. Then, I saw a beautiful young couple hugging and kissing when they left the building. The gorgeous woman turned and went away while the guy ran past my car, crossing the street. That was you, Declan! Why were you having breakfast with another woman the morning after you almost made love to me? After you asked me to go back to Dublin to give us a chance to get to know each other better. Why were you kissing her? Why did you do that to me?" Her voice broke off and she looked as though she had to make an effort to keep tears from falling.

Declan felt as if his heart weighed a ton inside him. What were the odds of Keira running into him at that particular moment? Was the universe conspiring against them? Was that a sign their relationship was doomed? Was it some kind of cruel trial the gods of love had conceived to test their resolve? Or was it his usual bad luck? He took a deep breath and put his sincerity and his feelings into his voice. He needed Keira to believe him.

"I wish I were beside you to look you straight in the eyes so you'd see the truth in mine. I guess this video call will have to do the trick. Jennifer is a very old and dear friend. I needed advice and she agreed to meet me for coffee."

"You kissed and hugged her. Do you kiss all your friends on the lips like that?"

"She's my oldest friend, Keira."

"So?" She raised an eyebrow at him.

That was a bad sign and he felt afraid she would be mad at him when she learned that he'd met with an ex-girlfriend. That was why he'd avoided the issue, but his explanations so far hadn't been enough. He hesitated before deciding she needed to hear the whole story. At least, the whole story regarding Jennifer.

"You deserve to know everything, but please, listen to me first. Let me tell you the whole story before jumping to conclusions. Is that all right?"

Keira just nodded.

"I've known Jennifer all my life. We grew up together. My brothers and I went through some pretty rough times when we were kids, which I intend to tell you all about, by the way, but I'd rather do it in person. Do you agree?"

"Yes."

He relaxed, because she sounded less distant and cold.

"Anyway, Jennifer was always there for me and helped me through a great deal. She also stood by me the first times I had my heart broken by girlfriends. Come to think of it, she did so every time, actually," he said with a laugh, and it sounded a little bitter. "She would offer her shoulder for me to cry on, some advice to help me get back on my feet, and wouldn't hesitate to kick my ass if I kept the pity party going for too long. Later, when she moved to Dublin, I was devastated. When things in my house got unbearable, I decided to try my luck in Dublin, and she offered me a roof and food for over six months until I was able to be on my own."

He stopped and waited for Keira to say something. When she didn't, he continued, "Well, you see, I kept trying to have a stable relationship with one girlfriend after another, and got disappointed every time. One day, I had the stupid idea that dating my best friend would be the answer. Up to this day, I don't know why the usually smart and sensible Jennifer agreed with me. We dated for a short while. It didn't work out and we almost destroyed our lifelong friendship in the process. She broke up with me, more than a year ago, and that morning was the first time we'd met since the break-up."

Keira seemed to ponder his story, but she took so long to do it that Declan worried. He thought the screen had frozen, or something. Then he saw her blinking and pushing her glasses up the bridge of her nose. Chills ran up and down his spine, because already he knew she did that when she felt nervous.

"Keira, say something, please. You're freaking me out."

"Why did you call her that morning? Why did you need her advice?"

This part of the story was potentially disastrous. He said a silent prayer, and hoped for the best before telling Keira the truth. "I got cold feet. I went jogging early that morning and started thinking about us—about the things we had going against us. I panicked."

Keira's face fell. "I knew it. You've got second thoughts, too."

"No, no. I *had* them. Past tense." Then her meaning sank in. "What do you mean by 'too'? Are *you* having second thoughts?"

It was his turn to get pale as her face got red. Keira seemed to struggle with her feelings. He had noticed her little insecurities before, but in that moment they were crystal clear. He saw when she took a deep breath before speaking.

"I was. Past tense, too. I called my sister, before I left Wicklow, and talked to her. She helped me see I had let my insecurities get the better of me when I jumped to conclusions. She pointed out that I hadn't heard your side of the story before calling you a cheating bastard."

"Ouch! That was mean."

He offered a bright smile in an attempt to lighten the mood. It worked. Keira smiled back. It was a shy smile as she pushed her glasses up her nose again. She was clearly uncomfortable.

"You can see why I thought so, though, can't you?"

"Yes, actually, I can, love." Although she kept a straight face, she looked to have softened a teeny bit. Declan continued, "I'd have done exactly the same. No, strike that. I would surely have done worse. I'd have punched the guy until I had rearranged his face."

Keira's jaw dropped and she stared at him in horror.

"That sounds horrible. How could you attack another person like that?"

Declan regretted his bluster, "I was just saying it. We Irish love to talk like that, but we're peaceful people. I wouldn't harm another person. Ever. I saw too many people getting hurt when I was too young to understand anything. I have a deep repulsion for violence. You'll understand it once I tell you about my childhood."

She studied his face and seemed satisfied with what she saw in his eyes. "I believe you." She gave him a sly smile before adding, "So, let me see if I got this right. You invited your ex-girlfriend out to ask advice about me. Is that it?"

His face burned. "It sounds awful when you say it like that, but that was pretty much what I did. Luckily, she gave me good advice."

Keira laughed. "What did she tell you to do?"

Declan's hopes lifted again and he smiled as his dark green eyes sparkled. "She told me to stop being an ass and go after the best thing that had ever happened to me."

"And what was that exactly?"

Keira smiled and the playful glint in her blue eyes made him wish he were there to kiss her until they were both out of breath. His eyes got darker and Keira seemed to read the intentions in their depths, because her own eyes got wider and her nostrils trembled a bit.

"You. You are the best thing that's happened to me."

Keira flicked her gaze downward—her cheeks burned. Declan decided to change the subject.

"Enough about me, love." His million-watt smile made a comeback. "How about your trip? Are you having fun?"

"Everything was perfect up until I left Wexford."

"Why? What happened?"

"Oh, it's a long story. Forget about it."

"No, you sound bummed out. I want to know what happened. Besides, I've got absolutely nothing better to do than look into your beautiful face and hear your heavenly voice," he said with an exaggerated, comical tone.

She rolled her eyes and told him what had happened during her trip, "Well, the trip to Wexford was quite easy. I stopped there because my great-grandmother was born in Kilmore—a tiny town. By mid-afternoon, I'd seen everything, at least twice. People started to eye the car from Dublin with suspicion."

"That's never a good sign." Declan winked.

"You bet! I thought they'd send the Garda after me." Keira's eyes sparkled with the memories. "After Kilmore, I started out towards Waterford, but the car broke down."

"I knew it. I knew something bad had happened. I should've done something."

"You couldn't have done anything. It was a mechanical problem. The engine sputtered for a mile or so. I crossed my fingers hoping to reach a gas station, but the car went completely dead before I got to one."

"What did you do? Did you call for help?"

"Well, there weren't any stores or houses around and the phone wasn't working."

"That's just great. It gets better and better. You shouldn't be traveling alone."

"Oh, you're starting to sound like my mom. That's not a compliment, mister!"

"I'm sorry, love. It's just that I've felt something was off these last couple of days. It was a strange feeling that I couldn't shake off and it drove me insane. Now you tell me you were in danger. I don't get it. Was it some kind of premonition? It's never happened to me."

"I wasn't in any real danger. Although I admit I was a little afraid. I left the car and walked to find a spot where I could use my cell phone."

"How long did you walk? It must have been dark. Did you get to a safe place?"

"In fact, a car appeared behind me."

"You're kidding me, right? Don't you know it's dangerous?" He felt upset and worried.

"I'm fine, aren't I? Nothing happened." She smiled. "Besides, there was this very nice couple in a pickup truck who helped me. No need to worry." She shrugged. "They took me to their farm. I called the rental company and they sent a tow truck. The driver was very polite and took me to Waterford in no time."

"Is that all, Keira? What aren't you telling me?"

"That's all. I got to the hotel too tired to call anybody. This morning, I took a tour I'd booked in advance. Did you know St. Declan founded a monastery in Waterford? He may have preached in Ireland before St. Patrick."

"Yes, I've heard these old tales." He laughed at her enthusiasm. "But, I'm no saint, love." He winked. "You must be exhausted, though."

"I am. Look, we've been talking for more than two hours and it's past eleven. We'd better hang up."

"Yeah, we should."

"Good night, Declan."

"Good night, gorgeous. Call you tomorrow."

"Okay."

When neither ended the call, Keira smiled.

"Aren't you going to hang up?"

"I was waiting for you to do it."

"Are you blushing, Declan Slane?"

"I feel like a teen again. It's embarrassing."

"Don't be embarrassed—it's adorable."

"Adorable is for puppies. I'm a twenty-six-year-old man." His face grew redder.

"Fine, I won't embarrass you any further." She winked. "Talk to you tomorrow."

"Sweet dreams, hon. I know I'll have them. I'll dream of you."

It was her turn to blush.

****

CHAPTER 4

After having called Declan, her doubts about the mysterious gorgeous woman had disappeared. She felt hopeful again and she looked forward to going back to Dublin and spending time with him. Those were her last thoughts before she fell asleep.

Keira dreamed of Declan. In her dream, she was back in Dublin and they went out to a fancy restaurant for dinner. She had the best time. He was a perfect gentleman and treated her like a delicate porcelain doll. At least, until they got back to her hotel room. When they got inside the room, he kissed her and she melted in his arms. He wasn't such a gentleman anymore, but Keira didn't want him to be one.

The best part of a dream is that the person can be anything. In Keira's, she was a bold woman who knew exactly what she wanted and how to get it. She wanted him to make her feel on fire again. She wanted his urgency, his desire. She lured him to the bed, crooking her hand in front of his nose. They laughed and kissed again as they tumbled together on the bed. Everything was perfect and Declan was a generous lover who took her to places she had never imagined existed.

* * * *

After hanging up, Declan stared at the phone for a while. He had worried about Keira for the last couple of days. Surely that was why he still felt uneasy after their phone call. He shook his head to clear it of gloomy thoughts and went to bed.

I'm overreacting. I don't like the idea of Keira being alone out there, but I can't do anything about it. I've got to let it go.

It took him a while to fall asleep and, when he did, his sleep was restless. He woke up early, feeling as tired as the night before. It was like he hadn't slept at all. He jogged, worked out, and thought about Keira every second. By lunchtime, he missed her so much he decided to text her.

"Hey, love. What are you up to today? Visiting more of my namesakes?"

"Not even close but having a great time. Call you later?"

They texted back and forth for the rest of the day. The messages were short. Sometimes they were sweet, sometimes sarcastic, but always funny. She spent the day sightseeing. In a way, it seemed like Declan was there with her because she shared all those visits with him through their messages.

* * * *

True to her word, Keira called him when she got back to the B&B. He picked up the first time the phone rang, "Hi, love. Missed you!" His Irish accent melted her bones.

"Hey. Are you at work? I don't want to cause you any problems."

"No, it's fine. I'm home. It's my day off," he answered, then added in a mockingly seductive way, "What are you wearing?"

"Nothing special, just my usual silk slip."

"Hmm, I bet it's soft and cool to the touch."

"As a matter of fact, it is." Keira giggled as she ran a hand over her old flannel PJs.

"Is it long or short?"

"Very short." This time, her voice was little more than a whisper.

"I wish I were there to run my hands up your gorgeous legs. Then, I'd lift the slip up your upper body until I reached your breasts. Would you let me do that?" His voice sounded seductive and a little out of breath.

She could easily picture them together since her dreams had been so vivid lately. Her heart beat faster and her throat went dry.

"I guess."

She sighed into the phone.

"I like how you sound. It's sexy. I'd cup your breasts and play with them until you sighed like you did just now. I'd catch your sigh with my mouth and kiss you until we couldn't breathe."

Keira blushed, not from embarrassment, though. Her cheeks were burning hot because of Declan's voice. The visions he wove made her blood boil. She felt like bursting into flames.

She heard his sexy laughter. "Keira, love, I could go on saying things like these all night but I don't think it would be a good idea. We'd end up frustrated and feeling bad."

"You're right. I'm already out of breath."

"Tell me about your day, then."

She did and they talked for hours. She told him about the places she had visited and he told her some funny stories about his clients at the bar. His coworkers were also very interesting people and good friends.

"What are you going to do tomorrow?"

"I'll go to Cork. It's not far, only a two-hour drive."

She tried to hide a yawn and failed.

"I hate to say goodbye, but you need to rest. Call me when you get in tomorrow."

"Yes, sir!" She laughed.

"Don't kid like that. I worry about you." He sounded hurt.

"I know you do. Sorry. You're cute for worrying, but I'm fine."

"I'll feel better hearing from you, though."

"Okay. Talk to you tomorrow."

"Sweet dreams, hon."

* * * *

The next couple of days were busy for Keira. She hired a tour in Cork and visited Blarney Castle on her first day. As she climbed onto the bus, she was surprised to see Sylvia and John Burtonderry, the owners of Burtonderry House where she had stayed in Wicklow. And Paul O'Hallon, the tow truck driver.

When she saw the couple, she sat across the aisle from them.

"Hey, good to see you again. What are you doing here?"

"We're celebrating our wedding anniversary."

"Good for you."

"Good morning, Keira," Paul O'Hallon said. "Can I sit here beside you?"

"Absolutely. Paul, these are Sylvia and John Burtonderry. This is Paul O'Hallon."

Once he'd sat down, he told them he was on vacation and the little group of four people spent the day together. The tour was amazing and Keira was actually glad to see familiar faces and to have people to share those wonderful moments with.

On the second day, Keira had planned a tour to Ring of Kerry. Sylvia, John, and Paul took the tour with her and they ended up having another excellent day.

Keira and Declan texted and talked a lot while she toured Cork and the surrounding areas. She had left Dublin nine days before, but it felt like an eternity for both of them. Their phone talks were getting hotter and naughtier. She missed Declan like crazy and she wished he were actually there with her— that he could hold her and kiss her. She wanted him.

Declan also seemed frustrated with their physical distance. If on one hand, the phone calls and the messages had brought them together—letting them know each other better—on the other hand, he said he was miserable when they hung up. He said he wished Keira were back in Dublin. Then, he would take her out, woo her, and make love to her until kingdom come.

After another of their phone calls, Keira went to bed. Unable to sleep, she looked up at the ceiling and counted the cracks. She rolled over and buried her head under the pillow.

This room is too quiet.

She stretched her arm out and turned on the radio alarm clock. A nice song filled the air. It was one of her favorite songs, about making memories. As the throaty voice of the band's lead singer invaded her mind, she closed her eyes, getting lost in the images that the lyrics evoked, which lulled her to sleep.

She dreamed she was in her bedroom in Boston, alone on her bed. She felt sad and wanted to cry. All of a sudden, as often happens in dreams, Keira wasn't in her room anymore. She was at her sister's house. Megan sat on her couch in the living room, staring into space. She looked sad. She could tell her sister had been crying because her eyes were red and puffy. Keira sat beside her and threw her arm around her older sister's shoulders.

"What happened?"

Megan ignored her and kept looking ahead. Their parents entered the room and hugged Megan but ignored Keira.

"What's going on here? Why don't you talk to me, guys?"

She got no answer from any of them.

Again the scene changed, and she was on a busy street, in a large city she didn't recognize. It looked European. She walked by a newsstand and glanced at the newspapers on display, trying to find out where she was. Her heart sank when a headline caught her eyes—"Young American dies in Ireland." On the front page, right below the headline, were two pictures: her graduation photo and one of Declan in handcuffs.

She woke up screaming and sitting on the bed, out of breath. It took her a few seconds to recognize the hotel room and figure out she'd had a nightmare.

85

She drank some water from the bottle that she kept on the night table and went back to sleep.

* * * *

It had been ten days since Keira had left Dublin, and Declan sat on his couch staring at his phone, trying to decide what to do. He checked his watch.

It's not even seven in the morning. If I call her again, I'll seem too needy. I don't want that. Maybe I should write something clever without showing her that I can't keep her out of my mind.

As he weighed his options, Jennifer's picture popped up on his cell phone's screen. He frowned and picked up the call.

"What's up? Is something wrong? Why are you calling me so early?"

"You tell me if there's something wrong, mister. You haven't called since our breakfast two weeks ago. I knew this time of day I'd get you before you went out to work. How did it go with the American? What's her name? Kim?"

"Keira. Nothing happened. She's still traveling. You caused quite an impression on her."

"Really? How so? We've never met."

"She saw us outside the coffee shop and thought I was cheating on her. She was so pissed off she hung up on me. It took her three days to talk to me again."

"That's great news!" Jennifer said with a squeak.

"Are you kidding me? I totally freaked out and you say it's good news."

"It *is* good news, silly. If she weren't falling for you, she wouldn't react like that."

"Well, you might be right. Can you believe she got a ride with a couple, complete strangers I might add, when her car broke down on the way to Waterford?"

86

"What happened, exactly?"

Declan told her the part of the story he knew, expecting Jennifer would agree with him that Keira had been reckless. To his surprise, she didn't see things the same way.

"What's the big deal? People do that all the time. There was no cell service. How was she supposed to call for help?"

"Would you have done the same?"

"I *have* done that and you know it."

"Really? When did you do it? I don't remember."

"When we were dating, I traveled to Cork for Christmas and you stayed here to work. I had two flat tires on the way. The first one, I changed myself. The second one was the problem because I didn't have another spare tire to replace it. My cell's battery had gone dead. I got a ride on a motorcycle. The guy dropped me at a gas station and I got somebody to fix the tires."

"Yeah, right. Now, I remember," Declan confessed, a little embarrassed. "I don't know, Jen. That was different. You're Irish. You know our roads well. Keira is a foreigner."

Jennifer laughed at his comment but stopped when she noticed he wasn't laughing.

"Are you serious? I'm sorry. I thought you were joking. That's the stupidest thing I've ever heard from you. And that's saying a lot because you're always saying stupid things."

"I'm not! Besides, I don't see why it's so funny. She could've been attacked or something. There are too many weirdoes out there, you know."

"It's funny, my dear blind man, because you can't see what's right in front of you. There's no difference between my story and Keira's. Except that you didn't freak out when I got that ride, even though we were dating at the time."

She waited for his reply, which never came. She sighed, and he could imagine her eye roll all too easily.

"Seriously, Declan. Nothing?"

"What do you want me to say? I don't follow you."

"Gosh, you're such a bright guy, except when it comes to love. You didn't freak out about me because you weren't head over heels in love with me."

"Get out of here."

"I'm sorry, my friend, it's official! You're so overprotective of Keira because you have feelings for her."

"I barely know Keira. How can I have feelings for her?"

She didn't say anything for a while and Declan thought she had hung up. He was about to say something when Jennifer talked again.

"I'll state the obvious here since it's clear somebody's got to do it. We'd known each other forever before we dated, yet that didn't help us fall in love with each other. We love each other dearly, but we were never *in love* with each other. Time means nothing when love finds us."

It was Declan's turn to be quiet, considering what she had said.

"I don't know, Jen. I don't want to rush things. It's too soon to say if either one of us is in love or not."

"Nobody rushes love. It just happens, sweetie."

That phone conversation haunted Declan for the rest of the morning. At work, he was distracted. Even though Harry and Màire had always gotten him covered, they were running out of patience.

"You've got to pull yourself together, mate." Harry said when Declan spilt the third drink over the counter. "Let me clean this mess up. Take some minutes out to cool off."

Declan went to the employee lounge where Màire was taking her morning break.

"What have you done this time?"

He plopped down beside her on the couch and closed his eyes.

"Nothing."

"Harry must be pissed off at you, if he's sent you away."

"How do you know he's mad at me? Maybe I just needed some time."

"On a busy morning like this? Forget about it. The bar's packed but he preferred to stay alone, which means you must have really gotten to him. Come on. Spill it."

Declan looked at his coworker, tempted to ask her advice. She was a good-looking and experienced woman. She could probably help him more than Jennifer because they hadn't been romantically involved.

"Is it the American beauty? I've got to tell you. You haven't been the same since she left."

"Is it that obvious?"

"Don't be embarrassed. Everyone feels stupid when they're in love."

Declan rolled his eyes. *Enough with this bullshit. I'm not in love with a stranger.*

Not wanting to offend Màire, he kept his mouth shut. It was useless because she didn't give him time to say anything. Her face got red and her eyes seemed to bore holes in his skull. She was pissed off at him as well.

"And don't you dare roll your eyes at me, mister. Maybe you don't see it, but there's clearly something going on with you. You've changed. That's a fact. Perhaps you should take some time off to get to the bottom of this— whatever 'this' is." Màire got up and stomped out of the room even though she hadn't finished her break.

"Apparently, nobody wants me around today

He stayed in the lounge for a while longer, considering the advice she had given him before he had found the courage to ask for it.

What if they're right? What if I'm falling for Keira? What should I do? She's too young and innocent. I have too much baggage. A lot of heartache and hurt in my past. Would I harm her beyond repair if I stuck around? Should I let her go before it's too late?

* * * *

On the morning of her tenth day on the road, Keira woke up feeling depressed and exhausted. After that horrible nightmare, she hadn't gotten much sleep. She crawled out of bed and dragged herself to the bathroom, where she took a shower while considering if she should call or text Declan for moral support, if nothing else.

After the shower she felt a little better, so changed her mind about texting Declan. He would only worry about her and, since he was miles away, he couldn't do anything to help.

As she went downstairs, she hoped she'd bump into Sylvia or John in the dining room, since they were staying at the River Lee Hotel. She could use a couple of friends to cheer her up. Even watching the stunning views through the glass windows from her table didn't work. While the waitress served her breakfast, Paul appeared at the doorway and spotted her. When he walked over to her table, a big grin lit up his handsome features.

"Good morning. Do you mind if I join you?"

"No, not at all. Grab a seat."

"So, what are your plans for today?"

"I haven't planned anything yet. I figured I'd do some shopping this morning. Tomorrow, I'll start my trip back to Dublin. I'd better take it easy today."

"Aren't you going to meet up with your friends?"

"I don't know what Sylvia and John are doing. I haven't talked to them today."

"Oh, I didn't mean those friends. I meant the ones you were supposed to meet with in Waterford. Remember?"

Keira felt puzzled. She had no idea what he was driving at. Before she could ask him what he meant, the waitress returned with his order of breakfast, and while she served Paul, it dawned on Keira.

On the way from the Wilkinson's farm to Waterford, she had told Paul she would meet with friends there. She'd been a little afraid of him then. Now that she'd gotten to know him better, the whole thing sounded silly. Not wanting to offend him, she stretched the truth a little further.

"Oh, yeah. We had a great time there, but they live in Waterford and couldn't leave work to come to Cork with me. I'm very happy for having met Sylvia, John, and you. Otherwise, I'd be alone here."

She hid her face behind the steaming cup of coffee, hoping he'd think her red face was caused by heat from the beverage, and not from her embarrassment. For a couple of minutes, Paul just stared at her and didn't reply. She felt uncomfortable under his penetrating gaze and thought she saw a dark shadow in the depth of his eyes, but before she could be sure of it he smiled and relaxed his features.

"Yes, of course. People have to work, right?"

He drank from his cup of tea but kept his eyes fixed on her face. For a split second, Keira thought his smile looked more like a smirk. His expression changed when he looked up and greeted John, who had just stopped by their table.

"Hey, mate! How are you today? Would you like to join us?"

John and Sylvia sat down to have breakfast with them, and Keira observed the three laughing together, having fun, and made an effort to push her recent dark thoughts aside.

91

Luck of the Irish

Gosh, I'm on edge today. I've got to relax. I'm on vacation. I'm anxious to see Declan again. That's it!

When she calmed down she ended up having a great time with her three new friends. John was a funny man and Sylvia a sweet lady. Keira already knew that, but she was surprised to discover Paul was a charming, intelligent man as well. He and John got along great and made Keira and Sylvia laugh so hard they couldn't breathe.

"Oh, stop, please. I can't take it any longer," Sylvia begged her husband, still smiling and wiping the tears from her eyes.

"You're killing me, here," Keira added, putting her hand over her chest. "I can't see straight. I've got tears in my eyes from laughing so hard at you guys."

"In that case, we'll behave," Paul replied with a playful wink. "You have a long drive back to Dublin tomorrow. You'll need to see straight."

"Also, I have to cross out some items from my shopping list today. If you'll excuse me, guys, I need to leave you."

"Oh, that's a shame you have to go, honey."

"Why don't you come with me, Sylvia? I'd love some company."

"I'd love to go with you, but we've got to go on this tour we've already booked." Sylvia patted John's hand and smiled adoringly at her husband. It was clear that skipping the tour was not an option for her. "Why don't you go shopping with Keira, Paul? Have you got any plans?"

"Actually, I don't. If you'd like some company, I'd love to go shopping. I have to buy some souvenirs for my family, too."

"Yeah, that'd be great. Tell you what, I'll go upstairs to grab my stuff while you finish your breakfast. We'll meet in half an hour at the lobby. Deal?"

He nodded. "It's a date. See you."

Sylvia stood up and turned to John, "I need to go up to our room. Take your time to finish your breakfast."

"I will." John winked at her.

Keira and Sylvia got inside the elevator and the older woman put her hand on Keira's arm and squeezed it a little.

"I'm glad to see you've found a fine young man for yourself. I was worried about you when you left my house. You looked so sad. But now you seem very happy."

"What do you mean?" Keira was surprised at the comments because she hadn't mentioned Declan to Sylvia.

"Paul, obviously. He's quite a catch. Don't tell me you're not interested."

"In fact, I'm not available." She winked, and then held the elevator door to get out of it when it reached her floor.

"Hmm, I see. There's a boyfriend waiting for you back home, eh? Good for you."

"Yeah, something like that. See you later. Have a great day, sweetie."

"You too."

Keira and Paul met at the hotel lobby and went for a stroll along St. Patrick's Street—or "Pana" as the locals called it. She admired the surrounding buildings and the curious, winding street. She had read somewhere that the street had been built over an arm of River Lee, which had resulted in its odd shape.

On a Saturday such as that, St. Patrick's Street was bursting with people. Keira didn't mind it, though. She had always loved watching people and in Ireland she could do that and hear their enchanting accent at the same time. She was walking on air.

They walked along the street for almost an hour as she bought things for her family: a silver and gold Triskele pendant on a delicate silver chain with matching earrings for her mother, a set of crystal wine glasses for her father, and a gorgeous designer purse for Megan.

After another half-hour or so, she hadn't found anything for Declan. She had stopped at countless windows. Nothing had gotten her attention. She wanted to buy something special for him, but didn't know what, exactly. They walked around for a while longer browsing more windows. Keira was having a hard time picking something up for him. In a street where one could literally find anything, she was on the verge of giving up when Paul stopped and turned to her.

"Don't get me wrong here, because I'm having a blast spending time with you. But we've been in and out of all kinds of stores and you haven't bought a thing. What exactly are you looking for now?"

"That's the thing, I don't know."

"Is it for you? Do you want to buy a souvenir from Ireland? There are many nice stores on the next block."

"No, it's not for me. It's a gift for a friend."

"Maybe I can help you out with it. Is this friend a man or a woman?"

"A man."

"Young or old?"

"Around twenty-five, I guess."

She blushed a little and looked around to try to hide it from Paul's piercing eyes. She had just realized she didn't even know Declan's age and wondered what else she didn't know about him.

"Well, I dare say he isn't a very close friend, if you don't know his age."

"He's a new friend."

He raised an eyebrow but didn't reply. They walked further down the street, and Keira still couldn't decide what to buy.

"There are some good clothing stores across the street. Would you like to check them out?"

She nodded and they started towards the stores. Keira still hadn't gotten used to crossing streets in Ireland, because the cars seemed to come from the wrong direction in her opinion. She hadn't wrapped her head around it yet.

"Watch out!" Paul shouted, and his arm went around her tiny waist and held her close to his warm chest, as a bus sped by them. The wind created by the huge vehicle pushed both of them backwards for a step or two.

"Gosh. I would have been run over by that monster bus if you weren't here with me." She steadied herself by putting a hand on Paul's chest before adding breathlessly, "Thank you."

"If I weren't here, you'd be paying more attention to where you were going. I distracted you." He held her in a loose embrace and stared into her eyes. "I'm sorry."

"Come on, it's not your fault."

Keira stepped back and he didn't try to hold her, although he looked disappointed.

"Can we agree to disagree on this one? Let's find a gift for this friend of yours."

He grabbed her hand as they crossed the street. She felt like a little girl, but the protection he offered was not entirely a bad thing.

"Look. What about that sweater?" Paul suggested as they approached the fourth store.

"It's beautiful. I like it. Would you mind trying it on? I think you and Declan are about the same height and have roughly the same build."

"Sure."

"Thanks," she said with a wide grin as she laced her arm through his, holding it close to her body. "You're a life-saver. Come on ... let's go inside."

Keira had grown fond of Paul in the last couple of days. She felt at ease with him, more than she had ever been around other men. When she was near Declan, for instance, she was on edge. She didn't feel the same with Paul. That was probably why she had grabbed his arm like that, so intimately. Either Ireland was teaching her to loosen up a bit, like Megan had told her to do, or she liked Paul more than she had realized.

He came out of the fitting room wearing the sweater and it looked perfect on him. Keira noticed how the design on the burgundy Aran sweater showed off his broad shoulders and strong arms.

"I think that'll do. Thank you, Paul."

As they waited in line to pay for the sweater, Keira said, "You're a life-saver. I know I said it before, but it's true. I don't know how I can thank you."

"Let me buy you lunch. It's our last day together and we're having such a great time. I'd love the company."

"You're right, we are having fun, aren't we?"

Although she agreed to lunch, she wasn't sure about letting him pay for it.

"Let's have lunch, but it's my treat. I don't want to abuse your friendship."

"That I can't accept."

"Let's split the bill, then."

"I pay for it or we won't have lunch together."

She closed her mouth without replying, studied his stern expression, and realized he wasn't going to back down on that one. It would be best to let the matter slide. She shrugged and offered him a broad smile.

"Only because you insist."

She paid for the sweater and they went out to the street again.

"Where would you like to go? Do you know any restaurants around here?"

96

"They're not as good as in my hometown, Limerick, but there are plenty." He winked. "Which do you prefer—Italian, Indian, Thai, or Chinese food?"

"Oh, I don't know. I love all kinds of food."

"You're not helping. Oh, I know. There's an Indian restaurant near here called Eastern Tandoori. Have you been there?"

"No, but I'd love to go. I've heard it's awesome."

"That's set, then. Let's go."

He grabbed her hand again and took her to the restaurant.

Paul turned out to be good company. They talked and laughed all through the meal. The noisy restaurant prevented her from hearing her cell phone ring. She ended up missing Declan's calls, which went to voicemail.

When they finished, she excused herself and went to the bathroom. She went through her things to find her lipstick, and spotted her phone flashing inside her bag. She checked her voicemail and heard Declan's message.

"Hi, baby. I miss you like hell every day, but today it's unbearable. I needed to talk to you. I did something stupid. It's just my luck I got your voicemail every time I called." He laughed, but a shiver ran down her spine. "Catch you later. I hope."

She pressed the icon on the screen to call him back but it went to voicemail. She hung up without leaving a message. When she got back to the table, Paul frowned.

"What's wrong?"

"I'm sorry. I'm fine. I've just heard a message on my cell phone and it distracted me."

"You look upset."

"Maybe I am upset. I don't know. I think I should head back to the hotel, though."

"Drink up your glass of water. You'll feel better."

"Good idea."

Paul signaled the waiter for the check, then said, "I'll walk you to the hotel."

"There's no need for that. I don't want to ruin the rest of your afternoon."

"Nonsense. It's almost five o'clock, and there's not much left of the afternoon, anyway." He smiled, took out his credit card to pay with, and handed it to the waiter.

"I hadn't realized it was so late. Thank you for a lovely day, Paul. I had a great time. I just want to get to my room and relax a little. I'll have a long day tomorrow."

They left the restaurant and took a taxi back to the hotel, which wasn't very far, but Keira felt too tired to walk there.

* * * *

A couple of hours earlier

Declan held his cell phone tighter against his ear, and would have smashed it to pieces on the floor in anger, if he didn't need the bloody thing. *Useless piece of crap.*

"Hi, this is Keira. I'm sorry …"

He hung up when he heard that for the umpteenth time. He didn't want to leave another message. It was a little after two in the afternoon, but the day had been so long and tiring, he felt exhausted—and impatient. Declan wanted to talk to her, not a machine.

When he arrived at the taxi stand, he got inside the car, gave the driver the address, and placed his hand on the older man's shoulder.

"Hurry up, old chap, please."

He leaned back against the smooth leather of the headrest and closed his eyes. He didn't need to see where he was going because he knew the

98

surrounding streets all too well. He also didn't want to think about what he planned to do next, because he was afraid he'd lose heart.

I need to do this for Keira. If we have the slimmest chance of making things work out right for us, as a couple, I have do this. Regardless of how I feel about the old bastard.

He gritted his teeth and steeled himself when he sensed the car slowing down. He paid the driver, got out of the car, and took a deep breath. His heart beat fast and he felt the adrenaline rushing through his veins. He'd only manage to do what needed to be done if he kept his cool.

The bile rose inside him, threatening to suffocate him, as he approached the front door of the run-down little house and knocked on it. That door used to be a bright, deep shade of red. Now, it was a dull-looking dark green, with the paint peeling off in many places. He noticed he had been holding his breath only when the door opened halfway and a bald, elderly man appeared behind it.

"Hello, Da. Can I come in? We need to talk." Declan felt both his throat and eyes burning from tension and suppressed anger.

He was so concentrated on keeping his reactions in check that he didn't notice his father's blank expression.

"Who are you, lad?" Peter Slane asked his youngest son, without a shred of recognition in his feeble voice.

Declan started picking up on the signs that something was very wrong in this picture. His father wasn't angry at him, or pretending he didn't know his own son. He sounded sincere. That was bewildering and terrifying at the same time. He opened his mouth to identify himself when an older woman appeared behind his father.

"I'm sorry, Mr. Slane isn't himself today. He shouldn't have answered the door, but he was closer to it than me." The woman put herself between Declan's father and him, as if to protect the old man from any harm. "You know how these things go. He has his good days and his bad days. Today's been a very bad one."

Tell me about it. When will this woman stop talking?

"I heard you call him 'Da.' Which one are you?"

"Declan."

"Oh, the young runaway." She laughed and the sound of her genuine mirth took the sting off her remark. "I'm Rose Michaelson—your father's caregiver. Do come in, please."

Declan was too stunned to say anything. He felt like he had landed himself in an episode of that old television show—Twilight Zone. Nothing made any sense at all as he followed the nice lady, in an impeccable white uniform, inside his childhood home.

This was the house where his worst memories had been born. The place where he would always go back to in his heart-stopping nightmares. The place he had run from a lifetime ago, and where he had returned to now, seeking closure in hopes of having a chance at a better future. *Will I find what I came here for? Where's that monster that has haunted me all these years?*

* * * *

Paul got out of the taxi, carrying Keira's shopping bags, but managed to hold the door open for her. They entered the hotel lobby and Keira turned to get her things from him.

"Absolutely not. I'll take these to your room."

"Thank you, but you don't have to do that. There aren't that many bags."

Keira regretted having drunk wine during lunch. Although she hadn't drunk a lot, she slurred a little and her movements came slower than usual.

"I know, my dear. But you look a tad tipsy. You don't want to break those beautiful glasses you bought for your father, do you?"

100

As they walked to the elevator, she nodded a couple of times but everything spun around her.

"You've got a good point, my friend."

They entered the elevator, and Keira felt dizzy again as it went up to her floor. She leaned her head against the mirrored wall and closed her eyes, trying to make the feeling go away. She hated being drunk. She had promised herself never to get drunk again.

"Are you all right, child? You look ashen," asked an elderly woman who was standing beside her.

"She had a couple of glasses of wine at lunch, madam. She'll be fine," Paul answered on Keira's behalf, putting his arm around her shoulders.

She was thankful for his support, because she didn't think she could move her head without getting sick. She wasn't in the mood for repeating her Dublin performance and throwing up in public, either. The elevator halted and the doors opened. Paul grabbed the shopping bags in one hand and Keira's elbow with the other.

"Throw your arm around my neck."

"I'm fine."

She took a step away from him, squared her shoulders, and walked with much difficulty towards her room without further help from Paul. She could see his smile out of the corner of her eyes.

I'm drunker than I thought. It looks more like a sneer than a smile.

She shook her head to clear it, opened her purse, got the keycard, and slid it inside the lock. When the green light flashed on, Paul opened the door and entered before she could do anything to stop him.

Faint alarm bells pealed inside her head. She wouldn't normally let a man she didn't know get inside her room like that. Uncomfortable, she left the door unlocked. Paul put the bags down on the table and turned to Keira—a smug grin curled his mouth up as he walked towards her.

She forced her brain to snap out of its drunken state, and managed to assess her situation better. It wasn't good. He looked threatening, and blocked her way to the door.

When he stood in front of her and framed her face in his big hands, Keira tried to step back but he held her tight by her hair. Any sudden movement would hurt like hell, so she stayed put. But those alarm bells were deafening by then, and her heart was beating all the way up in her throat. Panic gripped her.

"There's no need to be afraid, Keira," Paul whispered as his face came down towards hers. "Don't fight me and you won't get hurt."

His words took some seconds to penetrate her hazy brain, but her senses had already rebelled against his touch. She felt sick when his tongue invaded her mouth. It got worse when she realized his meaning, as his hands tore her blouse buttons apart in one single, violent movement. Keira shoved him away.

Caught by surprise, Paul moved backwards a couple of steps, but recovered fast and slapped her hard across the face. She stumbled. The sharp pain traveled through her body, and shook off the last effects of alcohol from her brain. She recovered her footing and sprinted towards the door. Paul grabbed her hair and pulled her back, smashing her against his hard body, his free hand squeezed her breast painfully. Her eyes filled with tears but she didn't utter a sound, not wanting to give him the satisfaction of knowing he had hurt her.

"I told you not to fight me. Now I'll have to hurt you." He threw her facedown on the carpeted floor. "I didn't want to hurt you. You've got such beautiful, smooth skin. I don't have a choice now."

Although the thick burgundy rug didn't cushion her fall, it rendered her frantic attempts to get away from under Paul almost useless. He straddled her, twisting her arms behind her back and holding her slim wrists in one hand. The more Keira fought him, the sharper the pain that traveled up her arms, but she couldn't give up trying to escape his vicious assault. She doubled her efforts

102

when he ripped her skirt off. She bucked, heaving and whimpering, but his strong legs kept her pinned to the floor.

"Get off me!"

"Shut up or I'll really have to hurt you," he threatened, covering her mouth with his free hand.

Keira bit down hard on it. Paul yelped and, for a second, she thought he would let go of her. The illusion ended quickly when she felt his leather belt around her neck. He used it to choke her and stop her frantic movements.

"No more dirty tricks. I'll gladly watch the last breath leave your body after I'm done with you, if you don't stop fighting me," he whispered against her ear.

Nausea threatened to get the better of her. She fought to keep lunch down, because she was afraid of choking to death if she threw up. Paul used his belt as a leash, tight around her neck. She didn't dare move. She felt dizzy from lack of air and despair. She didn't know what else to do to prevent the seemingly inevitable rape, when she felt his hardness against the small of her back.

"No, Paul, stop it. Please, stop this madness. I thought you were my friend," she cried out, appealing to his conscience.

He didn't seem to have any. She heard him opening a condom wrapper and laughing without any trace of humor.

"Friend? You are more stupid than you let on. You lied to me. You said you were traveling with friends just to keep me away, to play hard to get. I knew, all along, you wanted me to fuck you. Why are you fighting me now?"

Paul rambled on about how she had flirted with him, and how she had lured him into her room. He was clearly out of his mind. As he grew angrier, he squeezed the belt tighter. He had released her wrists, and Keira plucked at the leather strap, gasping for air.

She used her last breath to shout for help. The sound was stifled and weak. Her throat burned. Blackness crept in on her. Weightlessness didn't seem such a bad thing, since it meant she'd be unconscious and out of pain. She closed her eyes and welcomed that thought seconds before Paul's body slid off hers. She heard a thud and a crash and took a few precious seconds to recognize her savior's voice.

"Son of bitch! I'll kill you for this," Declan shouted as he grabbed Paul by the collar and threw him against the opposite wall.

Paul tried to punch back, but hit the air. Declan landed a blow on his nose. He doubled over and knelt in front of Declan who took advantage of Paul's position to jerk his knee up, hitting his chin, and making Paul fall backwards, sprawling on the floor. Declan straddled him, battering his head and face without mercy.

They had smashed a chair in their struggle and the pieces of wood lay around the floor. Paul's fingers inched towards the nearest one. Keira had gotten rid of the belt around her neck, so she used it to slash at his wrist as she stood up. She put her hand on Declan's shoulder to stop him beating an almost unconscious Paul.

"Declan, I'm fine. Stop it, please. He's not worth it."

"He deserves to die. He hurt you and he was going to do worse than that." He looked up into her eyes. She saw such hatred in the depths of his green stare that it frightened her a little. She understood his reasons, though.

"I know that, sweetie. But I don't want to lose you over this. If you kill him, you'll go to jail, and he'll be free, gone from this world. I want him to pay for what he did every minute of every day, for the rest of his miserable life."

* * * *

Declan hesitated then took the belt from her outstretched hand, and used it to tie Paul's hands. His knuckles were bruised and bleeding, but he didn't care. He had rearranged Paul's face and that was compensation enough for his own pain.

104

"You broke my nose, bastard! I'll make you pay for that," Paul shouted as he tried to kick Declan in the face.

Keira got a sheet from the bed and handed it to Declan.

"Good thinking," he thanked her as he tied Paul's feet and legs.

When he was sure the man didn't pose a threat to them any longer, Declan stood up and pulled Keira into a tight embrace. He buried his face in her hair and inhaled deeply as she sobbed against his chest. He fought his bitter tears and had a hard time keeping them at bay. His heart had stopped when he had heard Keira's shout from the corridor.

"Oh, Keira, my love. My world fell apart when I came in and saw him attacking you. I would've killed the son of a bitch if you hadn't stopped him." His blood was still boiling. Keira coughed and whimpered. She must have been in pain from the brutal assault. Declan let go of her with reluctance and took a step back to examine her, searching for bruises. He frowned when he found too many.

"Look at you, love. He hurt you badly. I *will* kill him."

She grabbed his upper arms when he turned to the spot where Paul sat on the floor.

"Hold me, please, Declan. Just hold me tight. I need to know you're real."

Unable to deny her heartfelt plea, he obliged. He folded his arms around her and cocooned her trembling body against his rock solid one, and soothed her nerves.

"I'm real, baby. You're safe with me, now. I'll never let anyone hurt you."

She closed her eyes and relaxed against his body.

He wished his warmth could restore her bruised body and battered soul, that his strength could restore hers. He needed to be sure she was going to be all right. As if she could read his thoughts, Keira ran her fingers through his soft hair and kissed his cheek.

"Thank you."

Her voice broke off and tears welled in her eyes before rolling down her bloodied face.

* * * *

CHAPTER 5

"Don't cry, honey." He kissed her eyelids closed. "I can't bear it, love. I'll kill the bastard if you shed one more tear."

"You're right, he doesn't deserve this satisfaction." She looked up into Declan's mesmerizing green eyes. "We have to call the police."

"Yeah, sure," he said and reached inside his back pocket for the cell phone. Still watching Keira, he thumbed in the emergency number. "Hello, this is Declan Slane. I want to report an attempted rape." He paused and listened to the other person. "My girlfriend. I don't know who the son of a bitch is. He's tied up waiting for you."

Keira knew that this wasn't the best time to feel happy just because Declan had called her 'his girlfriend'. The truth was she felt ecstatic and a warm sensation spread from her heart throughout her nerve endings.

When Declan got off the phone, Paul reminded them of his presence.

"So, tell me something, Keira, is this the boyfriend whose age you don't even know?"

Before she could say anything, Declan slapped Paul's mouth hard with the back of his hand. "You don't get to talk to her ever again, vermin. Shut the fuck up!"

"What are you going to do about it, huh, big guy? You heard her. She doesn't want you to hurt me. Why do you think that is?" He grinned. "She likes me. She's a liar and a cheat. You shouldn't believe a word she says. She begged me to tie her down and fuck her hard ..." He never finished the sentence because Declan's boot connected with the side of his head, and he tumbled to the floor, unconscious. Blood trickled from the gash that opened in his temple.

"I told you to shut up, sod."

"Declan, please, don't believe anything he ..."

"Come here, love," he held her in his arms again, kissing the top of her head softly. "Hush, baby. I know you. There's nothing he can say that will make me doubt you. He's a demented, sick man." He rocked her, running his hands along her hair, and her heartbeats returned to normal. "Now, put some clothes on. The police will be here any minute."

"Oh, gosh!" Keira looked down at her ripped blouse, realizing for the first time that she wasn't wearing much else. Tears clouded her vision as the enormity of what had just happened hit her hard. She sobbed, "I'm sorry."

"You've got nothing to apologize for. You're in shock. Unfortunately, you shouldn't take a shower—not before the police can examine you. Just sit down on the bed. Try to relax. I'll grab a robe from the bathroom for you."

His calm and patience soothed her wrecked nerves. She sat on the bed, staring into space. Horrific images kept popping up in her head and her mind threatened to shut down. She thought she heard somebody calling her name, but the sound was faint and distant. Her body shook. Then she realized it was Declan. He had put the robe on for her, without her noticing it, and now shook her lightly to call her back to reality.

"Keira, honey, the police are here. They need to talk to you, sweetie."

She blinked a couple of times until her eyes focused on two men wearing Irish Garda vests standing in front of her. "I'm sorry, detectives. I'm Keira Ashe."

"I'm Inspector Heller, Miss Ashe. This is Inspector Dwyer."

They shook hands and she asked the policemen to sit down. Only one chair remained intact, though. Inspector Heller took it. Declan sat beside her on the bed, a protective arm around her waist. Heller had a soft, soothing voice that matched his elderly countenance. Inspector Dwyer, on the other hand, looked much younger and energetic—in his mid-thirties.

"We're very sorry you had to go through such an ordeal, Miss Ashe. But, the two of you might have helped us catch a criminal we've been trying to

108

find for the last couple of years. I know it's going to be tough on you, but we need you to tell us everything you remember about the attack," Heller said, as a couple of ambulance men and a gardai took away a still unconscious Paul on a gurney.

* * * *

The next half-hour was a nightmare for both Keira and Declan. She had to relive the worst moments of her life, while Declan had to hear the details of what had happened to her when he wasn't there, and without reacting to the story. He cringed in horror.

"Have you known Mr. O'Hallon long?" Inspector Dwyer asked.

"I met him about a week ago when my car broke down."

"Wait a minute—was he the guy who stopped to help you? He's married, isn't he?"

"No, Paul didn't stop to help me. He drove the tow truck."

Declan opened his mouth to ask her why he was hearing that part of her story for the first time, when Inspector Heller interrupted him, "Do you remember the name of the truck company he worked for, Miss Ashe?"

"No. I have the car rental number, though. They can give you that information."

She got her cell phone, then gave him the number. Declan noticed she glanced at him out of the corner of her eye. He tried to keep quiet but he was royally pissed off. The fact that she had kept him in the dark hurt him more than he could bear. It was unfair of him to feel like that under the circumstances. Still, he couldn't help himself.

"Why didn't you tell me any of this before?"

"For your own good. You were already worried about me and, being in Dublin, you couldn't have done anything more than that—worry. I thought there was nothing to worry about. I was very wrong." Her voice sounded strangled.

"I'm sorry, hon. I'm an asshole." Declan squeezed her shoulder, feeling the part.

Inspector Heller cleared his throat as if to remind the couple of his presence.

"Did you see him again, miss?"

"No. At least, I don't think I did."

She hesitated and Declan held his breath as a myriad of emotions reflected in her blue eyes.

"What's the matter, Miss Ashe?" the insightful Inspector Heller asked. "Do you remember anything specific?"

"I'm not sure. Would it be possible to see things and not realize I saw them?"

"That's quite normal, actually. Tell me what you remember."

"In Waterford, when I was at the car rental getting a new one, Paul arrived with the tow truck. I didn't think much of it at the time. Now, it seems an odd time for him to deliver the other car. When he offered me a ride to the office, he said he had to go there early in the morning. I got there around noon. The next day, I thought I saw him on the other side of a street, but he had disappeared when I looked again. I dismissed it, thinking I'd seen someone who reminded me of him."

"Would you rather speak in private?" the detective suggested when she hesitated again.

"No, thank you."

"Keira, you know I'm here for you, no matter what. I told you that I know and trust you. If you feel more comfortable talking to them alone, I'll go out to get some air."

"Thanks, honey. You don't have to. When I arrived in Cork, I discovered Paul was a guest at the same hotel I was staying at. He took the same tours I did but, then again, so did a couple who owns a B&B where I stayed in Wicklow. I didn't think much of it."

"Apparently, he followed you down here. Don't worry, though. He's in custody. He won't do you any harm, now."

Heller exchanged a meaningful look with Inspector Dwyer before adding, "Judging from what you told us, I'd dare say he's really the suspect we have been looking for in connection to a number of rapes. We've been trying to find him for over two years. Unfortunately, we had little-to-no clues to follow."

He paused again, studying Keira's expression.

"You see, the few victims who survived the attack, never saw his face. The others were killed, leaving us without solid leads," Inspector Dwyer picked up telling the story. "We think he has used his position as a tow truck driver to choose his victims. He stalked the women traveling alone and attacked them. You were the first one with whom he tried to establish some kind of connection, Miss Ashe."

"I'm just relieved this nightmare is over. I want to go home and forget all about it."

The gardaí looked at each other again and Heller cleared his throat before saying, "Unfortunately, miss, that wouldn't be advisable. I mean, you're a tourist, so I can't hold you here against your will, but your presence during his trial would be crucial to our case. You are our only eyewitness. The other women might be able to identify him as the driver who towed their cars, but they didn't see their attacker's face."

Keira paled. "I hadn't thought I'd need to testify. I hadn't considered a future trial. I hadn't thought at all."

Declan put his arm around her shoulders, bringing her closer to him when she started to sound panicky. "Don't worry, love, we'll figure something out. Does she have to stay here in Cork until the trial?"

"No, not at all. We already have her statement. We'll conduct the investigations, which may take a while," Dwyer answered. "We ask Miss Ashe to stay around for a couple of days until we get all the lab results back and are sure we don't need to talk to her again. After that, she'll only need to be here again for the trial."

"Which would take place when, exactly?"

"That's hard to pinpoint, miss."

"Give me a ballpark number."

"Three to four months."

She moaned and dropped her head down, pressing her hands over her face.

"Keira, you don't need to think about it now. You can go home and return for the trial."

"It's not that easy. I saved money for years to come here in the first place and I don't have a job back home to be able to pay for another ticket soon."

He held her closer and kissed her hair, looking at the gardaí over the top of her head, "We'll find a way, officers."

"Our job is done here," Heller said as he stood up to leave. "Dwyer will write down your contact information, Miss Ashe, while I write down Mr. Slane's." He gestured for Declan to follow him, as he took a few steps towards the door.

When they were out of Keira's earshot, he spoke in a low voice, "Mr. Slane, she's been through one of the worst experiences of her young life. It may seem she has handled it well. In fact, she's still in shock and very vulnerable. She'll need all the support she can get from you."

"Unfortunately, I know that all too well from first-hand experience, sir. I thank you for your concern. Rest assured I'll take good care of her."

After the detectives left, Declan called the front desk, "Can you get us another room, please? I don't want Miss Ashe to stay in the room where she's been attacked."

"Certainly, sir. We'll send somebody to help with your luggage right away."

Once they'd moved to the other room and the bellhop had left, Declan and Keira sat on the bed. They didn't speak for a while, just held hands. When he couldn't stand the silence any longer, he took her hand to his mouth and kissed her palm.

"Keira, you should call your parents to tell them what happened."

"I don't want them to worry."

"The gardaí said they had been looking for this bastard for years. His arrest is bound to appear in the newspapers. Your parents will probably hear about it through the media and it'll be worse, don't you think?"

"You're right. If I call them they'll know I'm fine." But instead of getting her phone, she buried her face in his chest. "I don't want to talk about it all over again."

"I know you don't, love. I'll be right here by your side."

She didn't move for another couple of minutes. Declan nudged her and pushed her away until she looked at him.

"There's nothing to be afraid of. I won't let anything happen to you."

She still hesitated.

"What if we lay down together? Would you hold me while I talk to my folks? I'd feel safe, then."

"Your wish is my command, madam."

He lay down, opening his arms to hold her. She settled beside him, rested her head on his wide chest, and called her parents. Declan didn't say a word, just ran his hands slowly up and down her arms all the while she talked to them.

****

She managed to avoid the gory details. Nevertheless, there were many parts of the story when she had to stop and take a deep breath to keep her emotions in check. On these occasions, he kissed her head, laced their fingers together or squeezed her arms to remind her he was there for her. She smiled back into his eyes or blew him a kiss to thank him for those little gestures.

"We'll find a way to get to Ireland, honey. I don't know how, but we will. We won't let you go through this alone."

"There's no need for that, Dad. I'm not alone. Declan's here with me."

"That's not the same, honey. You've told us about him and he sounds like a good person. But, you need your family. You need us."

"I know you guys love me and want to protect me, but you don't have that kind of money right now."

"I shouldn't have remodeled the restaurant."

"Don't say that. You needed to do it. The restaurant had too many problems. It was an investment. It just takes time to get it back, that's all. You couldn't have known something like this would happen. Nobody could."

Her father went silent and Keira heard her mother's soft sobs. She had been listening to their conversation, too.

"I'm proud of you, honey. You sound very calm and self-assured. Much more than me or your mother." Her father chuckled and she knew she had convinced him she was fine. "And you're right, as well. We can't afford the trip."

They talked for some more minutes, and then she hung up.

"I'll call my sister tomorrow," she said and whimpered, hiding her face in the curve of Declan's neck.

"No way, lassie, it's going to be worse tomorrow." Declan pulled her away from him. "It's like ripping off a bandage. You should yank it off, not pull it off slowly."

"Oh, I know you're right, but it's so hard," she complained while she pressed her sister's number into her cell phone. "Hi, sis. Can you talk?"

****

Declan heard Megan's voice on the other side of the line growing louder and angrier as Keira told her what had happened. He couldn't make out her exact words but he knew too well how she felt. He kept soothing Keira while the sisters talked.

All of a sudden, Keira shouted into the mouthpiece, "No, I'm fine, Megan! I'm not alone. Declan's here with me. I've just told you he came in before anything happened."

She looked at him and rolled her eyes. He smiled and could only imagine what Keira's sister was raving about. However, he didn't need to guess for too long.

"Megan wants to talk to you." Keira handed him the phone.

"Why?" he mouthed as he grabbed the thing.

"I don't know," she mouthed back, shrugging and resting her chin on his chest.

"Hello?"

"You tell me the truth now, mister, or I swear to God I'll hop on the next plane to Ireland and I'll rip your heart out with my bare hands while you watch it," Megan shouted without stopping to breathe. "Is my sister unharmed? What did that motherfucker do to her?"

Megan was crying. She had probably held the tears back while she talked to Keira. He tried to calm her, "She's fine, Megan. She's shaken, obviously, but that bastard didn't have a chance to go through with his attack. I came in and knocked him unconscious. I would have killed the son of a bitch without qualms, but your little sister didn't let me." He smiled at Keira, and kissed her nose. "She was afraid I'd go to jail."

"That's so Keira," Megan took a deep breath and stopped crying. She whispered, "Thank you, Declan. We, my family and I, could never thank you enough."

"There's no need for that." It was his turn to choke up. "Do you want to talk to Keira again?"

"Yep."

While Keira talked some more with her sister, Declan caressed her arms and played with her hair but he got distracted. His thoughts traveled far away into his past. Dark memories clouded his face. Keira placed a cool hand on his cheek, and finally got his attention. He'd zoned out for a while. With it again, he looked down at her and smiled. "Hey, you! I didn't notice you had stopped talking."

"Yeah, I know. Where were you? Your mind was a thousand miles away, wasn't it?"

"More like a thousand years away, love." He pulled her closer and kissed her cheeks.

"You had a heavy expression," Keira said and closed her eyes. "Sad memory?"

"A quite disturbing one." He thought she was about to ask him for details, so he added quickly, "I'll tell you all about it, soon; but not tonight. We both need to rest."

Keira snuggled up to him and Declan sighed. They were both so exhausted that he hoped they would fall asleep fast. He closed his eyes, and felt his muscles relax for the first time since he had left his home in Dublin. Seconds later, he tensed up when Keira kissed a trail along his chest up to his throat, as she ran her hands over his skin. She played with his chest hair and breathed against a sensitive spot on his neck.

116

"Don't pretend to be asleep, silly. I know you're not."

He froze up and didn't know how to respond to her attempts at seducing him. It was wrong on so many levels. She wasn't ready for that and he knew it. On the other hand, she was emotionally fragile and if he weren't tactful enough she might feel rejected. It could get very ugly, very fast. He caught her hands in his, kissed their palms, and stared into her stormy eyes. Before he could say anything, she kissed his mouth.

"Kiss me, Declan, please," she whispered softly, against the corner of his mouth.

He was only human and couldn't deny her a little harmless kiss. He couldn't deny himself that, either. Keira took his receptiveness as encouragement and got bolder. She pressed her body fully against his, wrapped her hands around his neck, and pulled him down as she arched her back. He hesitated again, knowing too well things would get out of control soon if he let her go on kissing him like that. He pulled away and raised his head.

"Sorry, love. I don't think you're ready for this. It's too soon. Let me just hold you. We both need a good night's sleep."

She grabbed his shoulders and looked into his dark green eyes. "I need you tonight, Declan Slane. I need this to feel alive. I went numb after the attack. I'm afraid I'll freeze up inside." She held him closer, wrapping her arms behind his neck and plastering her soft body against his hard one.

She stretched up to reach his face and sprinkled light kisses over his stern features, as she whispered, "You make me feel alive like no other man has ever done, sweetie. Please. Kiss me. I need your warmth, your fire, to melt the ice in my heart. Help me forget what happened."

Declan resisted her seduction bravely up to the moment when her lush lips grazed the corner of his mouth. Her tongue tempted his lips, smashing down his already weakened defenses. He kissed Keira hard and urgently, taking control of the situation and moving over her to pin her gently to the mattress.

117

He also needed reassurance. He had been terrified when he saw Paul attacking her. He still felt shaken—afraid he would lose her forever. He wanted their passionate kiss to show her he was vulnerable, too. He had never wanted a woman more. He had never felt so afraid of his feelings, either.

Keira seemed to enjoy his hungry caresses, his thoughtful attentions, and he felt his body responding eagerly to her touch. Their bodies fit together in perfect symmetry. When she froze up in Declan's arms, he stopped kissing her neck and lifted his head to look at her. He had a pretty good idea why she had gone stone cold but had to ask.

"What's wrong, love?"

"I thought I could, but I just can't do this. I know you're not him, but I keep feeling his hands on me. I'm sorry," she babbled, on the brink of hysteria.

She rested her forehead on his chest—obviously to hide her tears. It was useless, because Declan heard them in her voice. He lifted her chin gently, until their eyes met, rubbing his thumbs over her cheeks to dry them.

"Keira, love, don't say you're sorry. There's nothing for you to feel ashamed of or to apologize for, silly." He kissed the tip of her nose.

"It's just that, in the short while we've known each other, I've cried in front of you more times than I've ever cried before in my life. You must think I'm a stupid little brat."

"That's nonsense, baby. You've been through hell tonight. Crying is a natural, human reaction." He rolled onto his back and pulled her into his arms again. He rested his chin on the top of her head, and soothed her, whispering in her ears, "It's okay. Everything will be fine."

When her arms closed tightly around his waist and the sobs raked her body, he closed his eyes to stop his tears from falling. He needed to be strong for her, despite his own fears. She needed him to support her, even though the ground seemed to have disappeared from under his feet and he felt like he was

118

falling from the top of a high building. His stomach sank with each of her sobs and he mentally beat himself up.

I should have thrashed the sod to kingdom come.

Gradually, her crying subsided and she got quiet. He kissed her hair and rubbed her back and shoulders all the while. Her breathing became even and deep. She had fallen asleep at last—although it would take him a long time to find sleep. He was too agitated, so he propped himself up on an elbow and watched her snooze. He brushed a lock of hair from her face, and ran his finger over her soft cheeks, which were still a little damp.

His heart shrank inside his chest and skipped a couple of beats. He had seen that kind of suffering before. All the pain—all the ghosts from his past—returned to haunt him. He had witnessed the woman he loved most in the world be brutalized. At that time, he had been paralyzed, unable to help her. He was terrified to think he might be useless now, as well.

What if I can't help Keira, either? I'd never forgive myself for that.

To see her sleep so deeply, so calmly, after all that she had been through, soothed his wounded soul and he dozed off. But it was restless and filled with nightmares that mixed images from his childhood and flashes of Keira's attack.

He woke up gasping and startled, and sat up on the bed. It took him a few seconds to understand where he was and remember what had happened the day before.

With a moan, he wiped his hands over his face before checking the time on the nightstand alarm clock—only seven in the morning. Keira wasn't in bed. Light came from under the bathroom door and he went there to check up on her. He raised his hand to knock on the door and stopped halfway, fist in the air, when he heard Keira heaving. He clenched his jaw—indecisive between giving her privacy and making sure she was fine. He went for the middle ground.

"Do you need help in there?"

"No, I'm fine," was her muffled reply, after a brief hesitation.

She sounded too weak for his peace of mind. He leaned against the door and strained his ears to hear what she was doing inside the bathroom. When he heard the shower, he went back to sit on the bed, facing the bathroom door. It didn't take long for Keira to get out. She wore her pajamas and was towel drying her hair. She flashed him a shy smile, as she sat beside him. "Good morning."

"I sure hope it is," he said with a dry laugh. "I don't mean to be rude, love, but you look awful."

"Gee, thanks." She play-punched his shoulder. "Just what a girl hopes to hear from a man in the morning."

"How are you, really?"

He kissed her cheek and she sighed, and stopped pretending to be light-hearted.

"You're beginning to know me too well." She stared down at her fingers, which she'd laced together on her lap. "I feel awful. Every inch of my body aches. It's like I've been run over by a semi-truck."

"Emotionally, you went through something worse than that, little one. Physically, it wasn't easy, either. I guess you don't want to go down for breakfast."

"Argh, I can't eat anything right now."

"That's not an option, young lady. Yesterday, I promised a very angry Megan I'd take good care of you. She threatened to rip my heart out of my chest if I lied to her. Somehow, I kind of believe she's capable of doing that."

Keira laughed at his feigned terrified expression.

120

"You know what? You'd better watch out, because I think she just might do something like that, if she thinks you've hurt me. She's always been overprotective of me. She'd chase off any kid who tried to bully me at school or in our neighborhood."

"I'll order breakfast, then."

"Just some fruit for me, please."

"No way. You'll eat a proper, healthy Irish breakfast."

She sighed and looked up at the ceiling when he turned away to talk to the person on the other side of the line.

"And don't roll your eyes, Miss Ashe," he told her, without turning around to face her, but covering the mouthpiece. "I know I can be an overbearing bastard when I want to be. This time, it's for your own good."

****

It felt comforting to Keira to have a person know her so well. She needed to feel safe to recover from the ordeal she had been through, and having Declan take care of her that way would hopefully ease the process. When he'd hung up, he turned and held her face, staring into her eyes as if he wanted to probe the darkest corners of her mind.

"Sweetheart, you know you can trust me, right? You'll tell me if you need anything, in case I'm too dense to notice it, please."

"I'll be fine. I am fine. You're taking excellent care of me, and I'll make sure to tell Megan that." She offered him a wide smile. "If nothing else, you're making me laugh. That *is* great."

He pulled her closer and she leaned her head on his shoulder. She relished the warmth and the feeling of safety that radiated from him, enveloping and cocooning her from any danger. She remembered something that had been hovering at the back of her mind since he had appeared in her room the day before. She sat upright to face him. Her eyes sparkled like a pair of sapphires.

"What the hell are you doing in Cork, Declan Slane?"

121

He laughed. "*Now* you ask me that?"

"Don't get me wrong. I'm grateful you're here, but I never asked you why you came down. I was just too relieved you did."

"Well, the answer to 'why' I came to Cork is quite a long one. The short version is that I missed you."

His hands tried to pull her back into his strong arms, but she resisted.

"Oh, no, mister. You won't distract me so easily this time. I want to know exactly what happened and we don't have anywhere else to go today."

As Declan searched for words to best explain his reasons to go to Cork, a knock sounded at the door.

"Room service," a muffled voice announced.

"I heard your sigh of relief, young man. You won't escape this conversation." Keira pointed an angry finger at him, then stood up and walked to the door.

Declan was right behind her. He got the tray while she signed the order and tipped the porter. Declan put the food down on the table by the bed, and she poured the tea. They started eating and she found out she was hungrier than she had realized.

"Well, Declan Slane, why did you decide to come down here?"

"I told you that my brothers and I had an awful childhood, remember? I said I'd tell you everything about that in person."

She nodded without taking her eyes from him. He sighed and hesitated.

"There are so many things about my past I want to tell you—so much pain. I don't know where to start."

"The beginning is usually a nice place to start," she whispered, and then encouraged him with a smile. "I understand if these memories are too painful for you. Just give me a short, less hurtful, version of the facts."

"I want you to know exactly what happened, though." He sighed, then put his cup down on the table.

122

Keira had finished her breakfast too, so they got comfortable sitting on the bed, resting against the pillows. He held her hands and she played with his fingers.

"My father was an alcoholic and a gambler. Luckily for him, his family had enough money to support his vices. When he met my mother, she was this sweet and beautiful young woman. Her innocence and grace attracted him, probably because they were traits he never found in the people surrounding him. The idea of him settling down and starting a family delighted his parents. They got a family started right away but never got to the settling down part. Even after my two older brothers and I were born, my father never saw himself as the provider. He relied on his parents' money for that, while he was too busy pursuing other interests, like women, gambling, and booze.

"My mother tried to work but he never allowed her out of the house for more than a couple of hours—time enough to run the household errands and return to the place 'where she belonged,' as he used to say. Don't get me wrong, Keira. My mother loved us deeply, but she wasn't a happy, fulfilled woman.

"Father would spend most nights out, in the pubs, drinking his family's allowance or losing it in the darts and on women. When he got home, hammered and broke, he was all too eager to take his frustrations out on us. My mother was his constant and favorite punching bag. He would beat her up and, if any of my older brothers tried to come between them, he'd beat them up, too."

Keira couldn't keep her indignation to herself. "How awful! I'm so sorry, honey."

"The worst part was that he used to make my mom think she'd done something wrong to deserve that kind of treatment. After a while, my brothers and I would run and hide whenever we saw our father clenching his fists. We would run to our bedroom and I would hide under my bed."

Keira held his hand between hers, taking it to her lips and kissing it.

"You don't need to go on, if it's too much. I get the picture," she said when his face screwed up and he seemed in pain.

"Thanks, hon, I can do this. I have to do this." He kissed her forehead and laced their fingers together. "One night, when I was six, my brothers were out of the house when the fighting started. I hid in my usual spot under the bed for a while. When I heard crashing sounds and my mom's screams coming from the living room, I ran there. I froze at the doorway when I saw mom lying on the floor in a pool of blood. He had thrown her against the crystal cabinet and smashed it to pieces. The shards of glass had cut her everywhere and she was bleeding. I didn't know what to do.

"Before I could move, my father heard me. He turned round and I thought he had a fever or something. His face was red and his eyes burned. He walked towards me while my mother shouted to me to go back to my bedroom. My limbs were heavy as lead, though. I couldn't move. Suddenly, something snapped in my mind. I lunged at my father, kicking and screaming. I was terrified my mom would wind up dead in his hands. I thought I could save her if I hit him hard."

He stopped and Keira threw her arms around his neck, pulling him into an embrace and holding him tight.

"Declan, please, stop it. I get it," she whispered, and kissed his damp cheeks.

"No, you don't. I didn't get it, either, at the time." He gave her the saddest smile she had ever seen. "It took me years to start understanding what happened that night. To be honest, I'm not sure I will ever understand it completely."

"You were only six. What could you have done?"

"I punched his thigh, which was the highest I could reach. He grabbed me by the neck and squeezed it. I gasped and heard my mom's weak pleas for him to stop. Then I passed out. Later, I found out that Jennifer's parents had

124

heard the commotion. They had come in just in time to take me from my father's hands. They called the police, but by the time the ambulance arrived, my mother had bled to death."

"Did he go to jail for that?"

"The police said there wasn't enough evidence to rule out accidental death. There were signs of a struggle, but no records of previous complaints. Mom had never pressed charges against him for the many times he had assaulted her. Besides, his family had a lot of money. I don't know how much effort the police put into finding out if he were a murderer."

"Oh, my God." She squeezed his hands. "I don't know what to say."

"Thank you, sweetie." He cupped her face and kissed her softly. "But it isn't over."

"What? How come?"

"Without mother around, he got worse. He drank and gambled more. A little after her passing, he brought women to the house, too—mostly prostitutes he paid to keep him company. They wore my mom's clothes and stole her things. It was painful for my brothers and I seeing our mother's memory defiled like that. Without my mom's protection, we became the ones he'd beat up whenever he felt like it. He didn't even pretend to have a reason anymore.

"After a couple of years, my father married a woman he'd met during a trip to London. Sally was Irish—from Limerick. My brothers and I thought things would finally improve for us because she was a great lady. I was almost nine when they married, and a little over eleven when she left him. First time he raised a hand at her, she was out the door."

"Smart woman."

"That was the thing—she was. She also tried to teach a lot of things to my brothers and me. We weren't an easy bunch to deal with, as you can imagine."

"I can."

"I was the worst one of all. I didn't want a new mother. I wanted my real mother back, which was impossible. I blamed Sally for that. She stayed patient and never gave up on me. Just when I started to trust her, open up to her, my father blew it and she dumped him."

"You must have been devastated."

"I was sad to see her go, but I was angrier at my father for having scared her off like that. Another effect of Sally's influence over me was that I admired her. When she left my father, that admiration led me to start questioning my mother's choices. I couldn't understand why she had stayed with a man like him. Not understanding her made me resent her, which made me feel guilty and even angrier."

"She loved your father. She also loved you and your brothers. She wouldn't have abandoned you."

"Yet, I felt as if she *had* abandoned me. I know it sounds insane, but deep inside I felt like she had made the worst mistake by sticking with him. I used to think that if she'd had the courage to leave my father, she would have offered us a better life away from all that we had to suffer in his hands."

"You don't know that. No one does."

"As a boy, I didn't know that, Keira. In fact, none of those feelings were clear to me, back then. I sorted them out as I grew older. At that time, I only felt the hatred and the frustration. Most of all, I hated the fact I couldn't do anything to fix my situation. So, I acted out. I didn't study. I hung out with the wrong crowd. Jennifer was the only person who saw my act for what it truly was—a cry for help. Luckily, she was also the only person I listened to and she always had a lot to say to me about my attitude. She saved me from myself."

Keira joked to lighten up the situation, "I have to remember to thank her for that."

"She'll love for you to do that. Well, long story short, after Sally left, my father didn't remarry but had a series of girlfriends, who got younger as he

126

got older. They only stayed until he started beating them up. My brothers left home as soon as they got jobs, but stayed in Cork. I wanted to go as far away as I could. Jennifer moved to Dublin to go to college. My life became unbearable without her around to keep me grounded. That's why I moved to Dublin when I was seventeen."

"Gosh, I'm so sorry you suffered like that. I wish I could make it all go away," she whispered, then pulled him for a quick kiss.

She meant to soothe his pain from those memories, but she forgot her good intentions as soon as her body reacted to his proximity. She ran her fingers through his hair. He held her close against his chest, splaying his big hands over the small of her back. Even through the layers of clothing, Keira felt his heart pounding. It was going as fast as hers. He savored her lips without hurry. She melted in his arms, feeling electric shocks traveling through her nerve endings. She kissed him back, hungrily, until they couldn't breathe. He released her mouth, and she gasped. He leaned his forehead against hers and smiled into her eyes.

"Believe me, Keira, there's nothing I'd like more than to let you make my pain go away, but not today. I'll gather the last shreds of self-control I still have, I'll get up from this bed, and I'll take a shower."

"But you still haven't told me why you came to Cork."

He stopped at the bathroom door, turned to her, and smiled. "I need to cool off. When I finish, we'll go out for a walk, and I'll tell you the rest of the story in a public place. I don't trust myself to be locked up in a bedroom with you like this. I'll end up doing something I shouldn't."

His meaning dawned on her as she heard him turn on the shower. She blushed and giggled as she stood up and opened the closet door to look for some clothes. She smiled at her reflection in the mirror, despite the marks on her face and neck, and held a dress in front of her body—it was perfect.

* * * *

"Thank you for convincing me to get out of that room. It's such a beautiful day."

"You've been lucky. Sunny days are rare in Ireland." He looked at her but Keira didn't notice.

They were lying on the grass at Fitzgerald Park, not too far from the fountain. The air felt warm and the breeze carried music and the sounds of children playing nearby. Declan propped himself up on one elbow, rested his head on one hand, and observed Keira for a while. She didn't move a muscle. He got a frond of grass and teased her nose with it. She fanned her hand in front of her face—probably thinking it was an annoying insect. When Declan drew the shape of her lips with the grass, she opened one eye and frowned at him.

"What?" He hid the frond, but his guilty expression gave him away.

"Are you for real? I was enjoying a bit of sun. Why did you have to do that?"

"I couldn't resist. You looked yummy." He leaned in and pecked her lips.

Keira sat up straight and moved to cradle Declan's head on her lap, playing with his hair.

"Are you ever going to finish telling me how you ended up at my hotel yesterday?"

"I guess I'll have to or you'll never let me be." He sighed, pretending to be upset, and laced his fingers through hers. "After you left Dublin, I was a wreck. I didn't sleep or eat well. I was absent-minded. I couldn't put a finger on why I felt like that and told myself I was worried you were driving alone. That was part of the reason. The truth was that I missed you, every second of the day. Harry, Màire, and Jennifer pointed that out to me a lot. Harry and Màire got really pissed off at me because I was messing up at work, and they had to do my job as well as theirs. They actually told me to get my act together or else."

"You didn't get fired, did you?"

128

"No. I had some overdue vacation days I'd planned to use when you returned to Dublin. I figured I'd better use them to come meet you and drive you back home."

"That was sweet." She kissed the back of his hand.

"Jennifer noticed I cared for you more than I would admit to myself. When she pointed that out to me, I denied it, but she convinced me. She also said I had to tell you."

"You care for me just as much as I care for you."

"I was terrified, though. I feared … no—I'm still afraid—that my past experiences would get in the way. I didn't want them to ruin our chances. So, during my flight here, I decided to stop by my father's house to confront him."

He stopped talking because Keira leaned forward and kissed him. It was a sweet kiss.

"It must have been tough on you, seeing your father, I mean. You're not close, right? When did you last talk to him?"

"Nine years ago. Not since I left for Dublin, to be more accurate."

Her jaw dropped. "Why talk to him now?"

"I went to his house looking for some kind of closure. I wanted to talk to him, not as a son talks to his father, though—I needed to talk to him as a grown man talks to another man, you know? I wanted to confront him about the horrible things he did to my mother, to me, and to my brothers. I wanted to put the past behind me, once and for all."

"What went wrong?"

He raised an eyebrow and smiled. "Now you're the one who's starting to know me too well, miss. It turns out my father doesn't remember much of anything."

"He's got Alzheimer's?"

Declan nodded and Keira sighed. "Oh baby, I'm so sorry."

"I won't deny that I was frustrated. There's a nurse, Rose, taking care of him. She's a nice lady, who made me go inside and sit down for tea. She told me my brothers never visit. Apparently, my grandparents had set up some trust fund for my father before they passed away. He benefits from it now. Rose said that's how she gets paid. The whole time I was there, my father looked at me funny, as if he was trying to remember who I was."

"Did he?"

"No."

"It must have been disturbing."

"I was pissed off—that's how I felt. The bloody bastard is screwing me up even now, I mean, being sick and all."

Keira ran her fingers through his hair for a while. "Maybe life is giving him what he deserves. Have you thought about that? I mean, Alzheimer's is a cruel disease. The idea of losing my memory creeps me out." She shivered.

"I think it's quite the opposite. It's a mean disease for the relatives who see their loved one fading away before their eyes. Scientists say people who have Alzheimer's, at a certain stage of the disease, barely understand what's going on with them. To people like my father, forgetting the past might be a blessing."

"I don't know about that. I do know that you won't be able to get the answers you wanted from your father. The best thing you should do is concentrate on your future."

Declan sat up and grabbed her face with both his hands. He stared into her eyes then kissed her. He couldn't let their kiss get too passionate in the middle of the day, in a public park, so he used all his self-control to keep the fiery kiss from consuming them both. She kissed him back with the same abandon and they were breathing heavily when he finally let go of her mouth.

"You don't get it, baby. If I want to concentrate on my future, our future, I need to understand my past. Now that I've found you, I can't risk losing you."

"Lose me?" She gave him a gentle smile. "Where's this coming from? Why would you lose me?"

"As far as relationships go, I have a terrible track record. I've told you I tried having a relationship with one girlfriend after another, and got disappointed every time. They told me I was afraid of commitment, but that wasn't true. I wanted to commit. I *want* to commit. But I'm afraid I'll become like my father …"

For the first time, Declan admitted to another person that he harbored those fears. For years, they weren't clear, even to him. He'd realized he had them when Jennifer broke up with him. Since Keira had entered his life, those fears tormented him day and night.

"Your innocence has captured my heart from the start. I wouldn't be able to live with myself if I destroyed it, like my father destroyed my mom's."

Keira knelt on the grass and laced her arms around his shoulders, then pulled him close. She held him in a tight embrace without uttering a word. Declan was surprised and confused, but didn't complain. When she let go of him, she sat on her heels and held his hands, keeping her eyes locked on his.

"Don't ever say such a thing again, please. You are nothing like your father—do you hear me? You are kind, caring, and patient. You are a good man. This is something nobody could say about your father. You've got qualities your father never had. Ones that convinced me I could trust you. I don't trust people easily. Today, I trust you with my life—completely." She lifted his hand and put it over her heart. "Do you feel it? My heart told me I could trust you. If you doubt yourself, don't doubt my heart. It knows you well."

Momentarily forgetting where they were, Declan crushed Keira against his chest and kissed her like he had never kissed her before—with his heart and

131

soul. He wasn't convinced he deserved her, but he was surely going to do his best to be worthy of her love.

Neither one of them heard Keira's cell phone ringing, because they were too wrapped up in the moment to notice such a mundane thing. Eventually, the annoying sound penetrated their cocoon and Keira reached for the phone.

"Don't bother with that," Declan pled, out of breath, grazing her lower lip and trying to take the phone from her. "The only people that matter in this world are right here, right now."

"Hello," she answered the call, chuckling, and wriggled out of Declan's strong arms. "Yes, this is she." She paused and listened. Her face turned ashen, and she shouted into the mouthpiece, "What? When? How did that happen?"

Declan waited impatiently for Keira to hang up, which she did without saying another word to whomever had been on the other end of the line. She slumped onto the hard ground and stared at him—sheer panic clouding her eyes. Her next three words had his blood run cold. "Paul has escaped."

* * * *

CHAPTER 6

"How did that happen?" Declan asked.

"They didn't say. Inspector Heller told me he's at the hotel, waiting for us." Keira stared into space. "I can't believe this."

"I'm here and I won't let anything happen to you, love."

After collecting their things, they ran out of the park and took a cab back to the hotel. When the car pulled over, a crowd of reporters surrounded it, all trying to get a statement from Keira, and all shouting their questions at the same time. Declan got out of the vehicle and pushed them out of the way to let Keira pass through the mob shoving microphones and digital recorders in her face.

"Miss Ashe, how long did you know Mr. O'Hallon before the attack?"

"Is it true he was your boyfriend, Miss Ashe?"

"Are you going to testify in the trial or are you going back to America?"

Keira had never been the center of attention, so she felt cornered and uncomfortable. Declan's arm around her shoulders gave her a sense of safety, even though his anger was evident by the swear words he mumbled under his breath. His muscles tensed up under his shirt and she noticed a bluish vein pulsing in his tight jaw.

"Miss Ashe, are you afraid Mr. O'Hallon might come after you now?"

Inspectors Heller and Dwyer met with them on the sidewalk, also pushing through the crowd, and tried to help Declan get Keira inside the hotel.

"Come on, fellows, leave the girl alone. She's been traumatized enough," said Heller, walking ahead of Keira and Declan towards the hotel entrance.

"Let us do our job," cried a young redheaded woman.

"We're just doing ours," replied Dwyer, who stood by Keira's right side.

"The public has the right to know what's going on," shouted an older man in a dark green suit.

Inch by inch, they fought their way through the crowd. When they were about to enter the hotel lobby, a reporter shouted, "Why did you help Mr. O'Hallon escape, Miss Ashe?"

Before anyone could move, Declan threw a punch at the man, his fist connected to the reporter's chin, who reeled from the sharp blow. Caught by surprise, the man lost his footing and sprawled on the sidewalk. Inspector Dwyer wasn't fast enough to hold Declan, who dove after the reporter, held him by the collar of his shirt, and kept beating him.

All hell broke loose with cameras flashing and rolling around them, and people shouting and shoving. Heller embraced Keira to shelter her, but she wriggled away to stand beside Declan.

"Stupid motherfucker, I'll kill you," Declan yelled, as his fist hit the man's bleeding nose again.

"Declan, stop it!" Keira shouted, and grabbed his upper arm.

He turned to her, his forest green eyes looked unfocused, and his face wore a mask of rage. For a spit second, he didn't recognize her, but she recognized the dark hatred in the depths of his tormented gaze for what it really was. She squeezed his arm to get his attention and shook her head, whispering so that only Declan could hear her, "He's not Paul or your father. He's just doing his job. He didn't harm me."

Her soft words wrenched Declan from the bloodthirsty trance he had fallen into. He shoved the poor man as he stood up. Looking down, he saw the front of his shirt was covered in the reporter's blood. His knuckles were bruised, but Keira felt sure his pride had taken the hardest blow. He seemed ashamed of the spectacle he had made of himself.

134

"I want this caveman arrested for assault and battery. You can't go about punching people for doing their job, mate."

"You wouldn't have gotten a black eye if you had done your homework. You were trying to rattle Miss Ashe with that question, Connor," Inspector Heller replied.

"I've got a picture that says otherwise, Heller."

He looked confident about the information he had gathered, and the investigators couldn't pass up a potential lead. Heller and Dwyer exchanged glances and the latter grabbed the reporter's forearm. "Not here, Connor. Come with us."

It was harder for them to move with the journalists in their way, but they ignored everyone as they entered the hotel. Heller went to the reception and asked the manager for a room with some privacy, and he offered them a meeting room.

While they walked down the corridor, Keira turned to Declan. "Are you okay, baby?"

He blushed and stared at her. "I should be the one asking you that. I'm such an ass. I can't begin to tell you how sorry I am for having put you through that."

"For defending me, you mean."

He stopped in the middle of the corridor and held her hands. He stared into her eyes. Didn't say a word. Just shook his head.

"What?" Keira asked when the silence got too uncomfortable.

"You amaze me. How do you do it? How do you see a good intention behind the Neanderthal-style stunt I just pulled?"

"Because I know your heart. It's in the right place," she said to him, putting a hand over his racing heart.

Dwyer came back for them and Declan didn't have a chance to say anything else. They sat down around a large oval table. Heller didn't waste any time. "What was that all about, Connor? I know you very well. You enjoy a bit of drama but you're a serious reporter. We know Miss Ashe hasn't been anywhere near that hospital today. You say you got a picture that says otherwise. Care to explain?"

Before Connor answered, Keira turned to the inspectors. "I haven't been there, but how do you know that?"

"We've followed you. I'm sorry about that, Miss Ashe." Inspector Dwyer ducked his head. "We were afraid you'd go back to Dublin or something. You're our only witness in this case. We couldn't risk losing you."

"I have to say that I don't like the idea of having the Garda spy on innocent people like that, Inspector," Declan replied on her behalf.

"You're not exactly innocent, sir. You put the man in the hospital in the first place," Connor stated, adding more fuel to Declan's already volatile mood. "You didn't do the same to me just now because we were in public."

Declan banged his fist on the table. "Shut the fuck up."

"Mr. Slane, if you don't get a hold of your temper, I'll have to remove you from the room. This is your last warning, sir," Inspector Heller said.

Keira squeezed Declan's thigh under the table and he turned to her. "Please," she mouthed. He visibly relaxed, sitting back on the chair. He didn't look pleased, though. His beautiful features were screwed up in a scowl, and he had crossed his arms over his chest.

"Connor, do you have the picture with you?" Inspector Heller asked.

The reporter unlocked his cell phone screen, then put it down so that everyone could see the picture. It was quite grainy; however, they could see a woman talking to the officer outside Paul's room. She resembled Keira. Inspector Dwyer used his fingers to enlarge the face. He whistled and handed the phone to Heller.

"Damn, she's a dead ringer to you, Miss Ashe. What do you know about this woman, Connor?"

136

"I don't know anything about her. I just got this from a fellow who works as security guard at the hospital. He owed me a favor and was on duty in the surveillance room. He sent this to me as soon as he found out O'Hallon had escaped."

"Thank you for your cooperation. We'll take it from here. You can go now."

Connor frowned. "Is that all? I don't get an exclusive or at least some info?"

"You've got plenty as it is. This is an ongoing investigation, you know."

"What about him?" Connor nodded towards Declan.

"What about him?"

"Aren't you going to arrest him?"

"We'll take him in for questioning. However, if you want to press charges, you'll have to come by the station later."

Heller waited for Connor to leave before resuming their conversation, "This doesn't feel right. It can't be a coincidence. Nick, the garda in the picture, never mentioned this woman."

"What happened exactly?" Keira asked.

"We know he attacked a nurse while he changed his bed sheets, then he stole his clothes, put them on, and sneaked out of the room. Nick knew O'Hallon couldn't receive visitors, so he wouldn't have let this woman inside the room. We need to find her," Dwyer replied.

"We'll relocate you to a safe house. We can't gamble with your safety," Heller added.

"Yes, of course," she said without hesitation—terrified.

"When can we leave?" Declan asked.

Heller cleared his throat, searching for the best way to explain the situation do the hotheaded boyfriend, and then Dwyer blurted out, "Slane,

137

you're not going with her. You'll come with us to the station. We'll book you for assault and battery."

"There's nothing we can do about it. You attacked Connor in front of cameras," Heller said.

"I knew I'd have to pay for my actions. But you'd better make damn sure nothing happens to Keira, or I swear I'll hunt you down. I don't care if you're the Garda or God Himself. That motherfucker slipped through your fingers. I don't trust your competence very much right about now."

Dwyer stood up and promised, "Don't worry about Keira. She'll be fine. … There's one more thing, Slane. I'll have to handcuff you—standard procedure. Turn around."

"Miss Ashe, pack your things. I'll send somebody to help you out and take you to the safe house," Heller told her.

Keira wanted to go with Declan, to offer him her support, but the detectives wouldn't allow it, so she decided not to cause any problems, even though her heart was torn to pieces. She stood up, holding Declan's face in her warm hands, and had to stand on tiptoes to reach his mouth to kiss him. She forgot the other two men in the room. The only person who mattered to her was in her arms.

The inspectors left the room to give them a little privacy. When Keira let go of Declan's face, he sighed. "What have we done to deserve this? We can't catch a break. You're still in danger. I'll spend at least a night in jail. We should be going back to Dublin. You should be having fun on your vacation, not hiding from a lunatic."

"Don't worry about me. I'll be fine. This is just temporary. The police will catch Paul again and we'll have all the time in the world to be together and have fun. I promise. Stay safe, Declan. Don't get in any more trouble. Come back to me soon."

138

They joined the others in the corridor, then proceeded to the reception, where a young female Garda met with them. She introduced herself as Katherine Murphy and she didn't look much older than Keira.

After the introductions, Heller told the two women he'd return in half an hour to take them to the safe house. Dwyer got hold of Declan and the three left the hotel. Keira saw the ever-growing mob of reporters swallow them up as the cameras flashed frantically, and the journalists shouted.

Her heart sank because those images reminded her of the nightmare she'd had—the one where Declan's picture in handcuffs appeared under a headline saying he had been arrested for her murder. She had never had premonitory dreams. And now wasn't a good time to start. She shook visibly at these thoughts and turned around to face Garda Murphy. "We should get going, right?"

"Yes, Miss Ashe."

They took the elevator to her floor and packed her things in less than fifteen minutes, which gave them enough time before their car arrived. Keira got her cell phone and unlocked the screen to call her parents.

"Excuse me, miss. Who are you calling?"

"My family. I haven't talked to them today. They'll worry when they hear about Paul's escape on the news."

"That's not a good idea, Miss Ashe. We can't tell anybody we're leaving. The department will take care of your check-out later. We'll have to hide you and leave the hotel undetected, so that we won't be followed. No one can know where you're going."

"I know you worry about my safety, but do you mean I can't tell even my own family where I'm going?"

The young police officer hesitated a little before answering, "I know it's a lot to process. Everything that's going on with you, I mean. I don't want to scare you further. You won't be able to tell your family where we'll take you because *you* won't know where we're taking you."

Keira furrowed her eyebrows together. "What do you mean?"

"It's for your own protection," Murphy whispered as Keira felt the burning sting of a needle in her upper arm. "I'm so sorry."

Those were the last words Keira heard before the world turned black as she lost consciousness.

* * * *

While Inspector Dwyer took Declan through booking, he couldn't remember the last time he had been in such a foul mood. He had been in trouble with the law before, but this time there was too much at stake. Keira needed him beside her and he had put himself in this helpless position and hated himself for it.

"Look, I know you're worried about Miss Ashe. She's in good hands," Dwyer told him as a Garda collected his fingerprints. "That bastard will never find her in the safe house and we'll get him before you know it."

A thousand different and colorful swear words warred inside Declan's head, all eager to come out of his mouth and describe to the man in front of him exactly what he should do with his reassuring comments, but he knew better than to make a bad situation worse. He owed it to Keira to control his temper. He took a series of deep breaths, swallowed those words up, and said, "I hope so. Keira's been through too much these past couple of days. She deserved to be relaxing somewhere beautiful and calm, not hiding away from a psycho."

They took him to a holding cell, which was surprisingly empty, while the other cells were crowded. He sat down on a hard bench and stared into space.

"Hey, Slane." He looked up to find Dwyer standing outside, holding a cup of coffee. "Take this. You'll need it."

"Thanks." Declan stood up to get the unexpected drink.

140

Dwyer grabbed his arm before he could sit down again. "I'd have punched somebody, too, if I were in your shoes," he said quietly so that only Declan could listen. "I sympathize but I can't do much about it."

"Yeah, I hear you. I appreciate it, though. The individual cell and the coffee, I mean."

"You bet." Dwyer winked, then left Declan alone to his gloomy thoughts.

He spent a sleepless night haunted by the events of the last days. His mind was restless and his body exhausted, yet sleep never came. The following day, Heller showed up, opened the door, and stood behind it, saying, "You're free to go. Connor didn't press charges. Quite frankly, you're much more useful out of this cell and with Miss Ashe."

"Couldn't agree more," Declan muttered. "When can I go to her?"

"Very soon. First, I need to take care of a few details."

They talked as they walked.

"Look, just give me the address and I'll be out of your way in no time."

"It's not that simple. We'll take you there, but you're not going to like it."

He frowned both at the comment and because the sudden brightness pierced his eyes as they came to the back door exit. To his surprise, Declan noticed they weren't on a street but rather at a yard. Dwyer stood beside a black sedan with tinted windows. He had a syringe and a black piece of cloth in his hands.

"Which do you prefer—wearing a blindfold or being knocked out?"

"Neither, but I'll take the blindfold, thank you very much."

They had been driving for a while when Declan asked, "How is Keira doing?"

"She is a sweet girl, that one. She's royally pissed off at us, though. She got angry because Garda Murphy didn't give Miss Ashe the choice we gave you. Truth be told, we didn't want to call too much attention to ourselves. We needed to get out of there quickly and I'm sure you'd have put up a fight if we had tried to sedate you."

"I suppose I should thank you for that, then."

Sarcasm dripped heavily from his words.

"Watch it, young man. I said you were useful, but I can as easily change my mind if you keep up with the attitude. We're on the same side here."

"I know that. It's just that I'm frustrated."

Declan leant his head back on the car seat and made an effort to control his emotions. He lost track of time as they drove in silence.

"Have you got any new leads on the case?"

"As a matter of fact, we found the woman in the picture," Dwyer replied.

"And?" Declan asked when the detective didn't go on. "What happened, man?"

"We'll fill you and Miss Ashe in on the details when we get to the safe house."

Declan felt impatient but kept his mouth shut until the car stopped. He took the blindfold off and got out of the car before the inspectors opened their doors.

At the same time, the front door opened and Keira came out of the cottage, running towards him, arms wide open. He caught her in his arms, kissing her like there was no tomorrow, like they were the only people on earth. She kissed him back with the same urgency. Their kiss was deep, passionate, but brief. She framed his face in her hands, angling her head while he grabbed her

142

tiny waist, then lifted and crushed her against his body, his hands roaming her smooth back, making sure she was real, her feet dangling in the air.

After both detectives cleared their throats loudly a couple of times, Declan reluctantly put Keira down, breaking their kiss. She kept her arms around his neck and gazed into his eyes. "I'm so happy to see you. I can't believe you're here. I'm so relieved."

"So am I, sweetheart. I was worried sick. Are you all right?"

"All things considered, I'm fine. I had a horrible night last night. I couldn't sleep. I kept searching for you in bed, stretching my hand to touch yours, forgetting you weren't there. Whatever sleep I got was filled with nightmares." She trembled. "Promise me you won't leave me alone like this ever again, Declan."

"I promise. I'm sorry I let you down." He hugged her and buried his face in her neck, whispering against her warm skin, "I'll never do that again."

"You didn't let me down, silly. I missed you, that was all. Come inside."

She intertwined her fingers with his, pulling him behind her as they crossed the little garden. The small white cottage looked cozy. It would have made for a perfect romantic getaway spot, if Declan hadn't been so worried. Two more gardai stood outside the house, which was completely isolated from any surrounding buildings. In fact, there were no buildings around the house at all. He had no idea where they were, but it was clear the safe house was remote.

The inspectors had given up waiting for the couple and had already made themselves comfortable in two big overstuffed armchairs in the living room. Garda Murphy stood by the door, which led to the rest of the corridor and the house.

"I don't know if I feel more at ease or more concerned to learn this place is so secluded," Declan told the detectives as he and Keira sat on the couch opposite them. He put his arm around her shoulders, keeping her close to him.

He needed to feel her body's warmth caressing his side. He needed to make sure she was safe and unharmed.

* * * *

"This is the perfect spot for a safe house. It's far enough that nobody will come snooping around or show up out of the blue. It's close enough to civilization that help can get here fast, if there's need for any. Rest assured, O'Hallon will never find you here," Heller wanted to give the two terrified young lovers some peace from the ordeal they were facing. He knew, too, what it meant to feel powerless when confronted by insane violence.

"By the way, you said you'd tell Keira and me about the case once we got here."

"We found the woman who tried to visit him." Heller noticed the way Declan hugged Keira closer, as if to protect her from anything alarming she might be about to hear. He couldn't hide a smile. "Her name is Ashling Green. Our IT guys traced her movements from the hospital to her neighborhood. Dwyer and I went there and found her house. She wasn't trying to hide from us or anything. Ms. Green told us she went to the hospital to visit O'Hallon because he's her cousin. She insisted with Officer Nick for a while, gave up, and went home. She found out about his escape later that day on the news."

"You didn't buy that, did you?"

"Not at first but her story checked out. We recovered footage from street surveillance cameras showing her leaving the hospital before O'Hallon. They never met."

"We doubt O'Hallon even knew Ms. Green was there," Dwyer added. "He took advantage of the nurse's presence in the room and got lucky when he got out of there. He'd have tried to talk to her if he knew she was in the hospital. She told us he's into her."

"How so?" Keira sounded intrigued.

"She didn't give us many details. I think she doesn't see O'Hallon for what he really is—a psychopath. O'Hallon's mother raised her after her mother died, when she was around four. He's like a brother to her and she doesn't seem to be aware of how dangerous he is," Heller explained, pausing to drink a little water.

"She thinks we caught the wrong man," Dwyer said with a snort.

"We've talked to some of Ms. Green's acquaintances, who told us the man is far more than into her. He's been obsessed since they were kids," Heller resumed his narrative. "They assured us she doesn't feel the same way. She told us she's fond of him, but she also said she feels uncomfortable around him because of his clinging behavior. She avoids him whenever she can. She went to visit him on account of his mother, her aunt. The old lady apparently called her, begging with her to go and check up on him. She couldn't say 'no' to the woman. You already know the rest."

"Don't you think he'd contact her if he knew she'd been to the hospital?" Declan suggested.

"My thoughts exactly." Dwyer sounded frustrated.

Heller scowled at his partner before answering, "We can't put her in harm's way. At this point, we don't know what this man is capable of doing. He's physically hurt, mentally unstable, and his violent nature may overcome any logical thinking he still possesses. We can't risk Ms. Green's safety like that."

A heavy, long silence settled on the group as each one of them racked their brains for a viable solution. Keira broke it first, "Use me as bait."

"Over my dead body!" Declan shouted.

"Sweetheart, think about it. Ms. Green is out there, unprotected. I agree she'd be in danger if Paul went after her. I'm the one living in a safe house, protected by all of you. He wouldn't have a chance to harm me." She pressed her hand on Declan's forearm. "We can control the situation. The police can

145

leak some key information to the press to lure him out of hiding. When he comes looking for me, they arrest him."

Dwyer nodded. "That's not a bad plan." He sounded impressed.

Heller frowned. "It's a great plan for disaster, that's what it is. Miss Ashe, I'm sorry. I know you're frustrated and want this to be over with but we can't do that."

Declan sighed with clear relief. Keira looked at him and he shrugged in response to her frowning expression. Heller guessed she was going to argue her case, so he went on. "We aren't totally empty-handed. Although my partner doesn't seem to agree with me, we've made some progress. Ms. Green told us about a place near Killarney, where they grew up and where his mother still lives."

"He told me he was from Limerick."

"He told you only part of the story. We know he was born and lived in Killarney until he turned nineteen, and he moved to Limerick after his father divorced his mother. Apparently, he had some distant relatives there who got a job for him. Ms. Green was born in Cork and moved in with the O'Hallons when her mother died. Nobody knew who her father was."

"He told me he had a bunch of sisters and brothers."

"Not true. He's an only child. Ms. Green gave us an address in Killarney, where he might have gone looking for shelter. It's not his mother's. We already had that one. I've talked to the Superintendent of the Garda Síochána there. He'll check the place out, talk to O'Hallon's mother, and let me know his findings."

"I'm sorry, detectives. I know you're doing your job but it's so frustrating to be here sitting on my hands. Yesterday, Katherine told me I couldn't even call my family back home. They must be worried sick."

"I hear you, believe me. We can't risk anyone—not O'Hallon or the press—tracking you down. I called your father. He's as frustrated as we are, but

146

he understands the seriousness of the situation. He knows these measures are for your safety. I promised to call him every day to update your family on our investigation and your well-being."

"I'm glad to hear that. Thank you. But, this just goes to show I've got a valid point. You wouldn't have to go through all this trouble if you caught the guy. Let me help you do that."

"Sorry." Heller offered her another bright smile. She reminded him of his younger daughter, Genna. Both were great kids but as strong-willed as they come. "Life isn't like the movies. There are too many things that can go wrong in a plan like the one you suggested. It's out of the question. Our psychiatrist has told us O'Hallon most likely sees you as a surrogate for his cousin. That would explain why you're the only one of his victims with whom he tried to create a bond. That also means he might get quite irrational about you."

"He did say some crazy stuff to me at the hotel room," Declan said. "At the time, I thought he was just taunting me. Now, I'm not so sure."

"Yes, you told us then that he said Miss Ashe liked him. We relayed your statements about the attempted rape, and our findings about Ms. Green, to the psychiatrist. He's convinced O'Hallon is on the verge of a psychotic break. This means anything can trigger a break from reality in him. Since our psychiatrist hasn't talked to O'Hallon in person, he couldn't give us a detailed assessment. He did give us a general prognosis, though. He can't be certain about what might actually trigger a break, or the outcomes of it. The causes could range from drug-induced depression to losing a loved one. As for his reactions, they could vary from harmless delusions to extremely violent acts. The bottom line is—we don't know what's going on inside that head of his. We should expect the worst and be prepared for it."

Aware each person goes through a different process of assimilating news, Heller watched Declan and Keira closely for any signs of trouble.

Keira looked far from reassured by his words and Declan stood up and paced the room. He seemed about to explode. Keira stood in his way and intercepted him. He gazed at her, and his expression changed immediately. Heller had also seen panic in her eyes. Declan made a visible effort to control himself. It was easy for Heller to deduce the young man was seething with anger and frustration, but he put on a brave face and opened his arms to harbor her.

"Come here, little one. I'll take care of you. I've told you I won't let anything happen to you, love." He closed his arms around her, kissed the top of her head, and looked at the two policemen—who had remained seated. "We won't, right?"

They stood up too, and Heller said, "We should get going. There really is no need for you to worry. We'll be back as soon as we can."

* * * *

A week passed by without much news. Keira and Declan established a routine of activities they did together and stuck to it—exercises in the morning, cooking lunch, reading in the afternoon, and sleeping early. Declan was a great cook and Keira was more than happy to leave him in charge of the stove. She helped with the cleaning up afterwards. They had a lot of fun preparing their meals—he cooked while she watched him. And what an eyeful! She never got tired of watching him.

Declan convinced Keira to join him when he went jogging in the mornings. The two male gardai followed them on these occasions. The safe house was set in a beautiful rural area, whose landscape offered a wealth of challenges for a fitness freak like Declan. However, Keira was a rookie jogger and he slowed down his pace to allow her to keep up with him. Regardless of the circumstances, they loved sharing those early morning moments. Since he had arrived, they spent each waking moment together and slept in the same bed.

"You're such a quick learner. I bet in another week or so you'll be outrunning me." He laughed as they entered the house, panting.

148

"I don't know about that. I just know I'd have a blast kicking your snob ass at jogging, Mr. Marathon Man." She play-punched his upper arm.

"I never said I ran a marathon. I won a couple of races in college."

Anticipating she would try to punch him again, he grabbed both her hands and held them behind her back. All playfulness left him when Keira nestled her soft curves against him, and his strong body reacted immediately to her heat. She smiled up at him, batting her eyelashes in the fakest innocent expression he had ever seen. While she rubbed herself against him, her smile broadened, and Declan hissed and closed his eyes. She stood on tiptoes, laced her arms around his neck, and pulled him down towards her expecting mouth. He stopped an inch away from it and raised an eyebrow. Two could play the teasing game she had started.

"You'll be the death of me, you know? I'm still out of breath from jogging and you want to steal what little air I have left."

"Don't worry, I know CPR," she whispered, then lifted her head and eliminated the distance between them.

He quivered as his rough tongue parted her soft lips, invading her in search of her eager tongue. He shuddered when her tongue slid against his then heard Keira's gasp when she forgot to breathe. He embraced her, sheltering her in the safety of his strong arms as he pushed her closer against the solid, wide wall of his chest, wishing she could stay there forever, where he knew she'd be safe. Her flesh seemed to melt against his but it wasn't enough for him. He wanted more and felt Keira did too when her hands tugged at his hair and their kiss got deeper and hotter.

If he followed his instincts, he would strip them both naked and ravish her there, in the middle of the living room, like the wild animal he felt raging inside his human frame. Although he knew better than to let the sexual beast inside him get the upper hand, he decided to ignore his rational side for a few more moments and indulge in the heat that was furiously consuming them.

149

Luck of the Irish

The sound of her whimpering when he broke the kiss to focus his attention on her face and neck, showering her with soft, quick pecks almost made him change his mind. He resorted to his willpower when she giggled and held tight to his shoulders for support.

"I could do this forever, you know," he whispered against her burning skin. He felt her heartbeat going wild as a vein throbbed under the tip of his tongue when he suckled a sensitive spot on the white column of her neck.

"I think we should," she replied while her hands found the lower hem of his sweatshirt and lifted it, exposing his torso.

When her cool fingers touched the bare skin of his abdomen, close to the waistband of his sweatpants, Declan felt a scorching wave of heat starting at the point of contact, radiating through his muscles, and exploding at his nerve endings. Shivers ran down his spine and he held her hands, preventing her naughty fingers from wandering further.

"You know we shouldn't."

He stared into the crystal blue depths of her eyes and felt their pull. Her allure was potent; not much different from the sirens in the fairy tales, but he had to resist it. He would one day drown in the sea of pleasure her eyes promised—no doubt about it. But not before she was ready for the plunge.

"We've had this argument before. As much as I'd love to rip our clothes off right now and lose myself in you, you're not ready for this. Not yet, anyway."

She gazed into his eyes for a long time, as if assessing his soul, before she replied with serenity and maturity beyond her years. "Our attraction is undeniable. Our feelings grow stronger by the day. Granted, we met a little over a month ago, but I feel like I've known you my whole life. You say you feel the same way. We've been through so much together. The difficulties we faced, and overcame, have strengthened our bond. It's much more than physical attraction. Why do we have to wait? I want you. You want me. Are you sure I'm the one

150

who's not ready? Sometimes I think you're the one running from these feelings."

He pondered her words over before opening his heart to her once more, "I love your candor, so I have to be honest with you, too. I'm terrified. After the horrible ordeal you suffered at the hands of that lunatic, I'm afraid you'll hate me for taking advantage of you at such a fragile moment, and I feel we should wait until all this is over and our lives are back to normal. First, I need to be sure you're safe." He took her hands, which had come to rest on his chest, and kissed them. "Besides, it's been only a few days since the attack."

"It's been over a week and it feels like forever to me, Declan. We've discussed this again and again over the last days. I don't want Paul to have this kind of power over me—the power to dictate how we make decisions. It's like he's winning, you know? It's like I'm a prisoner, or a hostage, waiting for him to decide my fate. I'll make my own decisions. I've decided I want you to make love to me." She smiled into his eyes.

Hers shone so bright with passion and love that he faltered. He scolded himself for his weakness and offered her a wide grin. "I don't want your first time to be hurried. I don't want it to happen in a safe house, while you're hiding from a psychopath. I want to romance you. You deserve candlelit dinners in fancy restaurants, and a luxury suite in a fashionable hotel with a bed covered in silk sheets."

She put a finger to his lips and silenced him. "You've already said that. I don't agree, but I respect your opinion. It's just that when you say these things you make me want you even more. You're so tempting." Her voice came out rough and low as she pressed her body against him.

He pulled away with a laugh. "No, no, no, young lady. You won't trick me that easily. You're the siren, and I'm the one who needs to worry about temptation."

He shook a finger at her, chuckled at her flustered expression, and then, with a wink, he went to their bedroom. He laughed dryly when he heard her frustrated sigh and a thud as she plopped down on the couch. Every day over the last week, they'd had that same argument. She wanted to take the next step, while he wanted to wait. So far, he had been able to evade her advances, but she was getting bolder and more practiced at reading his weaknesses. Truth was, Declan didn't know how much longer he could stand the frustration at keeping his desire under control. His only certainty was that he needed to overcome his lust for Keira's sake.

* * * *

A little after lunch, like they did every afternoon, Declan and Keira sat on the couch facing each other, leaning against the armrests, and reading their books. They didn't have much else to do because the gardai didn't allow them to use any electronic devices. In fact, all their things had been stored in Cork's Garda Station. Murphy had told them the police didn't want to risk anyone tracking them to the house, no matter how remote the possibility of that actually happening. Although the living room had a television set, they had no interest in watching it. They had tried to watch the news on their first night there, but the reporters seemed to talk only about Paul O'Hallon's Hollywood-style escape and Keira's disappearance. Most of what the journalists said was mere speculation. A few newscasters resorted to downright lies and innuendo since the police weren't commenting. Disgusted with what she saw, Keira had asked Declan to turn it off and they hadn't turned it on again.

Inspectors Heller and Dwyer, who came by the house every afternoon, were their only links to the outside world. So, when Keira and Declan heard an approaching car, they exchanged hopeful glances, put down their books, and sat upright.

Keira smiled. "Maybe this time the news will be good."

"I need it to be good or I swear I'll go nuts."

The expressions on the detectives' faces killed off any hope the couple might have had.

"What's wrong?" Declan asked before they could sit down on the armchairs.

"I'm afraid we don't have any news. We're stuck and it's driving us crazy," Dwyer said.

Declan grumped, "So you know how we feel trapped in here."

Keira petted his forearm and smiled at the policemen. She knew Declan well enough by then to read the signs, and could see he was about to lose it. His patience had worn thin and she didn't want to antagonize the investigators. "Have you talked to my family? How are they?"

Heller answered, "They're as fine as they can be, under the circumstances. Your father tells me every day he wants to come to Ireland and I have to convince him it would be a waste of time and money at this point. He wouldn't be able to see you. Your sister has been even harder to dissuade. Your mother rarely talks to me, but I know they're worried sick about you."

"My sister's quite a handful." Her smile held sadness because she missed them terribly.

Declan put his arm around her shoulder, pulled her close, and kissed her hair.

"Indeed, she seems to be quite a character." Heller chuckled.

Declan asked, "What about the hotel? Did you get in touch with Harry or Màire?"

"Yes, I called the hotel, but I talked to your boss, instead," Dwyer answered.

"Miss Jennings? Oh, my! I'm in trouble, aren't I?"

"She wasn't very happy to get a call from Cork Garda, I'll tell you that." Dwyer cringed a little, but smirked. "Once I was able to speak, she understood the situation and calmed down. She said she couldn't promise to

153

hold your job for you. But she did promise to offer you another position when you return to Dublin."

"Miss Jennings is a tough cookie but she's fair. Thank you, I owe you one."

"Don't mention it. Just doing my job."

When the detectives got up to return to Cork, Keira and Declan saw them to the car.

"We're in touch with the Killarney Gardai. They haven't had any luck investigating O'Hallon's ties there. We've got a couple of leads to follow, too. I said we're stuck, but we're not sitting on our hands." He nodded to Keira.

"We're doing our best," Dwyer added.

"I know you are. Thank you." She leaned forward to kiss Heller's cheek and shook Dwyer's hand in farewell.

The older man was a strong fatherly figure to her, while Dwyer came across as thoughtful. She trusted them with her life and she understood that feeling of being stuck because she felt the same way. It was disturbing, bitter, and disheartening. She laced her fingers through Declan's as they stood in the garden and watched the car disappear down the road. He squeezed her hand in return and she felt better. He had that effect on her nerves.

* * * *

Around nine o'clock that evening, Keira and Declan were both tired and restless. There was no reason for that so they gave up trying to relax and decided to go to bed even though it was much earlier than their usual bedtime.

As Declan brushed his teeth, he braced himself for what was about to come. Since he had arrived, they went over the same routine every night: Keira tried to seduce him or talk him into having sex with her ... he refused ... she got angry ... he got frustrated, and they wound up arguing. Her advances got bolder at the same rate as his self-control wore thinner.

It's a dangerous combination.

Besides, according to what they had learned from the police that afternoon, their lives weren't about to go back to normal any time soon.

I hope she gives me a break tonight. I won't last too long.

He squared his shoulders and went back to their bedroom. To his dismay and relief, Keira had already fallen asleep. He stood by the bed and observed her. Her breathing was even. She didn't move a muscle. He scratched his head and got under the covers, careful not to wake her. As sleep eluded him, he stifled the disappointment that crept up on him.

That was what I wanted, wasn't it?

****

A long time went by before Keira heard Declan's soft snore. When she did, she sat up against the headboard and studied his face. He was gorgeous, there was no doubt about that; but he was funny and intelligent as well as kind and protective. Although she'd had her doubts about him in the beginning, she had come to understand Declan better. She could easily picture the frightened little boy he once was as she ran her fingers lightly over his brow. She wished she could have cradled that boy in her arms, whispering in his ear that everything was going to be fine, and that he would grow into a good man.

At first, she'd had doubts about giving herself to a man she had met so recently, but she didn't have those doubts anymore—she had waited all her life for a man like Declan. A man who made her feel safe when he was around her, and made her see stars just from his touch. Her feelings for him had grown strong. She hesitated to say she loved him, because she had always believed she would have only one true love in her life—like her mother had. Although it was too soon to say that he was the one, Declan was a strong candidate. On the other hand, she had never planned on saving her virginity for Prince Charming. She just hadn't met a guy she wanted to sleep with—not until she met Declan.

Unable to resist, Keira leaned down and brushed her lips over his cheek. When he didn't stir, she moved down to his strong mouth. She didn't

155

want to wake him up, so she controlled the impulse to kiss him properly. It was hard but she changed her focus to the sheets that covered his wide chest. She pulled them down to expose the hairy expanse of flesh that fascinated her so much, and ran her fingers over the soft, curly hairs and down to the waistband of his sweatpants. She hesitated for a fraction of a moment before inserting her hand into his pants, searching for her prize. She found him, closed her fingers around his member, and stroked it gently, spreading open-mouthed, butterfly kisses on his chest.

He sighed and opened his eyes with a start. She stopped her explorations and waited. He was drowsy and took a few precious seconds to take in what was going on—to realize it wasn't another pleasant dream. When he moved to grab her hand and pull it out of his pants, she had already straddled him, trapping both their hands between their bodies.

"What do think you're doing?" Sleep—and something else—roughened his voice.

"Isn't it obvious, sweetie? I'm seducing you." She gave him a wide grin before leaning down and capturing his mouth. Not giving him time to reply, or stop her, she let go of his hardening erection to frame his face as she kissed him with passion and abandon, opening her heart to him, showing him how much she needed him.

****

Declan fought a losing battle against his treacherous body, trying to summon the faint shreds of self-control he still had about him. The resistance was short-lived before he surrendered with joy to the fire she had awakened in him without much effort. The truth was, he could have resisted their physical attraction, but that kiss bared Keira's soul to him. What he saw inside her mirrored and completed his own feelings. He had no doubt about where they were heading that night and it thrilled him to go there.

156

He grabbed her hips and pressed her down on him as he moved his body upwards. She moaned inside his mouth as delicious tingles started where their bodies were jointed together and spread through him. She kept playing with Declan's rough tongue and soft lips, biting them lightly. He moved his hands up and down her spine and kneaded her flesh. She undulated under his expert touch, which stoked his fires higher.

Her inexperienced movements made him harder and he fought to keep his body in check. He feared he would go off too soon if she kept going at that pace. He had to take control of the situation, so he broke the kiss, rolled over, and pinned her under him. He rested his forehead on hers to catch his breath. He laughed and the sound came out as a snort because he was panting. "Slow down, baby. I need a second here."

"I want you to make love to me, Declan."

"I've got that, sweetheart, but you won't have much fun if we rush things up," he said while he moved down her body.

His mouth covered her nipple over the rough cloth of her top and she writhed with closed eyes. She threw her head back in enjoyment. He suckled at the sensitive, hardening bud, and his tongue wetted the material and made it cling to her skin. She arched up to meet his demanding mouth, buried her fingers in his soft hair, tugged at it, and pulled him closer as he moved to her other breast to worship it in the same way. His expert hand wandered down her stomach and navel until he cupped her sex. She trembled and whimpered under his touch.

"You're so gorgeous—so responsive," he whispered. "I love how you sound."

"I love how you make me feel. Don't stop."

He raised his head to pull the wet top over her head. His eyes caressed her exposed, silken skin. She was a vision of innocent seduction. Her tousled

157

hair, flushed skin, and swollen lips evidenced their passionate kisses while her bright blue eyes shone with wonder. He rubbed a thumb over her lower lip.

"Keira, honey, are you sure about this? I need to ask while I can still control myself."

Instead of answering him, she raised her hips and slid her shorts down her legs, leaving her gorgeous body clad only in a flimsy pair of red lacy panties. He stopped her hand when she tried to remove them.

"Let me do it, please," he whispered, and then his voice caught at his throat.

His mouth went dry when he bent his head and kissed a scorching-hot, wet trail from the top of her breasts to her navel. She arched up, moving her head from side to side, and clenched the sheets in her fists when he grabbed the thin red material between his teeth to slide her panties down her body.

Next, he kissed his way up her legs until he reached the apex of her thighs. He spread them apart and smiled his wickedest grin before he dipped his head down and blew a cold breath inside her throbbing flesh. Before she could recover from the surprise, he covered her with his mouth. Keira closed her eyes and wriggled, moaned, and whimpered as waves of pleasure rippled through her. Out of breath, she whispered, "Please, Declan, this time I want you to make love to me, to take me. I want you inside me."

"Relax, love." He brushed his nose against her inner thigh, kissing her soft, trembling flesh. "We'll get there. I won't stop like last time, I promise."

He resumed his wicked ministrations but knew he shouldn't go much further because her passionate responses and total abandon drove him nuts. He ached to claim her. His throbbing erection threatened to explode inside his pants. He got rid of them and returned to her mouth, feasting on her sweetness, as he positioned himself between her legs. She crossed her arms behind his neck and pulled her knees up. He teased her lips with his tongue, mirroring the movements of his fingers inside her. Spreading her body with two fingers, he

158

shivered when she yielded to him and her flesh trembled beneath his fingers. He caressed her deeper, preparing her body for his much bigger member. When she appeared ready, he guided the head of his erection, but stopped at her entrance, and waited for her body to adjust.

"It's going to be uncomfortable, love. And it's going to hurt. I'm sorry."

"It's okay, I'm fine." She kissed his lips.

He grunted and moved further inside her body until he felt her natural barrier. She was so tight around him, but the feeling was so exquisite that he had to use all his willpower to keep from sheathing himself to the hilt. He needed to slow things down for her sake.

Keira gasped and buried her nails in his shoulders. Instead of pushing in, he pulled out. She opened her mouth to complain and Declan kissed her, muffling her cry when he pushed in again, past the barrier, and further inside her.

Declan's hands kneaded her sensitive breasts, and his mouth played with hers, to take her mind away from the quick, sharp pain she would've felt. Instead, he gave her a sea of pleasure. He set a comfortable rhythm for his movements—went in and out of her and stoked her fires. Her flesh trembled as the waves of pleasure rolled over her body, pushing her over the edge. She clung to his solid frame for support as she exploded.

Declan held his release back as much as he could while he watched her closely. He wanted to make sure Keira wasn't in too much pain. He hadn't expected her to climax her first time. He never dreamed it would be so amazing. Her body, wrapped around his, quivered from head to toe. She moaned, scratched his back, whispered his name, and grunted. He would love to go on watching her but he couldn't delay his pleasure much longer. He buried himself deeper inside her narrow passage one more time as he exploded, wailing her name. He couldn't remember the last time he'd had a mind-blowing orgasm like that. Most probably never. He moved in and out of her until his body stopped shaking. Spent, he plopped himself on the bed beside her, gathered her spent body in his arms, and kissed her hair.

"Thank you, love," he whispered, thinking she was asleep.

"My pleasure," she mumbled back, giving him her famous catlike smile, while she snuggled up against him and draped an arm across his chest. "I'm a very satisfied but exhausted woman. I just want a good night's sleep now."

He watched Keira closely, wanting to shout his love, his need for her, but held back. He didn't want to scare her away. It was too soon to say it, even though he had never been more certain of anything in his life. It was clear to him why he had postponed making love to her for so long. Deep down, he knew that once he claimed her, he would never want to let her go again. So, he held her as she slept until his eyes were too heavy and he fell asleep.

* * * *

CHAPTER 7

Keira woke up feeling sore and happy in equal parts. She lay quiet and motionless for a long time, listening to Declan's deep breathing and soaking up his warmth.

I could wake up to this every day, and it wouldn't be enough.

She snuggled up and fell asleep again. Next time she woke up, Declan was staring at her; his expression relaxed and a sexy smile curved his lips up, as his index finger traced a straight line from her nose to her belly button. She wriggled as he tickled her there.

"It's about time, Sleeping Beauty. How are you feeling? Too sore?"

"I'm sore, but I can manage." She returned his intent gaze, holding the hand he had forgotten on her navel. "Hmm, if this is another dream, I don't want to wake up. Ever."

"This isn't a dream, love. This is real. You are real." He gave her a lazy smile and leaned down—Keira lifted her chin to meet his tempting mouth halfway, but he stopped an inch before their lips touched. "I'm real."

"You're a real tease." She strained her neck and lifted her head, then grabbed his face with both her hands, pulling him down, and eliminating the distance between them.

She pulled his lower lip inside her mouth, then smiled when he sighed and she felt his hardness poke at her inner thigh. Declan's hands felt hot on her breasts when he cupped them, and then his lower body pinned hers to the mattress. She couldn't move her hips the way she wanted to, but she pulled her knees up and cradled his body between her soft thighs. He ran a hand from her ankle to the top of her leg, stopping there. As his tongue stroked hers, his thumb caressed the soft skin between her thigh and crotch. She sighed and let go of his mouth to take a deep breath. His intoxicating scent filled her nostrils. Keira threw her head back and arched up, releasing the air from her lungs in a mixture of a moan and a whimper.

"Hmm, you sound sexy."

"I feel sexy." She chuckled, but her voice got raspier when his thumb pressed against her trembling flesh, searching for her sweet spot. "Oh, *you* make me feel sexy."

He moved down her body, kissing her eyes, nose, and mouth until he found her breasts. He worshipped them as she moved her hips upwards to grind herself against his hard body. Declan took her breath away when he closed his teeth gently around a nipple, rolling it over his tongue. Keira arched her back again, but took advantage of his distraction to roll him onto his back. She ran her hands up his hard chest and grabbed his shoulders, straddling him, when he bit the soft flesh of her breast.

"You're getting very naughty, love," he whispered without letting go of her breast.

Delicious shivers ran down her spine as she moved over him, staring into his eyes and smiling. It was his time to moan and lift his hips, crushing his hard body against hers.

"Would you rather I stopped?"

"No way," he said, and his nails grazed the soft skin of her back when she leaned forward and kissed him deeply and for a long time.

Once again, their bodies found a rhythm of their own, timeless as time itself. Keira's softness surrounded Declan's hard angles, when her hand guided him into her expectant and ready body. He controlled her pace by gripping her hips, and moving her up and down as she swayed on top of him. She let go of his mouth and sat up to look into his green eyes. They looked dark and heavy with desire—a clear indication he wanted her as much as she wanted him. That was a heady sensation, a surprising realization—that she had that much power over him. She smiled at the beauty of that thought. When the now-familiar,

162

sweet desire coiled up deep inside her, spreading out from the point where their bodies were so intimately connected, awakening every muscle and nerve, she closed her eyes.

"Please, don't close your eyes, honey, look at me."

She made a great effort to comply with that simple request because her eyelids were heavy, too. She did open them and gazed into the wilderness of green that his eyes made.

"Thank you." He beamed and his gorgeous features lit up. "Your eyes are so expressive. I want to lose myself in them as you make love to me."

And she did exactly that. She rode the waves of pleasure, heard his elaborate breathing every time she pressed her body down on his, then let her hands roam up and down his chest, kneading his flesh, coaxing his responses, stoking their fire. His body trembled beneath hers, and he lifted his hips to meet her increasingly fast movements. Sweat slicked their bodies, and their hands hungrily explored each other's secrets, yet their gazes remained locked together.

Suddenly, Declan sat upright, holding Keira close to his chest in a tight embrace. She quivered, on the brink of another massive climax. His body was also about to explode. Their ragged breathing mingled, their arms fastened around each other's torsos, and yet they stared into each other's eyes without wavering. They didn't use words to communicate. Their emotions translated into sighs, gasps, and moans. Their feelings shone clearly in the sparks of light dancing in the depths of their eyes.

Declan kissed her, drinking in Keira's cries of pleasure, when he poured his essence deep inside her body. Her release was so intense she lost touch with reality, feeling as if she were spiraling through the night air, stars colliding all around her, and the only solid, real thing in her universe was Declan's hot body, around and inside her, keeping her from vanishing into thin air. She clung to his shoulders and her being expanded—endless, limitless.

Luck of the Irish

Declan locked his arms behind her back, pulling her closer, and kissed her deeply. Keira felt his heart beat fast against his ribcage. It seemed about to explode. They tumbled onto the bed. Their bodies sweaty, languid, and sated as they fell asleep.

* * * *

Keira and Declan spent most of the following week in bed, exploring each other's bodies, finding new ways to pleasure each other. There were no restraints—no limits for their imagination. She had never dreamed of a more generous, caring lover. He had always longed for the fiery, seductive partner Keira had become.

When they weren't making love, they explored other interests they had in common. Their morning jogging had become a treasured experience for both of them. The time they spent cooking, talking, and reading brought them even closer together.

The gardai that protected them had turned out to be an important part of their lives, as well. Although Katherine and Keira had started off on the wrong foot, she soon discovered the young officer was a sweet, funny woman. The three of them would sit down to play poker or blackjack in the afternoons, and not even the rain bothered them. Heller and Dwyer were in charge of buying the house supplies, but Murphy sometimes went out to buy female items, like shampoo and other personal hygiene products, for Keira.

Murphy protected the inside of the house, while James Morris and Nicholas Kerry, watched over the outside perimeter. Each one of the officers took turns of four-hour sleeping breaks, so that, during the day, the three of them would guard the safe house, and during the night, at least two would stay up watching over Keira and Declan.

Inspectors Heller and Dwyer had also become part of their routine. They would come by the house to visit every day, around the same time, bringing information about the investigation and Keira's family. Garda Murphy always had a kettle full of water at the ready to brew them some fresh tea, but rarely joined their conversation. One afternoon, at Keira's insistence, she sat down with them.

They had been talking and drinking tea for almost an hour, when Declan asked, "Inspector Heller, did you hear from the Killarney Garda Station yet? It's been over a week since you last mentioned them. Have they found O'Hallon's hiding place?"

"Unfortunately, they haven't. We had to go to Killarney yesterday because the gardai there haven't had any luck following the leads we gave them. As it turns out, the house we had thought O'Hallon might be hiding in has been empty and closed for a couple of years. It took the investigators a long time, and a lot of persuasion, to get a warrant issued to search the place. The judges didn't think there was enough evidence of probable cause to justify searching a third party's empty house. But there was no evidence of anyone having been in the house in a while," Heller answered.

"What about his cousin, Ms. Green? Has he talked to her?"

"We've been in contact with her. He hasn't shown up or phoned," Dwyer replied.

"Have you finished analyzing the footage from the hospital's security cameras and the street cameras?" Garda Murphy asked.

"We tried to retrace his steps after he left the hospital. The technicians finished their analysis, but they couldn't find him," Heller said, then hesitated, looking embarrassed.

"Why? You told us the other day that you had followed Ms. Green from the hospital to her neighborhood. You said she never met with Paul on the way, so I assumed you had followed him as well," Keira added.

Dwyer answered, "So did we. The footage isn't exactly high definition. There was a man, in uniform, leaving the hospital around the time O'Hallon escaped, who matched his height and general build. He moved slowly. We figured he was Paul O'Hallon because he was severely injured and wouldn't be able to move fast. The technicians followed this man to his apartment. He's a nurse and lives near the hospital. He walked slowly because he was texting his wife, who's on vacation."

"We even considered the possibility that O'Hallon had hidden inside the hospital for a while before leaving, so the techs went back to the recordings and examined the images from up to three days after he escaped. Nothing.

They were silent for a while, thinking. Katherine Murphy was the first to interrupt the pause, "They looked for a man leaving the place on foot, right? But he was badly hurt. You said so yourself. What if he got a lift out of the hospital?"

"We thought about that, too. There's a camera at the parking lot exit. We asked the guys to check it out, but there wasn't any image of O'Hallon leaving that way, either."

Another long silence fell on them, as they considered the various possibilities, until Garda Murphy's excited cry broke it again, "I've got it! He must have hidden inside a car, a big SUV or something. Have you thought about that?"

"Actually, we haven't," Heller admitted. "That's an excellent idea, Murphy."

"Happy to help, sir," she replied and promptly stood up to clean the cups and dishes.

Keira noticed her red cheeks before she escaped to the kitchen. The young officer might just have cracked the case, but blushed like a schoolgirl. She shook her head slightly and smiled, feeling sorry for Katherine—she could empathize.

"What?" Declan whispered in her ear.

166

"Nothing. Suddenly, I feel very old, that's all," she said, but added quickly when his eyes glistened with concern. "I'm fine. I'll explain it to you later."

She didn't want to embarrass their new friend in front of her superior officers. Declan frowned and hesitated, but finally accepted she wasn't going to say anything else.

"We should go and get the techs working on Murphy's theory," Heller said, standing up and offering his hand to Declan, then to Keira, in goodbye.

Declan shook it but Keira ignored it and kissed his cheek instead, as had become her habit. They said goodbye to Dwyer, too, and the two inspectors left.

* * * *

Keira woke up feeling feverish and nauseous. Darkness poured in through the little window, which told her it was the middle of the night. However, she couldn't recall where she was or how she had gotten there. She looked around and didn't recognize the place. It was a strange, small room. She found herself naked under the covers, but alone. The feeling there should be someone there lingered around the edges of consciousness. With a frown, Keira wrapped the sheet around herself, and got out of the bed to look for her clothes. As she checked the small closet, the door opened behind her with a creak that startled her. She turned around to find a man standing at the door. She didn't know him, so she felt embarrassed for being naked, under a thin floral sheet, in front of a stranger.

"Who are you? Where am I?" she asked, holding the long cloth to her chest as if it were a shield.

The man didn't answer, but his eyes traveled from her face down to her bare feet. His expression was hard to read because he withdrew to stand in the semi-shadows of the corridor. He lifted his hand slowly, pointed a gun at her, and pulled the trigger. She shouted when she saw the gun, but didn't feel any

167

pain when he shot it. Neither did she feel the bullet hit her. Instead, she felt her whole body shaking. A strange sensation. Somebody called her name from a far distance away. She knew that voice. She knew that man. He was supposed to be in bed with her. But he sounded so far. Where was he?

"Keira! Keira! What's wrong with you, baby?"

Declan's shouts echoed in the room but he got no response. She could only stare with unfocused eyes in a blank, expressionless face. Murphy entered the room, followed by Morris, both holding their guns. The sight of their weapons wrenched Keira from the strange catatonic trance. It took her a while to understand what was happening in the bedroom around her. When she did, her face flushed bright red and she pulled the covers to her chin to hide herself from the gardai's eyes. However, they didn't seem to have noticed her nakedness. They were too busy looking for the source of danger, the reason for the heart-stopping screams they had heard. Finally, she realized what had happened and her face turned a deeper shade of red. She felt mortified.

"Oh, gosh! I'm so sorry, guys. I had a dream. It was the strangest dream, actually. Did I shout? Did I wake you up, Declan?"

"You did, love, but that didn't scare me. I got terrified when you didn't answer me. You didn't see me. Murphy and Morris came because I screamed like a madman. Where's Kerry, by the way?"

"He stayed outside guarding the door. If you don't need me in here, I should get back outside."

"Yes, sure. Thank you," Declan said, absent-mindedly, searching Keira's face for any clues to what had happened to her.

"Are you all right, Miss Ashe? Do you want me to bring you water or anything?" Murphy asked.

"Thank you, Katherine. I'm fine. I'm just embarrassed as hell," she said and chuckled.

"I'll go back to my room, then. Call me if you need me."

Declan nodded and, when the door had closed behind Murphy, he framed Keira's face with his big hands and stared into her eyes. "What the hell was the dream about? You sat on the bed, screaming like a banshee. Then you fell into some kind of trance. It was spooky, Keira. I've never seen anything like that."

"I'm sorry I scared you. I don't remember much. I woke up in this room, but in the dream I didn't know where I was or how I'd gotten here. At first, I was alone and I missed somebody, but I didn't know who. I guess it was you." She smiled and squeezed his hand. "It would make sense, wouldn't it? There was a man, too. He appeared at the door. He didn't say a word. He pointed a gun at me and shot. In the dream, I didn't know who he was. But, in fact, I know him—it was Paul. He found me here and he shot at me." Her voice was strained.

* * * *

Declan noticed she was slipping away again. He held Keira's shoulders and shook her lightly to get her attention. When she looked up into his eyes, he spoke slowly and calmly, "Keira, it was a bad dream. O'Hallon won't shoot at you. I'd kill him first."

She stared back at him for a long moment, blinked, and sighed. Then she threw her arms around his neck, pulling him down to her. "I know you would, sweetie. That thought scares the hell out of me, more than anything else. I don't want you getting hurt, or in trouble." She touched his lips with hers, in the lightest of kisses, and Declan tasted the salt of her tears on them. He licked her luscious lips, wanting to kiss her worries away. He could accomplish that, at least for some moments, but hesitated because he didn't want to take advantage of her fragile state of mind.

As if Keira read his mind, she pulled away from his scorching embrace just enough to whisper in his ear, "I want you to make love to me like there's no tomorrow. I need you to erase this dream from my memory."

169

Luck of the Irish

"You don't need to ask twice."

Declan pulled the covers down her body. As each new inch of ivory skin revealed itself to his eager eyes, his desire grew stronger. His breathing became ragged when her glorious perfection was finally exposed to him. His emotions showed clearly, and he felt Keira's pulse rise. His passion fueled hers.

He cupped a breast in one hand, kneading the soft mound and rolling its tip between his fingers to a tight bud. At the same time, his hot mouth closed over the other peak, drawing her soft flesh into his wet cave, swirling his expert tongue around her hardening bud. She gasped, then hissed at the exquisite sensations he created. While grabbing his hair, she arched her back, desperately trying to eliminate any trace of distance between their fevered bodies. They were close, but he wanted them much closer, so he covered her soft body with his hard one. His legs pinned her down, but she managed to lift her hips to meet his, opening herself to invite him in, as her hand roamed down his chest, searching for his erection to guide it. However, Declan wanted to delay their pleasure for as long as possible. His self-control slipped through his fingers at the fast rate her naughty hands set. He caught her hand and lifted it to his lips, kissing her knuckles. She inserted her index finger in his mouth and shivered when he licked it with the moist tip of his tongue.

"Why the rush, baby? We have all the time in the world. Let me love you, sweetly and slowly," he whispered in the dark and her toes curled against his leg.

"That's a splendid idea. Let's try it some other time, though. I need you right now," Keira replied, and a naughty smile played on her kiss-swollen lips.

With her free hand, she gripped him and guided him to her hot entrance. Her body was more than ready. So was his. He didn't have time to argue his point any further before his treacherous body took control. His mind told him to slow their pace down, but Keira's movements beneath him made it clear she wanted him to go faster. She grabbed his shoulders, sinking her nails

170

into his flesh, and lifted her hips up so she could lock her feet behind his back, as her body tightened around him.

The familiar desire for her grew inside Declan, threatening to obliterate any thoughts, any control, he still had. It was useless, so he let go of it. The speed of his movements increased, matching her thrusts, and he gripped her hands and lifted them up over her head. He pinned her to the mattress with every downward thrust.

They cried out when they climaxed. Their minds shut the world out while their mouths sought each other, their tongues locked together—fingers and souls intertwined. Time stopped as they gradually slowed down their rhythm and sank into the bed, exhausted. Their skin and muscles tingled but the smiles they shared spoke of the immense bliss they felt at that moment and the deep, strong feelings budding in their hearts.

* * * *

"Are you going to town, Katherine?"

"Yes, madam."

"Please, call me Keira. I feel a hundred years old when you call me that." Keira laughed when Katherine's faced flushed. They had already had that same conversation a lot of times with the exact same outcome.

"I'll do my best, ma ... I'm sorry, Keira." She flashed a smile. "As you can see, it's going to be hard. Do you need anything in particular?"

"As a matter of fact, I'd like you to do me a huge favor. In a few days, it's going to be my sister's birthday. I thought I'd be home by then so I bought a purse to give her as a present. Would you mind going by the post office and mailing it to her for me?"

"Absolutely. Just give it to me with her address. I'll take care of it."

Keira shrieked a thank you and threw her arms around the officer's neck, then smacked a kiss on her cheek. "You're a lifesaver. I'll go get it."

Luck of the Irish

Declan came into the living room in time to witness Keira embarrassing Garda Murphy with her enthusiasm. He smiled when the young woman looked at her feet to avoid eye contact, and Keira zoomed past him towards their bedroom. Their voices drifted through the doorway, "Can you believe she thinks she's shy? I wonder how outgoing the rest of her family is for her to think she's the introvert one!" Declan said, in an obvious effort to mitigate the garda's embarrassment.

"I—I—Miss Ashe's a very sweet young woman, sir," Katherine stammered. "She's very generous and warm. Nonetheless, she doesn't seem aware of her many good qualities."

"That's right. She's completely oblivious to her beauty or her effect on the people around her. She always tells me her sister's the beautiful, confident daughter, while she's the brainy, nerdy kid. I don't agree with her assessment."

"She's mentioned something like that to me, too. It's indeed intriguing."

"What's intriguing, Kate?" Keira asked, as she came back into the room and handed the garda a box wrapped in brown paper, and a small card with her sister's address on it.

"You are, love." Declan laughed and hugged her tightly, kissing the top of her head, and inhaling the floral scent of her hair. He loved it so much.

"Me? What's intriguing about little old me?" She disguised her shallow breathing with a little giggle. Declan's proximity tended to jam her senses and cause them to overload.

"I don't understand why you think you're so shy and bookish when you've proven, time and again, that you're quite the opposite. You're gorgeous, warm, and outgoing. You captivate people around you with ease yet you don't see it."

"Yeah, right, wait until you meet my sister."

172

"See what I mean? You always do that, Keira. You undervalue yourself. Why?"

"Because …" She grinned and squeezed his hand, then turned to Murphy, who was still standing in front of them. "Talking about my sister, Kate, are you sure you don't mind going by the post office?"

"It's not a problem, madam … Keira. I'll get going, then."

"Thank you. Later, Kate."

Katherine left and Declan went straight back to the previous topic. The subject was uncomfortable for Keira and she avoided discussing it whenever he brought it up. But she cut his words off with a passionate kiss. Her arms circled his waist and her body pressed against his. When she let go of his mouth, he was panting, and wanting more.

"I was on my way to the shower. Join me?" her hoarse whisper invited him while a naughty spark in her blue eyes challenged him.

"I wouldn't miss it for the world."

She held out her hand, he grabbed it, and they hurried to the bathroom, shedding their clothes over the bedroom floor as they went. All thoughts about who was shy and who was outgoing in the Ashe family disappeared from mind.

* * * *

On the following morning, Keira woke up to amazing sensations: Her heart beat fast, her breathing came in labored gasps, and her flesh sizzled on fire. She realized Declan's long fingers were teasing her body in order to wake her. With a long stretch, she moaned and sighed. When he kissed a very sensitive spot behind her right ear and bit the lobe lightly, his chuckles came out all muffled. His big hands moved up her body to cradle her breasts. He squeezed them together and his fingers played with the hardened tips. His hot chest pressed her smooth back, his long legs were entwined with hers, and his erection throbbed against her backside. These signs made it plain for Keira how happy he was to have her in his arms.

"Good morning to you, too, sir." Her intention had been to tease him, but her coarse voice betrayed her excitement.

"I'm glad you feel that way, hon."

He didn't give her time to say anything else as his hungry mouth captured hers in a wild kiss. His hands left her breasts and traveled her body. One went south, splaying his fingers on her navel and holding her closer to his steaming hot body. His hardness poked the small of her back. The other hand held her face. She covered the hand on her lower body with hers, laced their fingers together, and pressed herself against him. She lifted her other arm and tangled her fingers in his hair, pulling his head closer to her. They ignored the awkward angle and devoured each other. When she tried to roll onto her back to face Declan, he tensed his muscles and held her in place.

"Please, don't move. I want to try something different," he whispered into her ear, while his tongue played with it.

"Something different? Different how?" She frowned, but stopped moving.

"Trust me," he said as his right knee moved between her legs and pried them open. "Just do as I say. Can you do that?"

She tried to answer but the air got caught in her throat when his expert fingers found her mound. She just choked and nodded. He laughed into her ear. "That's my girl."

Declan nibbled at her nape and shoulder as he inserted his digits inside her and played with her soft, moist folds. He knew her body well and touched her with the same reverence as a classical musician would touch a fine instrument. Her moans of pleasure sounded like the sweetest symphony. He pressed his fingers harder on her sensitive spots and her body answered quickly. Her flesh trembled under the tips of his fingers, and her back arched against his chest. She felt frantic.

"Declan! You're driving me insane," she wailed.

174

Her fingers grabbed his wrist and pressed his hand down harder—further inside her body. He smiled against the side of her neck and his body mirrored her hunger when his swollen member twitched against her smooth skin.

"Bend your knee a little," he told her.

When she complied, her body opened further and he glided his knee upwards and between her legs. He moved his fingers faster, in and out of her, to get her body ready as he positioned his own. He grabbed her hip to give her support when he penetrated her, inch by inch. He moved all the way in, then pulled back. He repeated those movements at a maddeningly languid pace. Even so, in no time, her flesh quivered around his hard body.

"Hold it off, Keira. Wait for me."

"I don't know that I can," she whispered back. She had difficulty expressing herself because she could hardly think. The position gave Declan easy access to her sweet spot, which he hit every time he thrust in and out of her.

"Yes, you can. Concentrate. I want us to get there together."

She closed her eyes and held her breath as his throbbing, hard member invaded her, again and again, and brought her the most exquisite sensations. She did her best to delay her satisfaction, and pressed her hand on the one Declan kept on her hip. She didn't have much room for moving, but she tried to meet his thrusts as well as she could.

Declan grunted from the effort to control his reactions, buried his face in her hair, and kissed and nibbled the soft skin of her neck at the same time as his fingers found and tweaked her hard bud. His body tensed when her inner muscles contracted faster around him. He used his powerful muscles to roll Keira onto her back to look into her gorgeous blue eyes when they at last climaxed together.

It didn't take long. He poured his seed deep inside her exactly when Keira's body writhed beneath him. He framed her face with his warm hands and kissed her. She buried her nails in his back and arched her body. Declan and Keira soared upwards and came crashing down at the same time. Their bodies lay tangled on the bed, but their minds drifted thousands of light-years away, in a place that only lovers know how to find. A place lovers go to when they share a perfect experience like the one Declan and Keira had just shared.

* * * *

When the inspectors arrived the following afternoon, Keira and Declan greeted them in the front garden. They had been out jogging later than usual because in had rained in the morning. The police officers looked worried. Declan defended he and Keira, "You know we go for a run, right? Either Morris or Kerry always follows us. There's no need to worry."

Dwyer exchanged a glance with Heller, who suggested, "We know that. It's no big deal. Shall we go inside? We need to talk." They followed his advice without another word until they were all sitting in the living room.

"What's going on?" Declan asked.

Keira held up a hand. "Wait up a second. I'll go get Katherine."

When the women returned and had sat down, Heller spoke, "We have finished analyzing the hospital cameras. We found O'Hallon breaking into a big pick-up truck. We followed the truck, using street cameras, until the driver pulled up at a supermarket and Paul left it."

He lifted a hand when Keira opened her mouth to speak. The gesture tapered off the excitement that had started to bubble inside her.

"Unfortunately, a big delivery truck hid him from view. By the time the truck moved away, O'Hallon was nowhere to be seen. We lost track of his movements."

"Did you run the plates, sir?" Murphy asked.

"We did and we found the owner. We paid him a visit. He wasn't very forthcoming, and he swore he hadn't seen anybody inside the truck or getting out of it. We checked out his story. He really has no connection to O'Hallon, and no reason to lie to us."

Dwyer continued Heller's explanation, "We searched the area around the supermarket but there wasn't any useful evidence left. Too much time had passed."

"What are you going to do now? Is there anything else you *can* do?" Keira asked, anxious and panicky.

"Murphy has told us about a hotline you've set up," Declan said as he draped his arm over Keira's shoulder. She needed that comfort because she felt at her wits' end. Declan continued, "You've asked people to call in if they have information on that bastard's whereabouts. Have you had any luck with that?"

The detectives exchanged meaningful glances again and Keira felt a shiver run down her spine as if a million ice-cold fingers were pressing down on her skin.

Heller answered, "Yes, we've set up a hotline. Unfortunately, it's hard to tell the serious calls from the pranks. A couple of people called saying they'd seen O'Hallon sneaking around the hotel where you stayed in Cork. At first, we dismissed them as prank calls because it didn't make much sense for him to return to that place. But a receptionist contacted me and said pretty much the same thing, except he told me O'Hallon had had the guts to come up to him and ask about you, Miss Ashe. We set up surveillance teams in and around the hotel, but he hasn't been spotted again. We didn't find him with the security cameras, either."

"Great, Heller. That's just perfect. This nightmare is never ending," Declan shouted. "Is this guy a ghost or something? Or are you all just plain stupid and incompetent? What the hell is wrong with you? Why can't you find him? We can't go on living like this. It's insane."

For the first time, neither detective replied. They looked mortified. Then Heller spoke, "You're absolutely right and we're sorry. I regret to say that

we have failed Miss Ashe and you yet again. However, there's still one thing we haven't tried." Heller hesitated before speaking again. "We'll need your cooperation if we decide to go on with this plan."

"What is it, Inspector? We'll do anything to help you." Keira felt desperate.

"She's right. We'll do anything to see that motherfucker behind bars," Declan said through gritted teeth.

"I'm still not convinced this is the best course of action, but my partner here has a very big mouth." Heller pointed his head at Dwyer. "He's blabbered to our superiors about Miss Ashe's idea."

Declan and Keira looked at each other. While her expression was hopeful, his was torn between terrified and furious. The last one won, "Do you mean to say you're going to use her as bait? No way, mister. I won't allow it," Declan snapped.

"That's the thing, Slane. Miss Ashe is an adult. We don't need your permission if she agrees to cooperate with us."

"Listen to me, son," Heller spoke to Declan, his tone reassuring, while his dark eyes sparkled with a glint of confidence. "We're on the same side here, and we want the same things—catching O'Hallon once and for all, and making sure Miss Ashe is safe. Even if you don't like this plan, helping us is in your best interest. Now, hold your horses or I'll have to ask you to leave. I don't want to do that. I want you on board because you're vital for this plan to have any chance of succeeding."

Declan huffed but didn't reply to the older man. He turned to Keira instead, "Are you sure about this, love? I think it's a bloody stupid plan, but I'll support your decision."

"We can't sit on our hands anymore. We've got to try something. Anything. This is the only idea we have right now. I think it's worth a shot. Please, help me out with it. I need your strength."

178

Declan hesitated, "My guts tell me this is insane. But when I look into your eyes … I can't say 'no' to you, Keira. I'd do anything to free you from this lunatic."

Keira leaned forward and stretched her neck to kiss his cheek. "Thank you."

They spent the next couple of hours laying out their plan. When Heller and Dwyer got up to leave, the mood was a bit more confident. The plan was that, on the following day, the older detective would leak information about the safe house to Connor, the reporter. He wouldn't give Connor the location, but rather would hint at the fact that Keira had been taken to a safe house somewhere around Cork and that the two inspectors visited it often. They expected to lure O'Hallon out of hiding, get him to follow Heller's car, and catch him before he got anywhere near Keira.

* * * *

That night, Keira and Declan decided to watch television to check if Heller had had a chance to put the plan into motion. When they turned it on, they found out Connor had been busy with their case, but not in the way they had planned. According to the host of the show they were watching, over the previous week Connor had tracked down O'Hallon's cousin and published an article about her on his newspaper column. His team of producers had invited Connor for a live interview to comment on the article and he had graciously accepted.

"What was the main reaction from the public to your article?"

"Most people emailed me saying they found it hard to believe that someone could grow up with a psychopath, like Ms. Green did, without realizing it. I'd like to point out that many studies show this is not a rare thing. I mean, sociopaths and psychopaths can lead pretty normal lives until the day they snap."

"You wrote, in your piece, that she visited him at the hospital on the day he escaped, but she wasn't able to talk to him and hasn't been in contact with him since then. We all remember quite vividly the commotion you caused in front of Miss Ashe's hotel when you accused her of having helped O'Hallon escape."

Declan fidgeted beside Keira when the scenes from that day appeared on the small screen.

"What can you tell us about that day? Have you been in contact with Miss Ashe?"

"Well, everything was chaotic after I said that she had helped her attacker escape, but you've got to agree with me that the resemblance between the two women is astonishing." The television director reinforced Connor's statement by splitting the screen in two to show pictures of Keira and Ashling side by side. Connor continued, "Anyone would have made the same assumption. I met with the investigators, gave them all the information I had, but nobody from the police has talked to me again. They say it's an ongoing investigation. Miss Ashe and Mr. Slane have disappeared from the face of the earth. Her family isn't talking to the press and his friends and colleagues swear they haven't been in contact with the couple. But, most importantly, nobody has a clue as to where O'Hallon is, either. It's a shame our police force hasn't been able to find this man yet."

"Heller won't be happy to hear that," Declan muttered. "Why hasn't he talked to Connor, though?"

Back on screen, Connor was still talking, "... To my surprise, I got a call from Cork Garda Station late this afternoon. I was on my way here and couldn't take it. I'll return the call after the show."

"That's interesting news. You might come back to our show tomorrow with an exclusive, huh?"

"I don't know about that, my friend. I think you'll have to read my column, instead."

"Thank you for your visit, Connor. I hope you return soon."

"My pleasure."

"We weren't able to get a statement from the police or Miss Ashe. As our guest has pointed out, they are unavailable to the press. We've also tried to contact Ms. Ashling Green to present her side of the story to you, dear viewer, but she didn't return our calls. If you're watching us, Ms. Green, we'd be honored to receive you in our show. Please, contact our team. This is Robert Kane—"

Declan turned the set off and looked at Keira, "I have the feeling we've started the plan off on the wrong foot."

* * * *

With time and constant practice, Keira had gotten bolder and more demanding in bed. She couldn't get enough of Declan's body. The same was true for him. Their feelings for each other had flourished and deepened. Still, none had said the three magical words. She thought it was too soon. He was afraid she wouldn't say it back.

They went to bed a little after watching the news program and soon their passion helped them forget about it.

In the middle of the night, Declan woke up from a naughty, but pleasant, dream. His muscles tensed and he sat up with a start, to discover Keira was responsible for his discomfort. Maybe it hadn't been a dream, after all. He raised an eyebrow at her mischievous expression and offered her a lopsided grin.

"Dare I ask what you've been up to, honey?"

181

"I'd rather show you than tell you," she answered before returning her attention to his lower body.

His body throbbed in response to her bold caresses, and at the same time he hissed and moaned. His legs trembled under her hands. She smiled when she looked up at him.

"Hold still, Declan."

"I wish I could. Come here."

Her soft curves fueled his desire as they brushed against his hot skin when she moved slowly up his body to meet his eager mouth. Her fingers didn't leave him, though, while their tongues dueled. He let go of her sweet mouth only because he needed to breathe. Soon, he lost the ability to do that, when she swiftly descended on his growing erection to show him she was a quick study. Her hands slid up his chest to find his nipples. She tweaked and played with them as her naughty mouth caressed him intimately. He arched his back and twisted his hands in the sheets. He groaned and had a hard time suppressing a yelp when she found a particularly sensitive spot. With good judgment on his reaction, she explored the spot, working his arousal, until he saw stars behind his closed lids.

With trembling hands, Declan held her shoulders and begged his sweet torturer for mercy, "Keira, love, I can't hold off any longer."

"So don't."

Her direct order made his body jerk even more under her touch. He never thought her mouth could be so innocent and tempting at the same time. He threw his head back on the pillows and braced himself. Keira had tried that before and he had managed to wrestle control of the situation from her. But he could see she was determined to go all the way this time and it was pointless to resist. He'd better surrender to the inevitable.

"Relax," she breathed against his skin. He was doomed.

His body swelled in contact with her hot tongue and lips and the sweet vibrations her voice had created. The last thing he saw, before he closed his eyes to reality, was the enticing sight of her fingers gripping him tightly as she bobbed her head up and down. He tangled his fingers in her hair in a last effort to keep his reactions in check, but the sensations were too overwhelming. They controlled his body and mind. Desire, lust, and passion pierced him, spurred on by her warm, wet caresses. Love and longing filled his heart and soul, nurtured by the abandon and selflessness with which Keira worshiped him. Her urgency stoked his fire and he soon reached the point of no return.

"Keira!" he wailed when her tongue swirled around him, teasing his senses, robbing him of the last traces of self-control, and his body exploded.

She caressed his thighs, trying to soothe his trembling flesh, but didn't let go of her prize. He bucked and writhed under her hands and mouth, yet she kissed him until there was no more energy left in his softening body.

She looked up at him, covered his body with hers, and seized his mouth in an endless kiss. He felt her tremors and closed his strong arms around her slender body. His lips played with hers as his emotions subsided, but hers grew stronger. He opened his eyes to watch Keira surrender herself and dive in the sea of sensations that she had created around them. It was an amazing sight to see and he reveled in it.

Their hearts returned to their normal rhythms, as their hands soothed and caressed each other. Keira lay sprawled over his body, resting her face on his wide chest. He breathed in the sweet smell of her hair, and kissed the top of her head. She sighed and smiled against his cooling skin.

"I love it when you do that," she said, sprinkling light kisses on his chest and then his throat.

"What? Sniffle your hair?"

She giggled. "No, when you kiss my hair."

"And I love it when you do that."

"What? Laugh hysterically?"

"No, sweep me off my feet." He squeezed her arms for emphasis.

"When did I do that?" She lifted her head and rested her chin on his chest to look into his eyes. "When I giggled like a stupid little girl?"

He traced her mouth with his thumb before answering. His expression was serious when he did speak, "No, Keira, when you made love to me like the beautiful young woman you are. You took my breath away in more ways than you could ever imagine."

Keira kissed the tip of her own finger and put it over his lips to stop him from saying another word. She looked spooked. "Please, Declan, don't."

He closed his eyes to hide his disappointment—he had so wanted to say he loved her, and she had hurt him. "I know it, Keira. I'd told myself not to say anything. I guess I got carried away."

"I'm sorry, sweetie. I'm not ready to hear you say it just yet," she said.

He admired the fact that she could be so poised despite being so young. He only hoped she would be ready soon to hear him say how much he loved her. The waiting was going to kill him.

He kissed her head again. "I hear you, honey. I don't want to pressure you. There's no haste. We have a lifetime ahead of us."

She snuggled into him. "Thank you."

With a warm grin, she rested her face on his chest again and threw her arm across his waist. He watched her fall asleep, which happened almost immediately, while his own sleep eluded him for a long time.

* * * *

Declan and Keira went for a run with Morris in tow. When they got back to the house, both Murphy and Kerry were at the front door. Murphy looked distressed and urged them inside.

Keira frowned. "What's wrong, Kate?"

184

"Ms. Green was found dead this morning. Apparently, a friend went to her house to check on her. He had called her cell phone the whole day yesterday, but she didn't answer or return his calls. He got worried."

"Inspectors Heller and Dwyer are going to the crime scene," Kerry added. "Dwyer called us on the police radio. He told us they'll come here as soon as they can to discuss our next moves."

True to their word, Heller and Dwyer went to the safe house straight from Ms. Green's murder scene, which was much later than usual. Keira and Declan spent the day glued to the television set, even though the reporters had little information to offer. They saw Heller trying to avoid the cameras without success.

"Please, fellows, I have no comments for you at this time. Let us do our job," he said as he left Ms. Green's house. He struggled through the crowd of reporters and walked half a block to the narrow alley, where he had parked his car. The reporters swarmed around it, shouting questions, and making it impossible for him to drive through them without running over somebody. He cracked his window open. "We'll talk to the press when we have more information. I swear it. Now, please, let me pass."

Declan and Keira discovered the footage must have been recorded earlier when they heard Heller's car seconds after the TV reporter announced a break for commercials. Dusk had already fallen, so the detectives wasted no time with idle conversation. They called Morris and Kerry to follow them inside in order to brief everybody on what was going on.

CHAPTER 8

When they entered the house, Heller dropped the bombshell, "We'll call off our plan."

"You mean, you won't use Keira as bait to catch O'Hallon? Hallelujah!"

"With all due respect, sir, I have to say I'm relieved too," Murphy added.

Keira frowned and said, "I thought it would finally set me free, but I understand the situation has changed. What about Connor? Does he know anything about the original plan? We saw him on television yesterday. He seemed pissed off at the police for leaving him out of the investigation."

"He won't be a problem. As it turns out, I wasn't able to reach him yesterday, which means, I didn't pass any sensitive information on to him or the press." He paused and stared at Keira before continuing. "My dear, things have escalated in a way none of us had anticipated."

Declan spoke up, "I beg to differ."

"I understand your frustration, Slane, believe me. However, we need to focus now on what's ahead of us. There's nothing to be gained by dwelling on past mistakes. I'll need your cooperation more than ever. Can I count on you?" Heller gave Declan a hard look.

"I'm surprised you have to ask. Of course, I'll do anything to help Keira."

"Good. We don't know what this psychopath is capable of in order to get what he wants. So, we can't risk exposing Keira at this moment. We'll have to relocate you."

"That's fine," her voice sounded thin, but she stared into the older man's eyes telling him, without words, she trusted his judgment.

His heart skipped a couple of beats at her unwavering trust because he hadn't been so sure of himself recently. He hadn't felt that insecure since his first big case. He was a green, rookie police officer back in the day, eager to prove to himself his reasons for joining the Garda in the first place had been right: bringing hope to desperate people; reuniting loved ones; catching the bad guys.

All his training hadn't prepared Heller to witness a little boy losing his mom. The horrible scenes he had witnessed over two decades ago and the nagging feeling of failure had haunted him through the years. They came back the moment he stepped into Keira's hotel room and talked to Declan.

Heller knew he had to find courage to make amends for his role in Declan's troubled past. He also knew he couldn't postpone that uncomfortable conversation for much longer.

But first, I've got to catch this bastard O'Hallon and set Keira free. If only fate would stop throwing me one curve ball after another.

His voice abandoned him so he acknowledged Keira's reply with a nod.

"The sooner, the better. When can we go?" Declan asked.

"Tonight. I sent Dwyer over to the other safe house to set things up."

"What happened to Ms. Green?" Kerry asked.

"Did O'Hallon kill his cousin?" Murphy added.

"That's the most obvious conclusion, although we need to work all angles. We're still sorting things out, collecting evidence, interviewing witnesses, but logic points blame to him. The first officers at the scene interviewed some neighbors. I haven't had time to get all of their intel yet."

"Did anyone see Paul at the scene?" Keira asked.

"Apparently, no."

Declan paced in agitation. "I tell you, this guy's a ghost. Nobody ever catches even a glimpse of him. He's either the smartest criminal around here, or he's the luckiest son of a bitch I've ever seen."

Luck of the Irish

"It feels that way," Heller said. "In my interviews with the people at the crime scene, I've found out the neighbors heard loud voices coming from Miss Green's house yesterday morning. They said there was some kind of argument between a man and a woman. Ms. Green has a boyfriend, who visits her often, and the neighbors assumed they were having a disagreement. They didn't want to interfere in the couple's affairs."

"How very polite of them." Declan sounded angry. "Meanwhile, a woman was killed. If people paid more attention to other people, more crimes could be avoided."

Heller felt Declan's words like a blow to his stomach. He was clearly hinting at his parents' situation and Heller's discomfort grew when Keira missed that clue and tried to make light of his worry. "Nobody likes a nosy neighbor. Would you like the police to come barging in every time we had an argument? Something tells me we'd keep them busy."

"I thought you, of all people, would get my meaning, love. If my neighbors had called the police, on any one of the many times my dad beat the shit out of my mom, things might have been different for her. Maybe she would be alive today."

"We don't know that. This kind of situation is very delicate. It's difficult to tell if you'll do more harm than good. My mother once called the police because she heard the neighbors having a fight. She even saw the husband striking the wife across her face. When the officers arrived, the woman told them she had fallen down the stairs. On the next day, she came by my house and told my mother never to interfere in her affairs again."

"I'm just saying. Sometimes, we think only about the proper thing to do and forget the right thing to do. But, I see your point. It's a tough call to make."

Keira looked at Heller. "Did the neighbors call the police?"

"No, because nobody heard any shots. Nobody heard any cries for help, either. I received a phone call from Denis Gentry, Ms. Green's boyfriend, earlier

188

today. He told me he had never trusted O'Hallon. He said he had told her many times that she should be more careful, but she dismissed his concerns saying the man was her cousin."

"She should have listened to him."

"Definitely. But, Mr. Gentry is a person of interest in our investigation, as well. Like I said, we can't rule out anything just yet. We need to explore all angles. We'll check his story, first. Yesterday, on the phone, he told me that he called her cell phone for most of the day, but she didn't return his calls. He was out of town and went straight to her house when he got back to Cork this morning. He thought there was something wrong, but he never expected to find her dead."

"How was she murdered?" Kerry wanted to know.

"Multiple stab wounds."

A brief silence fell on the group as each one processed the information.

"We watched Connor's interview last night." Keira broke the uncomfortable silence. "The host said his team had tried to contact Ms. Green, but weren't able to do so."

"Do you think there's a connection between her murder and Connor's article?" Declan asked.

Dwyer's arrival, at that moment, interrupted the conversation.

"Good evening, everyone." He nodded at Heller. "It's all set in the house." Then he glanced to Murphy. "I didn't have time to buy any food, though. You'll have to take whatever you have in here."

"That won't be a problem, sir."

"Thank you. Please, give Kerry the keys to the SUV. I'll drive you back."

"Don't you think we should take them to the safe house?" Dwyer suggested.

189

"There's no time for that." He lowered his voice, highlighting his frustration. "This lunatic has eluded us for far too long. We have to find all the leads he's left behind this time, while they're still fresh. It took the Garda years to find O'Hallon the first time. He eluded us for so long that we thought he must be some kind of criminal mastermind, but he was no bloody Houdini. I'll be damned if I let him get away with one more murder." He paused, and seemed to recover himself. He gave a sheepish look toward officers Kerry and Murphy. "Set the GPS with the address to the safe house. We've got a lot of work to do."

He turned to Declan to address his previous question.

"It's impossible to establish, for certain, if Connor's article had anything to do with Ms. Green's murder. We have no way of knowing if O'Hallon read the article or not. On the other hand, we can't rule out any theories at this point. And, that is a valid one." He glanced then at Dwyer. "We should head back to the station."

The two detectives stood up to go, and Heller turned to Keira. "Don't worry about your family. You know we've been in contact. I'll call them as soon as I get to the station to advise them of the change in your situation. I tried to talk to them earlier today—I was afraid they would read about Ms. Green in the media, but I couldn't reach them. Fortunately, the time difference between Ireland and the U.S. will work in my favor."

"Thank you, Inspector. I don't want them to worry about me more than they already do."

Heller nodded and cleared his throat. "Kerry, Murphy, Morris—you know the drill. Pack up the essential and leave the rest behind. Tomorrow, I'll send somebody to pick up whatever you leave here."

"Yes, sir," the three officers replied.

"Murphy, contact me when you get to the safe house." He looked at his watch. "It's a fifteen-minute drive from here. I'll give you half an hour to get there and call me."

190

"Understood."

"See you tomorrow, Miss Ashe. Slane."

Heller and Dwyer rushed out of the house, and Keira and Declan went to their bedroom to pack the few belongings they had with them. None of them wasted any time and everybody got busy.

"I'll pack the things in the kitchen," Murphy told her colleagues.

"We'll take care of the bedroom stuff," Kerry said.

Kerry and Morris opened the closet and threw things inside the bags without wasting time to arrange them properly. The first suitcase filled up in no time.

"Take this to the SUV, will you? I'll finish packing the other," Kerry asked Morris.

"I think we'll need another suitcase for Murphy's stuff. She's busy in the kitchen and won't have time to pack it herself."

"Good thinking. I don't think we have another one in here. I saw Murphy bringing some boxes in the other day. On your way in from the car, ask her where those boxes are, will you? We'll make do with them."

"I've got this."

Morris finished packing the second suitcase before Kerry returned with the boxes, so he decided to take it to the car and get the boxes himself. He passed Murphy in the living room as she was coming from the kitchen—her arms loaded with a huge box full of food and other supplies.

"Is Kerry in the kitchen with you?"

"No. I thought he was packing up things in the bedroom with you."

"He was. I told him to take some stuff to the car a while ago. He hasn't come back yet. I assumed he was helping you out, because I'd told him to ask you about some boxes."

They dropped everything to the floor as they realized something was wrong, and drew their weapons. A search around the room didn't produce any signs of an intruder, which didn't mean there wasn't one in the house.

"Check outside." Murphy lowered her voice. "I'll check on Miss Ashe and Mr. Slane."

When he moved to the kitchen, she explained, "I've already bolted the kitchen door. Nobody will come in through there."

"Fine."

"Be careful."

"You, too."

They went their separate ways. Morris headed off to check outside the house. It was dark so he crossed the small garden carefully, and got to the sidewalk. The SUV was parked in front of the house, but he couldn't see anybody near it. The trunk had been left wide open and Kerry wasn't there. Morris moved around the car and discovered Kerry lying unconscious, in the middle of the street, a few feet away from the car. Fresh blood pooled on the ground beside his partner. More blood oozed out of a gash in his lower abdomen.

Morris knelt down, put his fingers to his partner's neck, and checked his pulse. It felt slow and weak. His breathing was labored, too. He stood up and reached for his radio to call dispatch, when he heard a faint rustle of leaves coming from somewhere behind him. As he turned around, Morris felt a sharp pain in his lower belly.

He looked down to find a double-edged knife lodged there. He looked up just in time to see O'Hallon's sneer as he knocked Morris out with a punch to his right temple. He fell to the ground and blacked out.

192

When Murphy got to Keira and Declan's bedroom, she was relieved to find them still packing. She hesitated at the door for a second because she didn't want to alarm them, although she knew they shouldn't waste any precious time.

"Keira, we must go. Now."

"We've just finished packing our stuff," she answered without looking up at Katherine as she struggled with the suitcase zipper.

"Let me do that, love," Declan offered, taking her place.

"Isn't he adorable?" Keira taunted him, looking up at Katherine for support. Her smile vanished at the sight of Murphy's gun. "What's going on, Kate?"

"I'm sorry."

"What happened, Murphy?" Declan demanded. "Why are you here with that gun?"

The gardaí stood at the door watching the corridor and glaring at them as if cross they weren't doing what she told them to do. "We've got to go. Now. Kerry is missing. I told Morris to go out and look for him. I came in here to check on you guys. We can't waste time. Come with me. You'd better ..."

She never finished her sentence.

A shot rang out and Murphy fell to the floor of the corridor. Keira jumped forward to go to her, but Declan's strong hand grabbed her upper arm and pulled her back. He stepped in front of her, and before she could say or do anything, Paul O'Hallon appeared at the door, blocking their only way out.

"Missed me, gorgeous?" he addressed Keira, but aimed his gun at Declan. "Let go of her, Slane. Nobody else needs to get hurt."

"She's not going anywhere with you."

"That's a bold statement. You shouldn't underestimate her feelings for me. Now, get your hands off her and let her come to me."

"You'll have to shoot me first."

"That won't be a problem." He aimed at Declan's head and cocked the gun.

"Declan, please, don't do anything. He *will* shoot you." Keira moved to stand between the two men and faced Declan. "But, he won't hurt *me*. Please, let me go."

"I've told you a million times, Keira, that I won't let anything happen to you. I'll not let this vermin take you anywhere."

"Baby, please, let me go. I'll find a way to come back to you. I promise. I don't want to see you get hurt because of me."

"No way. You can ask me anything, love—just don't ask me to give up on you."

"I'm not asking you that. I'm asking you to have faith in me, in us."

Keira and Declan locked eyes, filled with conflicting emotions. His dark green gaze was full of determination and anger, while her blue eyes brimmed with tears, and her face screwed up into a mask of anguish.

With their feelings and senses so invested in their momentary battle of wills, Declan and Keira didn't notice O'Hallon moving inside the room, until he grabbed her upper arm and yanked her away from Declan's grasp.

"You heard her begging you to let her go with me. Keira belongs with me. You should have learned that by now, Slane. You took her away from me against her will." Loathing and spite glinted in his hard eyes as he pulled the trigger without batting an eyelash.

"No!" Keira's cry of desperation rang through the room, along with the blast from the gun.

Declan fell to the floor with a hand pressed to his stomach, where a stain of dark red spread across his shirt. Keira launched herself at Paul, screaming like an ancient warrior woman.

Deep hurt and churning hatred consumed her, but also gave her an unexpected strength to punch his chest and arms. Caught by surprise, Paul moved backwards a couple of steps. She followed him, sank her nails into the soft flesh below his eyes, and scratched at his face, hearing the gratifying sound of his high-pitched yelp of pain.

"You son of a bitch! Why did you shoot him? You didn't need to do that."

"Keira, I did that for us."

"I'll kill you for that."

Frantic, she looked around the room in search of something to hit him with, and missed his next movement. Sharp pain shot through her left temple when he hit her with the grip of his gun. Her sight turned hazy and she stumbled forward towards Paul. When he stretched his hands to hold her and stop her fall, she panicked.

"Stay away from me, you sick son of a bitch."

Keira couldn't stomach his hands on her again. She stepped backwards, away from Paul, trying to escape. She lost her footing with her sudden movement, fell backwards, and hit the back of her head on the ground with a loud crack.

"Declan ..."

His name was the last softly whispered word on Keira's lips before a silent darkness filled her mind and she lost consciousness.

* * * *

Declan's head felt fuzzy. Excruciating pain gripped his abdomen and clogged his brain, and allowed him to remember only bits and pieces, regardless of how hard he tried—gardai Murphy showing up, O'Hallon snatching Keira from his hands, then shooting him.

After he had fallen to the ground, he'd blacked out. When he woke up, he didn't know how long he had lain on the floor. Blood oozed out of the bullet wound, while crippling pain seared him when he made even the smallest movement.

He tried to shout for help, but his voice had deserted him. He moved his head, looking for Keira, and found her lying on the floor close to him. He felt utterly powerless when he heard the gut-wrenching sounds of bones breaking as O'Hallon continued to batter her already immobile body—just like he had felt when he was a child. He made a super-human effort to stretch his arm and reach them. He needed to stop the bastard, he needed to help her, but unbearable pain paralyzed him.

"Stop! You're killing her!" were the words he tried to shout, but no sound came out of his mouth.

He rolled onto his back. More blood oozed from his wound. Dizzy, sick to his stomach, and angry at himself for not being able to stop O'Hallon, he felt he had failed Keira. Just like he'd failed his mother as a kid. He couldn't live with himself if something happened to Keira because of him. He took a deep breath, bracing himself to try to move, but a sharp stab of pain pierced his chest, and he lost consciousness again.

* * * *

A series of loud beeps and painful moans broke the silence in the room as the nurse stepped through the doorway.

"Excuse me, ma'am," the nurse's gentle voice prompted Mrs. Claire Ashe to move away from the bed, where she had been standing since she had arrived.

The nurse checked the monitors, changed the IV bag of blood, and adjusted the one containing medication. She turned around to leave them alone,

196

stopped a few feet away from the door, and looked at Mr. Ashe, who sat on one of the two armchairs placed beside the bed, staring into space.

"We're doing all we can, sir."

He looked at her as if she had grown two heads, and squinted his eyes. After what seemed like an eternity, Rick Ashe replied softly, "Thank you, miss. You have Keira's eyes, you know?"

His dark blue eyes filled with tears and the young nurse scurried out of the room to hide her tears from a father who was going through a parent's most terrifying nightmare. The family didn't need an emotional nurse to make things worse.

* * * *

In the evening of the following day, Megan Ashe took her mother's place beside the bed. Careful not to dislodge the ventilator, she held the patient's hand, gave it a gentle squeeze, and whispered, "Stay with us. Do you hear me? Don't you dare give up now. We need you to catch that son of a bitch O'Hallon."

The sound of the hateful name was lost as the ECG monitor went crazy with fast, loud beeps, and a high-pitched alarm pierced the air. A hospital team rushed in, surrounding the hospital bed. They tried to stabilize the vital signs; but, when it was clear they wouldn't be able to accomplish that in the room, they quickly rolled the patient out.

"Where are you going?" Mr. Ashe asked.

"Back to surgery," the last nurse to leave the room replied without looking back at the family. Time was crucial. She couldn't waste it on niceties.

* * * *

When Declan opened his eyes again, he didn't know how much time had passed. The house was deadly quiet. O'Hallon was nowhere to be seen. Sluggish, Declan crawled forward and sat up beside Keira. He could barely breathe, due to the effort to move and the loss of blood, but he pulled her lifeless body onto his lap and held her close. He hugged her tight against his chest. He buried his face in her hair, which was covered in blood, and cried like he hadn't cried since he was a little boy. He felt like he was six again.

"Please, please, don't leave me, Keira."

His sobs filled the air. He balled his hands into fists, frustrated because Keira didn't respond. He couldn't face the evidence that she wasn't able to answer him.

"This is my fault, too. He wouldn't have killed you, if I had let you go with him."

He sat there, rocking back and forth for a long time, hanging on to her as if he could bring her back by sheer power of will. The thought that she was gone forever caused such burning pain in his chest, much stronger than the one from the bullet. He couldn't breathe.

"Please, don't go. I can't bear it if you leave me, too."

"I didn't want to leave you, but I had to go, sweetie. I wouldn't have left you, if there were any other way. Please, stop crying." Keira's voice sounded different. It seemed there was some kind of echo, like two people talked at the same time.

A soft hand rested on his shoulder. Declan looked up and couldn't believe his eyes.

"Mom? Is that really you? How? What happened? What are you doing here?"

"I came because you needed me, son. In fact, I've never really left you. You just couldn't see me."

He looked down to find Keira's body had disappeared. His mother stood in front of him. It was hard for him to look at her without squinting his eyes against the bright light radiating from her. She held out her hand and pulled him up.

198

"How is it possible? You're dead. It was my fault, too. I couldn't help you and you died. Just like Keira."

"Anything is possible here. Don't carry the weight of the world on your shoulders, son. I didn't die because you couldn't help me. And neither did Keira."

"I saw it. I stood there and watched father kill you. How isn't that my fault?"

"You were six. You couldn't do a thing. Besides, your father isn't a murderer. You were too young to understand what was going on in our house. You're an adult, now. You've got to forgive him. He needs you and your brothers."

"I'm sorry. I can't do that, mom. My brothers can't, either. He killed you."

She lifted an almost transparent hand to tap his. There was so much love, so much compassion in her eyes, that he felt like those same emotions filled his body.

"I've forgiven him, love. Why can't you and your brothers do the same?"

She paused and waited for his reply. When he didn't say anything, she smiled.

"Besides, nobody really dies. I mean, we cease to exist as corporeal beings, but we don't cease to exist. In this sense, I've never abandoned you. I'm here now, aren't I?"

A thick white fog wrapped them up and cloaked everything else around them. He couldn't see a thing.

"Where are we?"

"At the hospital. You're undergoing surgery."

Iris Slane swept her hand in the air in front of them, the fog lifted, and Declan saw they were standing in the middle of a brightly lit room. A group of people worked around an operating table. He had to strain his neck to see over their shoulders. His body lay on the table. He didn't question the fact he could see his own body a few feet away, but rather wondered about Keira.

"Where's Keira?"

Iris didn't answer. She preferred to hug her youngest son instead.

"What happened to her, mom?"

"It's going to be all right, Declan."

"How can you say that? I saw her on the floor. Her face was covered in blood. Her body was battered. She wasn't breathing."

"I know what you saw, dear. It's difficult for you to understand it. You've got to have faith, son. You've got to believe your love is strong enough to lead her back to you."

"I don't know if I can do that, mom. I'm so tired. I'm tired of everything."

"Don't say that, love. You're too young to say such a thing."

"Keira's been through so much. Both of us have. I can't take it anymore. I'm just so very tired."

"Don't give up. You must fight back this weakness."

The monitor in the operation room sounded a high beep. Declan had flatlined. The doctors and nurses hurried around the operating table, trying to revive his motionless body.

"Go back, Declan, and I promise I'll find Keira," her mother told him. "Know that I'll always be by your side."

As the team shouted orders, he felt light-headed. At the same time, his mother seemed to get more ethereal, slowly vanishing in the air. All of a sudden, he couldn't see her anymore, and everything turned quiet around him. All the pain had disappeared. He didn't feel anything.

* * * *

Morning dawned gray and cold over Cork before the Ashe family heard again from the doctors. When the door opened, they expected to see somebody from the hospital team, but Inspector Dwyer entered, followed by two young men.

"Any news?" Dwyer nodded towards the empty bed.

"Not yet," Megan replied.

"My I introduce you to Colin and Brandon Slane? They're Declan's older brothers."

Before they could say anything else, two doctors entered the room. They looked exhausted—their facial expressions impossible to read. Claire and Rick held hands, while Megan braced herself for whatever they were about to hear, although she doubted her numb senses could take more bad news.

"We stopped the internal bleeding, which alleviated the pressure inside the chest and allowed the heart-rate to return to its regular rhythm. I have to be honest with you, though. It was touch and go for a while. We thought we had lost him a couple of times because he had already lost a great amount of blood from the bullet wound, and during the first surgery. But, he showed remarkable resilience and stamina."

The little group exchanged meaningful glances and their relief was evident as they released a collective sigh. Inspector Dwyer broke the silence, "When can we see him?"

"Mr. Slane is in ICU now, so we can monitor his recovery. He will remain there until he can breathe without the ventilator," one of the doctors answered. "We advise you to go home and rest. All of you. He won't be able to receive visitors before noon. We aren't sure he'll be able to talk even then, inspector."

"We need to talk to him as soon as possible, doctor. Please, let me know it when he's fit for questioning."

"That may take a while, sir." The younger doctor glanced around the group, then said, "Rest assured, we'll do all we can to get him there fast."

"Thank you, doctor, we'll do that," Rick said and the doctors left with a brief, respectful nod towards Claire and Megan. Rick turned to Inspector Dwyer, "Could you give us a ride to the hotel? I don't think I can manage looking for a cab at this point."

"Absolutely, sir." Dwyer anticipated the next question the Ashes were bound to make. "I'm sorry to say we don't have any news on Keira's whereabouts, yet."

Claire dropped her head to her husband's shoulders and tried to muffle a sob. She didn't succeed. Megan wanted to scream at the detective who had let her family down far too many times over the past weeks. However, the oppressive emptiness that had filled her chest and head, had also rendered her uncharacteristically listless.

On the other hand, Dwyer's expression of utter misery and chagrin made it clear that there wasn't any more blame for her to throw at him that he hadn't already thrown at himself.

"We'd rather stay here at the hospital. We'll call you if there's any news," Colin told Dwyer as he and Brandon sat down to wait for their baby brother's return.

* * * *

Declan opened his eyes to find a beautiful woman looking down at him intently. She reminded him of Keira, except her eyes were brown. His head swam and he wasn't sure where he was or what had happened to him. His mouth felt dry and his throat burned.

"Rick, come here. He's awake," the woman called somebody over her shoulder.

He frowned and opened his mouth to speak. Nothing came out of it. He cleared his throat and was about to try again when the woman said, "Calm

202

down, Declan. You shouldn't exert yourself. Here, drink a little water. You'll feel better."

He did feel better but was still confused. He was in a hospital, hooked up to a lot of machines and IV bags. He felt so weak he didn't even try to sit up. Scenes popped up in his head and he squeezed Keira's mother's hand.

"Where's Keira? Is she all right?"

"We don't know." Her father came to stand beside his wife. "We had hoped you'd help us with information to find her."

"How long have I been out?"

"You were shot three nights ago. You've undergone two surgeries, and you've been in and out of consciousness since then. This is the first time you've spoken with any sense at all."

Declan frowned at Mr. Ashe, who added, "I mean, you said some pretty crazy things in between surgeries. At some point, you appeared to be talking to your deceased mother. Then, you accused somebody of murdering 'her.' We weren't sure if you were referring to your mother or Keira. You were probably hallucinating, but we were terrified you meant Keira."

Declan didn't remember any of that. He closed his eyes and tried to concentrate. His head hurt like hell. Some things started to come back to him. He opened his eyes again.

"O'Hallon came to the safe house when we were packing to leave. I don't know how he got inside undetected. I didn't hear anything until he shot Garda Murphy. He threatened to shoot me in order to make Keira go away with him. She tried to convince me it would be the best thing to do. I obviously didn't agree with her. He took advantage of our distraction to pull her away from me, then he shot me before I had time to do anything." He paused, fighting tears. "I heard Keira screaming before I blacked out. Everything after that is a blur."

"He stabbed two police officers outside the house, then shot you and the young female officer inside it. He took Keira away in the car you were going

203

to use," Megan said. "The investigators believe he hid inside their car because the police didn't find any other vehicles in the area or any footprints coming in from the road to the property."

"How did he manage to do that?"

"Earlier that day, Inspector Heller had parked his car in an alley, near Ashling Green's house, when he went there to investigate her murder. They believe that's when he hid inside the trunk of Heller's car."

"If he escaped from the safe house in the police SUV, they'll be able to track him down in no time."

"That's the thing, Declan. O'Hallon has disabled the GPS."

"Motherfucker!"

"No argument there."

"How are the officers doing?"

"Morris and Kerry lost a lot of blood. They are still unconscious, but the doctors say they'll recover. Murphy didn't make it."

"I'm so sorry to hear that." A lump in his throat strangled his voice for a couple of seconds. "She was a sweet girl. She died protecting us."

"You almost didn't make it yourself. Although the police got there fast, you had lost a lot of blood from the bullet wound. You were in very bad shape. Unfortunately, they couldn't save Garda Murphy. O'Hallon shot her in the head, and she died instantly."

"How did the police get there so fast?"

"They knew there was something off when the officers failed to contact Inspector Heller at the time they were supposed to call."

"Lucky me, … he probably wanted me to die slowly and make me suffer," was Declan's humorless reply. "How did *you* get here so fast, Mr. Ashe?"

"We grew tired of waiting in Boston. There was nothing we could do, either at home or here. We were aware of that, but we decided we should come.

204

We wanted to be near Keira when the police found that monster and set her free."

Megan spoke with bitterness, "Back then, we still believed these cops were capable people. A fat lot of good it did us, huh, dad?"

Declan answered, "We're all frustrated and worried, but the police officers are doing the best they can under the circumstances. O'Hallon is a certified lunatic. However, he's no moron. He eluded the police for years before he attacked Keira. Besides, I know they'll find her."

A brief silence fell in the room. The Ashes held their breaths waiting for Declan to explain himself. When he remained quiet, Claire grew impatient.

"What do you mean? How can you be so sure?"

"Honestly, I don't know how I know it. I just know it. You can call it intuition, or wishful thinking, but I'm sure Keira will come back to us soon."

* * * *

Another long silent pause stretched itself before Megan broke it.

"Now who's the lunatic? Or is it the meds talking?"

Declan didn't answer her petulant remark because he had fallen asleep again.

"Well, that answers my question, doesn't it?"

"Megan, go get some air, will you? You're driving us crazy."

She was about to tell her mother off when she realized she had been pretty unreasonable since Keira had been attacked. She couldn't help it. She loved her little sister too much and would never forgive herself if anything happened to Keira. After all, wasn't she the one who had convinced Keira she should go on that damn trip? Hadn't she told Keira, time and again, she should be more adventurous, more self-confident? She hated herself for having said those things. Now, there was nothing she could do to change that.

* * * *

Luck of the Irish

When Declan woke up again, half an hour later, he was surprised to see Dwyer, Colin, and Brandon sitting down and waiting to talk to him.

"How are you holding up, little rascal?"

"Wow, it took us a deadly wound to reunite the Slane brothers, huh? Do me a favor, Brandon. Next time you want to see me, get yourself shot, will you?"

The two older brothers managed to hug Declan without knocking over any of the medical apparatus surrounding his bed. It wasn't an easy feat. Although they joked about the situation, Brandon and Colin told Declan they were worried sick since they had heard about Keira's attack on the news. They had contacted the Gardaí early on and had been updated about all developments. The brothers might not have had time to meet often over the years, but they never lost touch. They loved one another deeply.

Declan grinned at Brandon. "How is my new sister-in-law doing? When was that, two years ago, right? It's about time she realized the mistake she made when she married you."

"Sod off. She's blissfully happy with me. And it's been almost four years."

"Wow, that long? Congratulations, brother. I mean it. When are you going to give me a nephew? I'd love to have a niece, too. Or several." Declan laughed at his brother's terrified expression.

"God forbid I should have a bunch of daughters. I wouldn't know what to do with them."

Colin spoke up, "That's true. I have two and they're a handful. You wouldn't survive a house full of them."

"How are Iris and Allyson, by the way? I miss them so much. I'm sorry I haven't been down as often as I should."

"Nonsense. You have your life, and your work, in Dublin. Erin and I know that well enough."

206

Declan asked, "Why didn't you tell me about father's disease the last time we spoke?"

"You never ask about him. I don't blame you for that." Colin raised a hand to stop Declan's argument. "I know your reasons. I respect your decision to wipe father's memory out of your life. I preferred a different approach. I also don't want to have anything to do with him, but I had to keep in touch with his nurse. I manage his expenses, remember? Last time I spoke with Mrs. Michaelson, she told me he wasn't doing so badly, considering his disease."

"When was that?"

"About six months ago."

"What about you, Brandon?"

"I kept my distance from the bastard, much like you did. Colin told me about the old man's disease once, when we went out for dinner. I think he's got what he deserves."

"What about Kim? Does her family live in Cork, too?"

"No, she's from Galway. We have a few friends here, but to be honest, except the occasional dinner or lunch with Colin's family, Kim and I prefer to keep to ourselves—enjoy our married life before the children start coming, you know?"

"Wow, brother. You sound like you're hoping for a big family."

"Yeah, I want a lot of kids, but not only girls. Don't change the subject. Why do you ask about father? Have you seen him? Have you been to the house?"

Declan just nodded.

"You swore never to set foot there again. What made you change your mind?"

"Yeah, I said that, and a bunch of other stupid things. I was younger and dumber. Keira made me change my mind. Well, not exactly her, … more like the possibility of losing her if I didn't do anything about my relationship issues. That's a long story. I'll tell you about it some other time."

The Ashes came back at that point.

"What aren't you telling your brother, young man? Don't you know it's a bad idea to postpone telling people things you want to say to them? You never know if you'll have another chance to do it in the future." Mrs. Ashe wagged her finger in mock severity.

"You're right. I'm sorry."

It surprised him that she was able to tease him at a time like this. However, underneath her light tone, her words sounded true and reminded him of the last night he had spent with Keira.

"That story is really too long and I'm tired. I can wait for a better time to tell it to them. There are other more important things I regret not saying when I had the chance. Like telling Keira I loved her. I had the chance and chickened out."

Claire patted his forearm and smiled into his eyes. "Don't worry, son. You'll have plenty of time to tell her that, once the police return her to us. I agree with you, it'll be soon."

Declan returned her stare in silence for a moment. He was speechless. Claire Ashe wasn't a fragile flower. She was tough as steel. Even in the middle of her grief and pain, she found it in herself to cheer up her daughter's boyfriend—a person she barely knew. Keira must have gotten that trait from her mother.

Her words stirred a dormant memory in the back of his mind. A conversation he'd had with a woman, but he couldn't recall it properly. It seemed more like a dream than a real conversation and he let it go. He looked at the detective, who stood a couple of feet away from the small group, while they talked.

208

"That's quite a vote of confidence, Dwyer. I can't say I agree with Mrs. Ashe about your role in Keira's return."

"I don't blame you, Slane. Believe me when I say we're doing all we can."

"Have you found out anything else?" Rick asked.

Everyone sat up a little straighter and looked at the detective. Any news would be welcome, even bad news. It's the not knowing that can be the hardest to deal with.

The police officer replied. "We had hoped Declan could give us more details about what happened in the house, since he's the first witness to regain consciousness. But, you told us what he said when he woke up. Unfortunately, it didn't add much information to what we already knew. We've recovered O'Hallon's DNA from the trunk of Heller's car, which confirms our initial suspicion that he hid inside it to get to the safe house."

"How did he do that, by the way? You were at a crime scene, for heaven's sake!" Indignation rang loud in Megan's voice.

"I've told you already that Heller parked his car in a small alley near the house." The detective sounded defensive. "The place was swarming with reporters and police officers. None of us thought O'Hallon would have the guts to stick around after his crime, let alone pull a stunt like that."

Declan cut the officer off. "This story is beginning to sound a bit fishy to me. Was it part of that stupid plan of yours? Heller said the Garda wouldn't go along with it after the murder. Now, you say nobody saw a man getting inside Heller's car in a place full of people."

"I didn't say that. I said the car was in an alley. The alley wasn't full of people. The street was."

"Wait just a second. What plan?" the accusation in Megan's tone was unmistakable.

Declan spoke when the inspector failed to, "Using Keira as bait to lure O'Hallon out of hiding. I said that was the worst idea I had ever heard."

"Come again? I didn't hear you right."

"Oh, yeah, you heard me fine, Megan."

Dwyer glared at Declan. "Since you remember saying that, Slane, you should also remember that Heller told Miss Ashe he wasn't comfortable with that plan. Does it ring any bells?"

Colin intervened, "Guys, guys, calm down. This is not going to get us anywhere."

"You're right," Declan said with a sigh. "I'm sorry, inspector. You know I'm quick-tempered."

"There's no need to apologize. We're all tired and frustrated. You were almost killed. I should have known better." The detective took a seat again, and the atmosphere in the room eased.

When Megan spoke, her voice was gentler, "Before we came to Ireland, you told us this man was obsessed with his cousin and that was probably why he had stalked my sister. We're talking about a psycho here, but it wouldn't make much sense for him to kill Ms. Green to get to Keira, if he wanted his cousin in the first place. Even so, do you think he killed his cousin to get you there and find out where Keira was?"

"That wouldn't surprise me," Dwyer said. "But we interviewed a couple who lived next to Ms. Green. They weren't home when she was found dead, so we didn't talk to them until recently. Their house shares a wall with Ms. Green's. They told me they heard part of an argument between a man and their neighbor. Now, I'm sure the man was O'Hallon. They said he begged Ms. Green to run off with him, to marry him. He said they belonged together, and that her boyfriend was the one keeping them apart, spoiling their happiness."

"They didn't know O'Hallon?"

"They had moved to the neighborhood recently and didn't know Ms. Green very well. They didn't call the police because they believed it was a lovers' spat."

"Did they hear what she said? I remember she didn't think he was obsessed with her when you first talked to her." Declan asked.

"Exactly. My guess is she realized, too late, that she was wrong about her cousin. The neighbors said her voice was difficult to hear, but it seemed she was trying to calm down her visitor. We think that, most likely, O'Hallon was threatening her with the knife and she was trying to talk some sense into him."

"She underestimated her cousin," Rick said.

"It's not that uncommon. All her life, Ms. Green had chosen to ignore the signs that showed something was clearly wrong with a person she thought she knew. She had grown up with him, and certainly shared many fond memories with the man. Our forensic psychiatrist believes O'Hallon snapped when Ms. Green refused to play her part in his fantasy."

"She didn't agree to elope with him and he killed her. Just like that?" Megan asked.

"You said it yourself, miss—we're discussing a psychologically damaged mind. The rules that apply to our behavior don't apply to O'Hallon's. Ms. Green had always been nice to him because it was in her nature to be kind. He probably mistook her kindness for love. If she loved him, she would want to be with him—would want to marry him. In his fantasy world, his cousin represented the perfect woman who would be happy to be his perfect wife. All he had to do was ask her to marry him. When reality didn't match his fantasy, he lost it and stabbed her to death. I'll spare you the gory details, but the number of times he stabbed Ms. Green substantiates the psychiatrist's theory of a psychotic break."

Megan gave it some thought, then nodded. "It's logical to assume that once he killed his future wife, he turned to the surrogate he had already found—my sister."

"Unfortunately, you're right. That's why we are employing all our manpower, and have asked the neighboring cities to send us more officers, to find O'Hallon. We're looking into a couple of new leads we can't discuss with you at the moment. I assure you, we'll rescue Keira before he can harm her."

He's had her for three whole days. Declan shivered at the thought of what O'Hallon might have done to Keira in that time.

Just then, Dwyer's phone rang. When he answered the call, his expression gave Declan new hope. He announced, "That was Heller. They've found the SUV. I've got to go."

* * * *

CHAPTER 9

Three days earlier

Paul couldn't believe his eyes when Keira recoiled from his touch. Something was very wrong with her. She was his soul mate. Why would she be afraid of him? Surely, that bastard Slane had poisoned her against him. God only knew the kind of lies he had told for Keira to turn against him like that. He was glad he'd shot Slane. He deserved to die for trying to keep Keira and him apart.

When Keira fell to the ground, the loud cracking sound her head made as it hit the floor horrified him. No doubt she had cracked a bone or two. He rushed to her side and knelt beside her, cradled her motionless body in his arms, and rocked her back and forth.

"Don't worry, love. You'll be fine. Everything will be all right. I'll take care of you."

He looked down to admire her heart-shaped face, then frowned when he noticed her usually rosy cheeks were deadly pale and her lips were turning blue. He put his ear to her mouth. She wasn't breathing.

"Keira, stay with me."

The tow truck company had given Paul CPR training, so he applied a vigorous massage to Keira's chest. He bent down again to check her breathing. Nothing. In desperation, he pounded her chest, over her heart, repeatedly. Finally, Keira gasped and opened her eyes for a brief moment. They looked unfocused. She moaned in pain and closed her eyes again.

"Keira! Talk to me."

She mumbled something incoherent, tried to open her eyes, but they didn't obey her. She stretched her hand in the air, grasping at something invisible to Paul. Then, she let it fall by her side and her body went limp. She looked exhausted but breathed regularly. Her face was still ashen, although her lips had returned to their normal red coloring.

He ran a thumb over her lips. "I've got you, Keira. Slane can't hurt you anymore."

Paul scooped her up in his arms and took her to the SUV parked in front of the small cottage. He lay her down on the back seat and fastened the seat belts around her waist and chest, as best as he could due to her awkward position. He didn't want to risk her getting hurt while he drove them home.

Those damn police officers wouldn't take long to appear. While he had hidden in the back yard, waiting for the best moment to rescue Keira, he'd heard Inspector Heller telling the gardai to contact him. He was running out of time. He had been two steps ahead of those dumb officers so far. He couldn't risk being outsmarted at this crucial moment. Fortunately, he had towed a car to this area a few months earlier, and knew it well. A little dirt road, not far from the house, would give him the hideaway he needed, but he needed to move fast to clear out of the driveway before the police arrived. The shortcut led through a neighboring farm, and was hidden from the main road.

He disabled the GPS system, jumped behind the steering wheel, and sped the SUV down the cottage driveway. He reached the farm gate and disappeared up the little dirt road seconds before the sirens broke the quiet of the chilly night. In the rearview mirror, he saw the first garda patrol car zoom past the gate. He sighed in relief, but didn't slow down.

An app on his cell phone would allow him to avoid the main roads, so he typed in an address and discovered they were going to take around two hours to get to Youghal. Their final destination was a small white cottage that he had rented, through a website, under an assumed name—Kevin Riordan.

Paul had been using this identity for years to avoid the police getting in the way of his quest for true love. Unfortunately, he hadn't been very lucky in that department until recently. Sometimes he wondered whether he was too demanding when it came to finding a suitable woman. But it wasn't his fault if

214

he knew exactly what kind of woman would make him happy and went for what he wanted.

He'd known it since he was a boy, although he couldn't have her. And had suffered so much growing up next to her, unable to express his true feelings. Many a sleepless night had been spent lusting over her—the forbidden fruit, lying awake in bed, daydreaming about the possibilities. Deep down, Paul knew society would never accept their love. She seemed to suffer in silence, as well. Ashling clearly loved him, but his mother wouldn't understand it. Ashling would never intentionally hurt his mother so she kept her feelings to herself.

When he had gotten the tow truck job, he realized he was like a knight in shining armor, who drove a truck instead of a powerful steed, and traveled around saving damsels in distress. It fitted his romantic side. Intuition told him that, one day, he would find his better half in one of his clients.

In fact, Paul had met a couple of candidates over time. They seemed very promising at first but, before long, he would find out their true character. They were petty, unkind creatures, who thought they were better than him. Paul couldn't stand pompous people and found that trait disgusting in women. He *had* to give them a lesson. They would never humiliate another man after he showed them what a real man could do to a heartless woman.

Keira, on the other hand, was perfect. He knew she was the one the first time he laid eyes on her. She was as kind, gentle, and beautiful as his Ashling. All of a sudden, Paul realized he had dreamed of marrying Keira even before they met. Fate had brought them together. An odious villain had tried to steal her away, but Paul had taken care of Slane. He looked over his shoulder to check on Keira. She slept peacefully. The poor dear must have been exhausted to sleep so soundly while the car bounced along the narrow dirt road.

"Don't worry, love. We'll be there soon," he told her when the app showed him they were ten minutes away from their new home.

215

Luck of the Irish

His heart beat faster when he saw the house. The online pictures hadn't lied. It looked perfect. Paul had dreamed of living in a place like this all his life—a small white cottage fenced in by an old stone wall, halfway up a hill, in a cul-de-sac overlooking the sea.

He would be happy here with Keira. Only the two of them. Nobody else around to bother them. Nobody to get in their way. He'd taken care of that. The nearest neighbor lived miles away. He had also asked the owner of the cottage to take away the television sets, radios, and phones. Nothing would interfere with their retreat.

He parked, carried Keira inside, and carefully lay her down on the bed. He didn't want to leave her, but he needed to ditch the car. He hesitated briefly before deciding to give her a little something to guarantee she wouldn't wake up while he was gone. He carried a sedative with him everywhere he went, hidden inside an innocent bottle of liquid painkiller for children. The strong tranquilizer had been very handy on many occasions. He gave a tablespoon of it to Keira, pinching her nose to ensure she swallowed everything. He stood by the bed for a while until he was convinced it had worked.

* * * *

As Keira watched Declan's lifeless body fall to the ground, she lost her will to live. She would have gladly killed Paul out of revenge, but when she had cracked her head on the floor, she'd welcomed the darkness and the silence, hoping they would take her away from the pain. She wanted to die to be with Declan again. However, she couldn't find him. In fact, she couldn't see anything because of the blinding light that surrounded her. The pain had gone and she felt weightless. It was as if she were floating in the air.

A soft hand touched her shoulder. Keira turned around in surprise to find a beautiful redheaded woman standing beside her. She appeared to be medium-height, slender, and wore a long white robe that reflected the bright light. She looked like an angel. Her dark green eyes reminded Keira of Declan's, as did the woman's gentle smile.

"I didn't mean to startle you, child. Forgive me."

"Where are we? Am I dead?"

"No, Keira. You're very much alive."

Keira's chest ached, she couldn't breathe, and she heard a male voice calling her. It sounded distant, although she knew he was nearby. She peered around but couldn't see much past the white glare of light, except for the silhouette of a man kneeling beside a body lying on the floor.

"I'm dying, aren't I? Did you come to take me away?"

"I'm no angel. I'm just like you, except I live in a different dimension."

The agonizing pain returned, filling Keira's head, and made it impossible to process information. Only one thought stood out.

"Where's Declan?"

"I'll find him. Don't worry, sweetheart."

Keira wondered if that voice calling her was Declan's. He sounded desperate. All of a sudden, Keira felt a sharp pang in her chest and gasped as a strange force pulled her towards the body on the ground. Feeling as heavy as lead, she managed to raise a hand to the woman who had begun to fade away.

"Please, don't go. Take me to Declan."

Her hand almost touched the woman's before Keira blacked out again.

* * * *

Paul relied on the backwoods where the cottage was located to make his task easier, and looked for the remotest spot he could find to get rid of the car. Once he was done with it, he walked back to the house as fast as he could. Life had dealt him a good hand for the first time. He wouldn't waste it. Surely, he and Keira would need to keep to themselves for a while, until people forgot about them. On the other hand, wasn't staying away from others and concentrating on themselves expected of newlywed couples? With a smile, Paul realized he wouldn't have any problems with that part—he looked forward to it.

As the house came into view, while Paul climbed the gentle slope, it glowed under the moonlight. A few lazy wisps of cloud, scattered over the starry sky, didn't shield the cold moonbeams in the freezing night. Those rays of insubstantial light, focusing directly on the little spot he had chosen for his new life with Keira, seemed to bring a kind of unearthly blessing to their union. Even though he wasn't a superstitious man, Paul welcomed any blessings that came his way, no matter how eerie.

When he entered the house, he went straight to the bedroom where Keira slept peacefully. He sat on an armchair and watched over her sleep for an unmeasured length of time. Paul felt so happy to finally have her to himself. Eventually, physical exhaustion prevailed and he fell asleep on the chair.

* * * *

Dawn wouldn't tinge the sky with orange and red for at least another hour, when Keira woke up. As usual, it got darker before the sun rose, so she couldn't see anything inside the room, which would help her understand where she was. Waves crashed in the distance and gave the only clue she had to figure out her odd situation. They didn't help much.

Her throbbing head didn't help matters either. The world tilted sideways before it spun out of control when she sat up. She closed her eyes, prayed for the dizziness to stop, felt queasy, and had to swallow hard to keep the bile from coming up her throat. A long series of deep breaths later, the nausea subsided yet the pain didn't. On the contrary, the harder she attempted to remember what had happened to her, the stronger the pain became.

She ran her hands down her body to discover she was dressed in jeans, a top, and a woolen coat, which did little to protect her against the chilly night air drifting in through the open window above the bed. Why she'd slept in her clothes was another mystery.

When her eyes adjusted to the dark, she distinguished a few pieces of furniture. In addition to the large bed, she recognized a vanity, a closet, a door, and a night table on each side of the bed. One had a lamp on it, while the other had an alarm clock, which displayed five thirty in the morning.

On a chair by the bed, somebody slept. That realization startled her. She couldn't muffle a gasp, and sheer panic froze her from the inside out when the man stood up and approached the bed. Wide shoulders like those could only belong to a man. He bent down to turn on the lamp near her. The amber light cast over his face did nothing to taper off her panic. It wiped away all traces of hope from her heart and made her utter doom clear.

"You look pale, love. Are you feeling all right?" He touched her cheeks with his fingertips and she shuddered.

"I'm cold, nauseous, and have a killer headache—other than that, I'm just peachy. How are *you*?" she burst out. "More importantly, though, *who* the heck are you?"

He frowned at her reply. It was out of character for Keira, "What do you mean, love? I'm Paul. Paul O'Hallon." He turned on the overhead lights. "Don't you remember me?"

"No, I don't. I also don't know where I am or who I am, for that matter."

He spun around with a look of surprise and studied her expression carefully. Keira wasn't joking. Fate was the one playing a cruel prank on him, robbing his beloved of her memories of their time together.

"Don't worry. I can answer all your questions, Keira. I'll tell you all about you, about us, but it'll take a while. There's a lot to tell, angel. You said you were cold, nauseous, and had a headache. Why don't we take care of those problems, first?"

219

Although he sounded gentle and concerned, she didn't trust him, which shouldn't be surprising because he was a stranger to her. If she didn't remember him, she didn't know him. No amount of sweet endearments on his part would make any difference to her at that point. How could she trust him if she didn't know who she was?

"You doubt me, love. I get it. Let me help you up. You can take a shower while I fix us breakfast. We'll talk as we eat, huh?"

She looked at the hand he had stretched out to her. To judge by her body's reaction when she'd sat up, she would need a steadying hand to be able to stand up. She held his hand and Paul pulled her up, but her legs gave out from under her with the violent fit of vertigo that came over her. She grabbed his upper arms for support and closed her eyes.

"What's wrong?"

"I'm dizzy," she answered through gritted teeth. But closing her eyes didn't make the pounding headache go away—only gave her the illusion of it. "Just give me a minute."

When the sensation slackened, Keira opened her eyes and squared her shoulders.

"Let me help you out of your clothes," he offered, and his fingers unzipped her coat.

A new wave of panic hit her, threatening to destroy her hard work to keep the nausea under control. She stopped his hands.

"I don't know what kind of relationship we had. Right now, you're a stranger to me. I can undress by myself. Thank you."

His eyes betrayed his exasperation.

"I guess you're right," he said with a sigh and released her coat.

"I'll need a hand to get to the bathroom, though," she admitted with reluctance.

220

He offered his arm, but once they stepped across the threshold she let go of him.

"Thank you. I'll be fine, now."

"I'll be in the kitchen. Call me if you need anything."

With a nod, she closed the door, locked it, and leaned against it. She felt hollow, but couldn't give in to desperation. She tore herself off the door, walked to the sink, and looked at her reflection in the mirror, hoping that it would jolt her memory.

Not knowing who she was had seemed unbearable enough until she looked at her face. A purplish-blue mark swelled in her left temple, which hurt when she touched it. Although her head throbbed everywhere, a focal point pointed to where the pain seemed to originate. She couldn't see it in the mirror because it was at the back of her head, but her fingers found the spot. There was a huge swelling there, too.

"What the heck happened to you, woman? While we're at it, who are you?"

When her reflection didn't answer her humorless jokes, Keira turned on the faucet to fill the bathtub, while she shed her clothes. A bath sounded less risky than a shower. If the dizziness returned, she didn't want to slip and add a third bump to her already injured head.

Keira stepped inside the tub and slid her battered body down until the water covered it. She leaned her head back against the tiled wall, closed her eyes, and felt her muscles gradually unwind under the relaxing effect of the hot water. However, for the healing process to be efficient, she needed to rein in the million thoughts scattered inside her head. That wouldn't be easy though, so she chose to put them aside and concentrate on one step at a time. Instead of exhausting herself trying to guess what had happened, Keira should listen to what Paul had to say and trust her instincts to judge if he was truthful.

* * * *

"It smells good. What is it?"

"A family secret recipe for omelet. Eat it and tell me what you think."

Paul had finished cooking breakfast and had set the table while Keira took her bath.

"It's delicious."

"Thank you."

They ate in silence until Keira couldn't stand the wait anymore, "What happened to me? I've got two huge bumps on my head and countless bruises everywhere."

"You may not like what I have to tell you, love, but I've got to be honest with you. You were kidnapped."

"Me? Kidnapped? Why? How?"

"Well, I guess I'll have to start from the beginning."

"You said my name was Keira. What's my surname? Where am I from? Where's my family?"

"All right, I get it." He laughed and raised a hand to stop her. "Your name is Keira Ashe. You're American. You don't have a family. You were an only child and your parents died in a car accident last year. You were so devastated by your loss that you decided to come visit your grandparents' country in search of solace."

He paused for her to process the information. Despite not remembering them, her stomach churned at the idea of having lost her parents. She guessed they'd been close.

"It's weird. I don't remember them, yet I miss them."

When they'd finished their breakfast, Keira told Paul she wanted to take a walk. Maybe the ocean breeze would help her recover faster. Paul offered his arm but she refused it. She wanted to test her limits. She walked slowly and he resumed telling Keira about her life according to his imagination.

"Well, you arrived in Ireland a little over two months ago. We met on the beach, not far from here. You told me you had come to Youghal because your grandmother was born here. We fell madly in love and got married in less than a week."

He reached for her hand and laced their fingers together. A jolt of energy made her jump when their hands connected. He laughed. She felt surprised that the touch of her alleged husband made her skin crawl. Maybe her head injury was causing the nausea.

"But, like any other great love story, ours had a villain. There was this guy in the hotel where we spent our wedding night. He's sick, and sneaked into our room and tried to rape you while I was downstairs."

He paused. A deep crease had formed between Keira's eyebrows as she concentrated. "For a second, I thought I remembered it," she said with a hopeful expression. "Then it was gone."

"I returned in time to save you. I threw him to the ground and punched him within an inch of his life. You stopped me. I would have gladly killed the bastard."

Keira came to an abrupt halt and squeezed his hand.

"I remember that!"

She closed her eyes and saw vivid images of two men fighting. Although she couldn't see their faces, she saw broad shoulders, which looked exactly like Paul's. The height was a match, as well.

"I can see it," she exclaimed, a little before the scene vanished from her mind. Disappointed, she opened her eyes. "It's gone. It's a start, though, isn't it?"

"Yes, sure," was his weak reply. "You look pale."

"I'm not feeling well. I'm sorry. Can we go back? I guess I'd better rest."

Paul frowned, but agreed, "Absolutely. You'd better save your strength for later. I've got plans for tonight."

All that information had made her head spin. She wanted to lie down and wait for the dizziness to stop.

* * * *

As it turned out, Keira was more tired than either of them had anticipated. She slept through most of the day, skipped lunch, and didn't respond to Paul's numerous attempts to wake her. In the early evening, he paced the floor in the living room, waiting for her to recover. He feared her head injuries were causing the lethargy, but he couldn't risk taking her to a hospital. He rushed to the bedroom as soon as he heard her moving inside it.

"Hey, Sleeping Beauty. Feeling any better?"

Keira had opened the closet and was going through its contents. She had found linens, blankets, and pillows for the bedroom as well as towels for the bathroom.

"Where's my stuff? I wanted to take a shower and change into fresh clothes. I couldn't find any."

"Sorry about that, love. I haven't told you the rest of the story. You see, this isn't our house. I brought you here in a hurry to hide from that lunatic Slane. But, I'll go out and get you something. I won't be long."

"Just get me a new top, then. We can go to town tomorrow and buy more things."

They couldn't do that. He'd find a way to get that idea out of her head later.

"Nonsense—what else do you need?"

"If you insist, I'd love to wash my hair. Would you bring me some shampoo?"

224

"Sure. I'll be right back."

It took Keira by surprise when Paul bent down and covered her mouth with his. She froze. His hands on her back pulled her against his body as his tongue searched for hers. She yanked herself free from his embrace, covered her mouth with a hand, and ran to the bathroom.

Paul started to follow but stopped at the sound of Keira hurling. He couldn't stand the sight of that. He'd never been able to see people throwing up without feeling sick as well. Instead, he went out to get her stuff.

Frustration and anger boiled inside him as he stomped out of the house and down the road. Why did Keira reject him like that? He loved her, but he wouldn't take that kind of behavior. Not after having sacrificed so much for her. He had risked his freedom to get her back and now how did she repay him? She denied him—recoiling from a simple kiss as if he were a repulsive vermin or a snake.

Paul shook his head to clear it from those gloomy thoughts. Keira was different. She loved him. She had invited him to her hotel room in Cork and begged him to make love to her. She had stopped Slane from killing him then, hadn't she? She had begged Slane to let her go with Paul the night before, hadn't she? Slane was the problem. That bastard had kept her against her will. Otherwise, she would have visited Paul at the hospital. Later, when Paul had tried to rescue her, Slane hit her temple. Her head injury caused the nausea, not being repulsed by him.

That's right. It's Slane's fault that she's sick.

While mulling over Slane's role in Keira's changes, he had arrived at the nearest house without noticing it. He peered through the kitchen window but couldn't see anything. He moved around the house, checking the windows. The lights were out. Apparently, there wasn't anybody in, which made it easier for him to get what Keira needed. Going to town was out of the question, so Paul needed to be creative. Luckily, the backdoor was easy to pick and it didn't take him long to find a top that would fit Keira and—his luck held—a full bottle of shampoo. He put them inside a plastic bag and hurried back to their house. Even at his fast pace, it took him a long time to get to the cottage.

* * * *

When Keira stopped throwing up, her head pounded with the intensity of a thousand church bells. She couldn't keep her eyes open because of the splitting headache. She stood up slowly, washed her face and mouth, then searched the medicine cabinet for something to relieve the pain. There wasn't anything.

Sluggish, she moved to the bedroom and tried the drawers there, without any luck. She stumbled through the narrow corridor, leant against the wall, and stopped many times along the way, and eventually got to the kitchen. There, she opened the cupboard doors until she found a bottle of a painkiller. She couldn't read the label because it was torn and she wasn't wearing her glasses. It was stuff for children, so she figured she should take double the dosage. She filled a tablespoon with the red liquid twice and swallowed it.

Keira retraced her steps to the bedroom and plopped herself on the bed. She felt too exhausted to go on fighting to keep her eyes open. She closed them and couldn't avoid thinking about what had happened. Her reaction to Paul's touch had surprised and confused her. Why had she married him if she felt that away about him? Maybe she was too depressed and lonely after her family died and had fallen for the first nice guy she had met.

That sounded wrong. Despite her bruises, when Keira studied her reflection in the mirror, she saw a beautiful young woman. Certainly, she'd had many other boyfriends before meeting Paul. On the other hand, he was a handsome man. It wasn't so hard for her to believe she had fallen in love with him. A strange lethargy came over her and her train of thought became unclear. Keira tried to focus on Paul, but another man's face popped up behind her eyelids. He was

226

gorgeous. His green eyes shone with the most wonderful light—love. She knew him. She tried to remember who he was, but his name eluded her. *Who are you?*

* * * *

When Paul returned, Keira was sleeping deeply. He sat beside her on the bed and watched her for a while. She was so beautiful. He could hardly believe how lucky he was.

"Keira, love, wake up," he whispered in her ear.

No answer ... no movement at all. He leaned closer, kissed her cheeks, cupped her shoulders, and shook her lightly. When she didn't open her eyes, he spoke louder.

"Keira?"

She still didn't move. Paul grabbed her shoulders, pulled her up, and shook her. It was useless. Her arms hung slackly by her side, and her head dropped back. Paul let go of her and stood up. In panic, thinking she had passed out from the head injury, he looked around the room searching for something strong for Keira to smell. He needed to wake her up.

He found nothing in the bedroom, so ran to the kitchen looking for vinegar or some other strong-smelling product. He found the bottle of tranquilizer on the table, instead. It dawned on him that if she had taken a spoonful of the sedative, she would sleep until morning.

Paul swore a string of colorful terms, under his breath, as he returned to the bedroom. His plans for the evening were ruined. All through the day, he had planned their night, counting the minutes until the moment he would have Keira in his arms. He was going to show her how a real man treated a woman. He leaned against the door, watching her. A scorching desire burned in his guts, turning his insides to aches. It was almost painful.

He didn't mind a little pain, though. It added a touch of spice to a relationship. A slow smile curved his lips up as he envisioned Keira's sweaty, naked body writhing under his strong hands, her wrists bound over her head,

227

while she begged him for a breather. He was going to take good care of her and she would to love it.

For a split second, he contemplated carrying on with his plans regardless of the fact she was asleep. But he wanted Keira to be alert to appreciate his skills. He lay down beside her, embraced her narrow waist, and pinned her legs under his. He spent a long time running his fingers up and down her arms and playing with her hair until he fell asleep.

* * * *

Early in the morning, Keira woke up feeling hot and trapped. She could hardly move and didn't know where she was. All of a sudden, it came back to her. Paul was her husband. He had rescued her from a crazy man who had kidnapped her. It all sounded far-fetched. It was hard to believe something like that would happen in real life.

She remembered her dream—she had seen a pair of dark green eyes staring at her with so much love. Those eyes had also been filled with rage, yet she knew it wasn't directed at her. Although she didn't remember the face, she knew those eyes belonged to a very handsome man. It was impossible to explain how she knew that—she just did.

In the dream, he had talked to her, calmed her down, and said everything would be all right. She had believed him. Now that Keira was awake, she couldn't remember the conversation they'd had, but she had the impression it was important. It felt like he had told her everything she needed to know about herself.

It was just a dream, silly.

With a glance out the window, she saw it was dark outside, which meant it was early. There was no need to wake Paul. She slipped out of bed, as carefully as she could, so as not to disturb him. She found the top and the shampoo he had brought the night before, and took them to the bathroom with her. Without thinking, she locked the door behind her.

228

All the while Keira washed her hair, flashes of images came back to her. They were pretty confusing, like scattered pieces of a puzzle. She remembered watching the police take a man away, in handcuffs, as her heart sank. He wasn't Paul. She remembered a man forcing her against her will as she struggled with him, but she couldn't see his face because she was lying on her stomach. Another man arrived and the two men fought. She saw Paul's face covered in blood as she begged the other man to stop beating him. He had his back turned to her, as he straddled Paul, so she couldn't see his face. She reached her hand out to make the man turn around when she heard somebody turning the doorknob.

"Keira, are you all right in there?" Paul shouted when the door didn't open.

The memories vanished and she cleared her throat to answer him.

"Yes, I'm fine. I'll be out in a minute."

"I'll fix us breakfast, then."

While they ate breakfast, Keira feared Paul would bring up her reaction the night before. Instead, he talked about the weather and other unimportant things. Even though she was relieved, she wanted to know more about herself. So, she was happy when they sat down on the living room couch and Paul resumed telling her what had happened.

"As I told you yesterday, that lunatic Slane attacked you in our hotel room, but I saved you before the police came. When the gardai arrived, I'd already overpowered the bastard. They had only to take him to the station."

"I remember seeing a man in handcuffs." She nodded enthusiastically as Paul talked.

"After the attack, you were so shaken up that you asked me to get rid of the TV sets and the radios in the house. You wanted to avoid the news about it."

229

Something stirred at the back of her mind. That sounded familiar.

"Is that why there are no TVs or computers here?"

"Well, not exactly. It started that way then we got used to it. I mean, hell, we were on our honeymoon. Not having any distractions around us gave us a sense of isolation. We were everything to each other. We didn't need anything else."

"I remember that," Keira interrupted him and sprung to her feet as he leaned to kiss her.

"You do?"

A strange sense of déjà vu came over her.

"I remember being cut off from the rest of the world. I know that feeling." She paced the living room. So many emotions clashed inside her that Keira couldn't sit down. She had a hard time sorting them out and expressing herself.

"You're pale, love. Why don't you sit down and try to relax?"

"I can't. I remember the feelings but I can't remember details. It's so frustrating."

The story was starting to sound plausible to her. She remembered the isolation he described. She also remembered feeling protected by someone who loved her very much.

"Paul, there's something that doesn't add up, though. I remember hiding from imminent danger, needing protection from some harm. If the police arrested this man, why would I need protection from him?"

"He was released after a short while. We didn't understand it. Maybe he bribed somebody. The fact is he was out and you feared he would come after you."

"That's familiar, too."

230

Keira heard bits and pieces of conversations in her head. She stopped pacing, closed her eyes, and pressed her temples. Angry voices argued about her safety. She couldn't make out what they were saying.

"Did we argue about it?"

"We didn't, but I told the police officers off for being incompetent jerks."

"I know you did. I remember it."

"He eventually found our house. He got in one night and kidnapped you. He must have cocked me in the head with a gun or something because I didn't hear or see anything. You've got to believe me, love." He grabbed her hands in his and stared into her eyes. "I would never have let him take you if he hadn't knocked me out. I swear it."

"I'm sure you wouldn't." Her voice came out in little more than a whisper.

She felt dizzy from the intense emotions and her struggle to retain the elusive images and sounds in her head. Her eyes glazed over and she fainted.

Keira came to with another splitting headache. She sat up on the couch and the room spun around her. She was tired of feeling sick all the time. She was even more tired of the blanks in her memory. She hated not knowing who she was and not remembering what had happened before the last two days. Once the dizziness settled, she stood up and went to the kitchen to get the painkiller. It wasn't there. She was going through the living room furniture looking for it when Paul came in.

"What's going on here?" he asked her when he saw the contents of the drawers scattered over the floor.

"I need something for my head. It's killing me."

His features tensed. "I might have something, but it's in the bedroom. Let me get it for you."

"It's fine. I've got it." Keira showed him the painkiller bottle she had used the day before.

"That's for children. I'll get you something stronger."

"Nonsense. It worked like a charm yesterday."

He tried to take it from her but she turned around and walked towards the kitchen in search of a spoon. He went after her.

"Keira, give me that. You shouldn't take it." He sounded furious for some reason.

They stood in the middle of the kitchen, and she frowned as she turned to him.

"Why's that?"

"Don't be childish. Just do as I say. Give me the bottle." His voice rose and his face went red. He was losing it.

"I'm not acting out. I just want to know why you don't want me to take something that helped me yesterday."

With one stride, he snatched the bottle from her hand and yelled, "What's your problem? Can't you follow one simple instruction without whining? Are you dumb or what?"

She blinked several times and flinched away from Paul, fearing him as he let his mask slip away and showed his true nature. Paul grabbed a glass and poured a generous dose of the red liquid.

"Here. Take it. Do you want to kill yourself? Go ahead. Take all of it, for all I care."

He shoved the glass in her hand and Keira stared at it. She didn't have a clue what he meant. His actions were beyond her comprehension. In fact, the whole scene felt too surreal. Besides, her pounding head didn't seem fit for thinking too hard. She took a gulp of what she thought was a painkiller and sat the glass down on the table.

"Happy now?" he fumed.

"I don't know what you're getting at, Paul. You're not making much sense. Then again, my head is throbbing. I can't think straight. I'll lie down. I hope we can talk this through when I get up."

She went away before he could say another word.

* * * *

Keira didn't know how she had gotten to that beautiful garden. Color filled it and the flowers in bloom smelled delicious. Among the flowerbeds stood a tall, redheaded woman. Her expression looked serene and inviting. Keira knew her.

"Who are you? I think I know you but I can't remember. Do I know you?"

"Not exactly. We've met before but I wouldn't say you know me."

"I've seen you before. I don't know where. I've been confused lately. I'm sorry."

"No need to apologize, child. You've been through a lot. I know it. I was there."

"Are you my mom? I can't remember anything and it's driving me mad. I hate this feeling of helplessness."

"I know what you mean, but I'm not your mother, Keira. I'm Iris Slane. Your mom is alive, you know. Your whole family is alive and they worry about you. They love you very much. Paul's been telling you all kinds of lies, sweetie."

Keira felt relieved and anguished at the same time. Her family was safe and she wasn't alone in the world. On the other hand, what kind of man was Paul? Why did he tell her such vicious lies? She couldn't trust him.

"You're right to question him. He is a very dangerous and sick man."

"Can you read my mind?"

"We can do anything here, child." Iris smiled sweetly at somebody standing by her side. Keira couldn't see the person. "I brought somebody to see you. He was about to give up because he thought you were dead. I had to promise him I'd find you to convince him to go back."

Keira's heart skipped a few beats when she laid eyes on the gorgeous man beside Iris.

"Declan!" She threw her arms around his neck, laughing and crying. "I know who you are. I know who I am, now, too."

Everything came back to her—emotions, people, facts, places, and feelings. Dizziness overcame her, but his strong arms around her narrow waist were all she needed to keep her safe.

"I've got you, love. Nobody's going to hurt you anymore. I'm here."

Declan kissed her hair, her moist face, and her mouth with so much love and tenderness. Their tears mingled as they kissed, as they whispered the sweetest words to each other, and the world around them ceased to exist.

In the evening, as the effect of the sedative wore off, Keira didn't want to wake up from that dream. She was afraid she wouldn't remember it. To her surprise, her memory was intact when she opened her eyes and stared at the living-room ceiling. However, with those memories came the fear that Paul would discover she knew her real story. She needed to tread carefully. She sat up and looked around. He wasn't there and dead silence filled the house.

Maybe he ran away.

She laughed at her own joke. She hadn't been that lucky so far. Why should she start counting on luck now? She had an idea and went to the kitchen to put her plan into motion. She found the cooking utensils and the food she needed to prepare dinner. When Paul returned, she was setting the table for

234

them. She had found candles and a candlestick, which she'd just placed in the middle of the table when he entered the dining room. He looked dumbfounded at the sight.

"Would you do the honors, honey?" she asked.

"What?"

"Can you light the candles while I bring the food?"

She didn't wait for his answer, which never came anyway. Paul just sat down at the table, with a puzzled frown on his face. Then, his expression changed into one of hunger.

"If I weren't starving, I'd suggest we skipped dinner and went straight to bed. I can't wait to have you to myself. But you haven't eaten much and you'll need your strength, hon. I've planned a long and fulfilling night for us."

She noticed the way he salivated while watching her set a sizzling bowl of stew in the middle of the table and guessed his reaction had nothing to do with the meal. Her skin crawled at the thought of Paul touching her and she controlled herself to avoid pouring the contents of the bowl over his head.

"I hope you like stew. I can't remember my own name but I knew how to cook this. Don't ask me how."

She sat down and took a little bite from her plate of food while Paul attacked his.

"Hmm, there's too much salt in it," she said.

"I think it's perfect, honey."

"Really? I don't like salty food." She got her plate and stood up to go to the kitchen. "Are you sure you'll eat that?"

Paul just nodded, swallowing another spoonful of her stew.

Once in the kitchen, away from his eyes, Keira threw away the food and filled the plate up again with the stew she had left in the pot on the stove. The one in the bowl was laced with the tranquilizer Paul kept in the painkiller bottle. She had figured it out when she woke up that evening. All the pieces of

235

the puzzle had come together. She understood why she had felt dizzy that day in the restaurant. Paul must have put it in her food or wine when she had gone to the bathroom. She had also slept most of the previous day after she had taken it, thinking she was taking something for her headache.

She returned, sat down again at the table, and resumed eating her meal. It didn't take long for the drug to knock him out because she had poured the whole bottle into the bowl. She barely had time to move his plate to the side before Paul collapsed on the table. Her first impulse was to accommodate him on the couch, but she reminded herself that she needed to move fast.

She grabbed her coat and ran out of the house. No moonlight was visible in the dark overcast sky and the streetlights shone too dimly for her to see ahead. She slowed down her pace and waited for her eyes to adjust. She had no idea which way to go. She only knew she had to put as much distance between Paul and herself as possible, so she walked up the road to the top of the hill, but without finding a soul. Desperation threatened her resolve when she looked around—there were no houses for miles. The only light she was able to see was too far for her to make out what it was. It could be a house. It could easily be a store, in which case, it would be closed at that time of night. Her heart sank and she sat on a nearby rock, contemplating her options. They were limited at best. In truth, they were quite slim.

She could walk aimlessly around the dark and cold countryside, looking for help, hoping a Good Samaritan would show up out of the blue. But the odds of that happening were against her, and she would end up freezing to death. Her coat was too thin.

She could go back to the house, pretend nothing had happened, and wait for another chance to escape. Paul was crazy but he wasn't stupid. She wouldn't be able to deceive him for too long. She needed to use her head. A crazy idea came to mind. It would be risky and dangerous to pull it off, but she was running out of options.

236

I'm sorry, Declan. I can't see another way out.

She sent him a silent prayer as she stood up and dragged her feet back to the cottage. She had no doubt she loved Declan deeply and that he loved her with the same intensity. She could only hope he would forgive her for what she was about to do.

When she got to the kitchen, she found everything exactly as she had left it. She had a hard time getting Paul up and carrying him to the bedroom but she managed it. Stripping him off proved to be another ordeal for her. She was sweaty and out of breath when he finally lay on the bed in his underwear. Fortunately, the sedative was potent and he didn't stir a muscle. She also figured out he would be out of commission at least until noon. That would give her some time to rest and prepare herself for the next phase of her plan. She took a blanket and a pillow from the closet and went to sleep on the couch.

A little while later, Keira woke and took the chance to clean the kitchen up, getting rid of all possible incriminating evidence from the night before, in case Paul suspected something and went snooping around the place. Once she was done with it, Keira sat on the living room floor and forced herself to remember the time she had spent in yoga classes as a teenager. She used that knowledge to calm herself down and pass the time.

Around noon, she tiptoed to the bedroom. Paul's clothes were scattered around the floor. She added hers to the mess. It suited her plan. Leaving only her bra and panties on, Keira slipped under Paul's arm and lay on her back. His proximity threatened to undo the positive effects of the yoga exercises, but she conquered the urge to hurl.

While she stared at the ceiling, she realized it had been only three days since Paul had taken her from Declan, but it felt like three thousand. She braced herself for what was to come before she could be with him again. Her love for

237

Declan was strong enough to get her through one more ordeal and lead her back to him. She prayed his love would be strong enough to accept her if he ever discovered what she had to do to find her way back to him.

CHAPTER 10

As Paul stirred in his sleep, slowly regaining consciousness, Keira took a deep breath and said a final silent prayer. She had to act fast if she wanted to take advantage of his momentary confusion before the last effects of the drug wore off. She lay on her side and kissed Paul's chin, neck, and chest, while her nails scratched the skin on his thighs. When he opened his heavy eyelids halfway to look at her, Keira smiled up at him in the best imitation of a seductive smile she could muster under those circumstances. Her survival depended on her ability to deceive Paul. That much was clear to her and the thought kept her going. In fact, her will to survive combined with her wish to go back to Declan drove Keira on.

"Good morning, stud. I hope you didn't wear yourself out last night."

A confused expression clouded his face as he creased his eyebrows and his unfocused stare fell on her. Ignoring the unspoken questions, Keira wove her tale, "We had a pretty wild time last night. The best I've ever had. You taught me a trick or two."

Keira leant her head down to hide her disgust, then scattered open-mouthed kisses on his stomach, moving slowly downwards, until she reached the connection between his abdomen and hips. She grazed the skin over the hard bone there and heard his sharp intake of air as he dug his hips in the soft mattress. She raised her head to look at him when her warm palm found his hardening body. With a soft gaze into his eyes, she licked her lips.

"I have a couple of tricks of my own to teach you, too, you know? Can I show them to you, Paul?"

"Yes, yes." His eyes glazed over and Keira knew this was her best shot.

"Good." She straddled him without removing her hand or slowing down its rhythm. "I don't want anyone interrupting us, though. I want to have you all to myself today. I have big plans for us." She squeezed his hips between

239

her thighs for emphasis. "Are we isolated enough from any nosy neighbors, hot stuff?"

Paul closed his eyes and buried his head in the pillows when she increased the speed of her hand caressing him.

"Yes," was his breathless reply. She felt his heart beating like crazy beneath her other hand. "I took care of that. The closest house is a thirty-minute walk down the road towards town. Nobody will come up this steep hill just out of curiosity." She increased her pace and he went silent.

She closed her eyes and thanked God for her blessings. Paul had given the information she needed much sooner than she had anticipated. With a sigh of relief, Keira let go of his member and sat down on his stomach. His body shook from head to toe and his frustrated gaze flew to her face.

"Don't stop, woman. Are you out of your mind?"

Instead of answering him, she bent down until her mouth touched his ear, where she whispered, "I want you, Paul. I want you so badly it hurts. I want to make you feel the way you made me feel last night."

He smiled up at her with a smug expression, then put his hands on her waist. "You sound impressed, my darling."

"I am. You amazed me. I never thought you'd be like that." Keira grabbed his hands, raised them above his head, and pinned them to the mattress. "You like it kinky, don't you?"

"Yes." He wiggled under her and his gaze dropped to her chest, half-clad in her lacy bra, and he licked his lips.

"Me too," she said. "I loved it when you blindfolded me." She produced a scarf from under the pillows. "It was so hot. I want you to feel that, too."

She squeezed him between her thighs again and Paul closed his eyes. Keira found a spot on his neck and sucked at it as she tied the scarf firmly around his head.

240

"You little vixen. You love it when I ride you hard."

"Yeah, and when you tied me down, too." She splayed her hands on his chest, scratching his skin lightly. Keira used Paul's obvious delusional fantasies about the two of them to trick him into thinking he would have his way with her. "Let me do the same to you, stud," she whispered into his ear and recoiled from his touch when he turned his head searching for her mouth.

Paul smiled and licked his lips.

Keira got the scarves she had stashed in the nightstand drawer earlier and tied his hands to the bed with them. She took a second to admire her handiwork. They wouldn't hold him for long, so she gathered her courage to take the next step.

Blindfolded and lost in his make-believe world, Paul's body reacted to Keira's proximity when she bent over him. When her breasts brushed against his cheek, he turned towards them, open-mouthed, and tried to kiss the globes but she took them away from his reach. He laughed.

"You want to play hard to catch, do you? I can—"

Before he had a chance to finish his sentence, Keira hit him with the heavy metal lamp from the nightstand. She used all the hatred that had been boiling inside her to swing the object up in the air above her head before directing its base to Paul's temple. She smiled and allowed herself to revel in a brief moment of triumph when he gave a guttural grunt and a thick stream of blood poured out of the gash she had opened on the side of his head. His body went limp under hers and Keira knelt on the bed beside him, heaving, still holding the lamp in one hand, and looking like a vengeful Celtic goddess.

"Good! Now you know how I felt, you sick son of bitch."

Adrenaline pumped through her veins, and Keira jumped to her feet and used the wires she had gathered around the house that morning to tie his feet and hands to the bed. Although she wasn't planning on sticking around for when he woke up, she also didn't want to risk Paul escaping before she called the police.

Since the walk to the nearest neighbor took at least a half-hour, she couldn't take any chances.

When Keira was satisfied with the results, she stood by the foot of the bed for a brief moment and looked at the man lying there. Just then, the enormity of what had happened in the last month came rushing at her, threatening to crush her spirit. Keira shook her head to fight the gloomy feelings. This wasn't the time to doubt herself. Despite her best efforts, she wasn't able to conquer the sudden fit of nausea that gripped her. She barely had enough time to run to the bathroom before hurling the contents of her stomach.

When it had emptied completely, she washed her face and mouth then hurried back to the bedroom to put her clothes on. She needed to get to that neighbor's house down the road to ask for help before Paul came to, and she was running out of time.

As Keira left the cottage through the front door, she collided with a solid, warm male body. With a startle she looked up and found detective Heller's eyes. She squealed in a mix of delight and relief, threw her arms around the older man's neck, and buried her head in his ample, fatherly chest.

"Oh, thank God, you're here! I can't believe you've found me!"

Heller held her tightly in his arms and kissed Keira's hair while she sobbed loudly and clung to his bulky frame.

Detective Heller patted her and repeated countless times, "It's all right, child. Everything is going to be all right. I've got you." He motioned for the gardai to enter the house and search for O'Hallon as he rocked her back and forth until she calmed down.

Keira wiped the tears from her face, then pushed away from the detective—mortified when she realized how improper her behavior was.

"I'm so sorry, sir. I shouldn't have thrown myself at you like that." She looked up at him, embarrassment written all over her bright red face.

"There's no need to apologize, my dear. It's a natural reaction." He winked at her to lessen her discomfort. "Besides, beautiful young women don't generally cry for joy when they see me nowadays."

She laughed and her face felt less hot. "Oh, gosh, detective, there's so much I've got to ask you. How is Declan? How are Murphy, Kerry, and Morris? How did you find me? Where are we?"

"Calm down, Keira. I'll answer all your questions." He cupped her shoulders. "But first, you've got to go with this nice lady, here. Her name's Shannon and she's a paramedic. She'll check you over."

Keira noticed a short, sturdy woman beside Heller. A warm smile curved her lips, changing her expression completely when she noticed Keira's apprehension.

"It'll only take a moment, my dear. I know you want this to be over soon. Who could blame you?"

"Can you at least tell me how Declan is, detective?"

"He's swearing at me, Dwyer, and the whole Garda for letting O'Hallon take you. So, I guess you can say he's fine."

"Thank God he isn't hurt."

"He went through a couple of surgeries, but he's doing okay now. He'll tell you all about it once we get you to Cork."

"I'm sorry he had to go through that alone."

Heller smiled then said, "He wasn't alone. Your parents and your sister came over and his brothers also showed up at the hospital."

With no words to express her relief, she squeezed the inspector's hand then sat on the ambulance's rear step.

"I have so many questions to ask you right now, detective," she said with a bright smile. "But I'll be a good girl and behave until Shannon finishes her job."

"You do that. Do you mind it if I stay? I can get your statement while Shannon examines you."

"Absolutely."

Heller stood in front of Keira, by the open door of the ambulance, while the paramedic checked her blood pressure and temperature, and looked for injuries. She suspected that he had deliberately blocked her view of the house so that she wouldn't have to see O'Hallon again as the police officers rolled the gurney out of the house and into another ambulance. Two officers climbed into the other vehicle and it set off for the hospital. Surely, this time, O'Hallon would stay in custody for a long time.

While Keira told Heller everything that had taken place since O'Hallon had attacked them at the safe house, Shannon examined her cuts and bruises. The older woman held Keira's head gently between her hands and looked closely at the injury on her temple.

"This looks ugly but it's clean. There isn't any risk of infection."

Keira winced when Shannon pressed her fingers on the bump.

"How did you get this?"

"Paul hit me in the head."

"Did you faint? Did you feel dizzy or nauseous?"

"All of the above."

"Did you have any other symptoms?"

"Well, I blacked out when he hit me. When I woke up the next day, I didn't remember anything."

"When did your memory come back to you?"

"Yesterday."

"We'll need to take you to the hospital to run some scans and check for internal injuries," Shannon stated as she removed her gloves.

"Is it necessary? I feel fine now. Can I go to a hospital when I get to Cork, instead?"

"I can't release you without a thorough exam, Miss Ashe. I'm sorry."

"I guess you're right," Keira said and sighed.

Shannon took Keira's disappointment for concern, "Don't worry, Miss Ashe," she said. "Head traumas may cause temporary amnesia, which doesn't mean you had any serious internal injuries. The doctors will be able to know it for sure after they examine the scan results."

"Oh, I'm not worried about that. I mean, I feel okay. I just wanted to go see my boyfriend, and my family."

"I understand you're anxious to go to them, but there's nothing I can do about it, Miss Ashe. Now, I've got to ask you, my dear, did O'Hallon hurt you in any other way? Did he try to rape you again?"

"No, he didn't."

Keira looked at Inspector Heller when he let out a deep sigh.

"You've got no idea how relieved I am to hear that, Keira. I wouldn't forgive myself if he had hurt you. Neither would Declan or your family."

Not listening to Keira's pleas to let her ride with Inspector Heller to the hospital, Shannon made her climb into the ambulance and climbed in after her. Keira had hoped the detective would call Cork while they drove to the hospital, and let her talk to Declan and her family. Although she knew the paramedic was doing her job, Keira felt like a time-bomb, ready to explode if she didn't hear Declan's voice soon.

At the hospital, she wanted to scream in frustration but, in spite of that, she went through the endless scans displaying remarkable resignation. Inspector Heller stood by her bed as they waited for the young doctor in charge of her case to return with his findings.

"Could you call the hospital in Cork again, Inspector Heller? I'd love to talk to them."

"I've called Dwyer's mobile twice but it went straight to voicemail. Let's wait for the doctor to give us his feedback, then we'll have more information to relay to them."

"This might take forever."

Keira sounded whiny but she really didn't care at that point. She would do anything to talk to Declan and her family.

Heller and Keira turned to the door when it opened, expecting to see the doctor. She shrieked, got of the bed, and ran to hug Declan, who entered the room in a wheelchair pushed by Dwyer. Aided by the investigator, he stood up to take her in his arms, and held her close to him, burying his face in her hair.

"Thank God you're alive, Keira. I thought I had lost you."

"So did I."

He framed her face in his big hands, caressed her cheeks with his thumbs, and stared into her blue eyes as if probing her very soul. When he spoke, his words came out slowly and clearly, "I love you, Keira. I love you more than my own life. I couldn't live without you."

"I love you, too. I can't tell you how much I love you. I guess I'll spend the rest of my life repeating it to you."

"Promise me you will, and I'll be the happiest man on earth."

Instead of using words, Keira laced her arms around his neck and offered her mouth to him. Declan feasted on her sweetness until they were both breathless. As their hungry mouths sought each other, their eager hands grasped, clenched, and caressed each other's flesh. Both of them needed to make sure the other one was real; that they were together once more, against all odds. They shut the rest of world out of their bubble of happiness, and whispered sweet words into each other's ears. Their hearts swelled as they gazed into each other's eyes, resting their foreheads together and catching their breath before resuming kissing again.

****

While the couple celebrated their reunion, Dwyer offered Heller an apologetic smile as the other man shook his head. "Don't ask," the young officer answered his senior colleague's unspoken question. "It was either bringing him along or throwing him in jail for public disorder and assaulting a couple of police officers. Present company included."

"Did her family come too?"

"They'll get here soon. They stayed behind to wait for confirmation from me that you had found Keira. Garda Dean is driving them."

"I take it Slane didn't want to wait, eh?"

"That's the understatement of the year. An army wouldn't have held him down. He demanded to come with me. The hospital staff refused to let him go, saying he was too weak to travel. He threatened to get out of there without their permission. They finally agreed to release Slane into my care, only after he signed the waivers, and only if we came here in an ambulance. He's still in recovery, you know. He's a nutcase, if you ask me."

"That bad?"

"You know me. In all these years with the police force, I never came so close to punching a victim in the nose as I did with Slane earlier today. The man drove everyone crazy until he got the hospital staff to do his bidding. He was relentless."

"You didn't tell them we'd found out O'Hallon had rented a house here, did you?"

"I most certainly didn't. I know better than to share such sensitive information. I wouldn't divulge it prematurely and risk giving them false hope. I just said the gardai had found the car. Slane insisted that he knew we would find

Keira and that he wanted to be here for her. I don't know how Slane knew it, but he was right, after all."

"Watching them together now, can you blame him?"

"I can't," he said and gave a grudging smile toward the couple, who remained wholly engrossed with one another.

****

Young doctor Green's return to the room put an end to Declan and Keira's passionate kiss, but not to their embrace. They didn't want to let go of each other for fear of waking up from another pleasant dream. Declan kept his arm around her shoulders and she hugged his waist as they sat on the bed to listen to the Doctor. All the while, they exchanged little tender gestures, quick kisses, and feathery caresses.

"The scans showed no internal injuries, no broken bones, and no brain injuries."

"That's excellent news," Keira said.

"Indeed it is. There's a small concussion on your temple, but you have nothing to worry about, Miss Ashe."

"Was that why I had amnesia?"

"You did? Oh, we have so much to talk about, love," Declan said as he kissed her cheek.

"We do, sweetie."

"No, Miss Ashe, but it probably caused the loss of consciousness."

"Why did I lose my memory, then?"

"Since the amnesia wasn't related to a physical problem, as the tests showed, I can only assume it was caused by a psychological one. Judging from your report of events, it's safe to say it was caused by shock."

Keira frowned and looked as though she was about to say something to the doctor when Heller interrupted.

248

"You had plenty of reasons to be in shock, my dear. You saw your boyfriend being shot and thought he had died. You were kidnapped and taken to a strange place. To top it off, you had to deal with a former aggressor, who also happened to be delusional and a well-known serial rapist. You're strong, Keira, I'll give you that, but you're not a superwoman."

"I'm not as strong as people think."

"You're much stronger than *you* think, little brat."

"Megan!"

Keira leapt to her feet, and her parents' and sister's arms swallowed her up when they hugged her in a tight embrace. The emotional reunion of the Ashe family brought tears to Declan's eyes. He had witnessed their distress first hand and, now, it delighted him to be able to release Keira into their welcoming arms. He sat on the bed, watching the family hugging and kissing Keira, at last. Everybody laughed, cried, and talked at the same time and he wondered how they understood each other.

Doctor Green discreetly called the detectives over to a corner of the room, but Declan overheard their conversation.

"I'll sign Miss Ashe's release papers. She doesn't need further treatment, but I advise you to take Mr. Slane back to the hospital in Cork as soon as possible. He's doing his best to put on a brave face, but I can tell he's in severe pain. His paleness worries me, too. I understand he's lost a lot of blood recently, which means his body is most likely still compensating for it. If he goes into shock again, he could have a heart attack or other vital organs may shut down."

"Keeping him in the hospital might turn out to be a little difficult. He's one stubborn fellow," Dwyer said with the conviction of somebody who had dealt with that stubbornness and lost.

"At any rate, it's getting late, doctor," Heller said. "To drive him back to Cork tonight wouldn't be advisable, would it? What if you kept Slane here overnight for treatment? We can arrange for his transfer back tomorrow morning."

"I'll see what I can do about that, detectives. Mr. Slane needs medical assistance and that's a fact. The hospital administration can't argue against facts."

"Thank you, doctor.

* * * *

It proved much easier to keep Declan in the hospital in Youghal than anyone had anticipated. After all, he was so glad to be with Keira again that he didn't care where he stayed, as long as she stayed with him. The Ashes and the detectives had gone out to buy something to eat and to give the couple a little privacy, so Keira lay beside Declan on the hospital bed, resting her cheek on his chest. He had been hooked to the monitors and IV bags again.

Keira played with the buttons on his shirt, and talked without looking up at him, "I have to tell you something. I don't know how, though. I'm afraid of your reaction."

The fear in her voice frightened Declan to his core. He could deal with most things, except the fact that Keira might be afraid of him at all. He cupped her shoulders for emphasis. "Keira, love, look at me, please." He waited for her to lift her gaze to his before he continued. "Whatever you think of me, I beg you, don't fear me. I can't stand thinking you're afraid of me. You know I could never harm you, don't you?"

"Of course. I'm sorry. I know you would never hurt me." She offered him a weak smile. "I'm not afraid of you hurting me. It's the other way around, in fact. I—I don't want to hurt your feelings."

"Why? How would you do that?"

She looked at her fingers, which rested on his chest, and absent-mindedly tugged at the thick hair there.

"Keira? What happened?"

250

She looked up and her eyes met his dark green gaze. Then she tried to change the subject, "It's so comforting to feel your heart beating under my hands like this." She caressed and kissed his chest. "I thought I'd never be able to do it again."

Unable to fight the effects of the drugs, which were beginning to take their toll, Declan closed his eyes and rested his head on the pillow, clenching his hands in her hair. He tried to focus, to stay alert, but it proved so hard. He hated the weakness he felt.

"You're making no sense, love. It must be these painkillers. They're making me dizzy. I don't want to sleep. I don't want to waste time sleeping. We've spent too much time apart."

"Hush, Declan. You need to rest."

He lifted his head and opened his eyes, but his eyelids weighed a ton each. He couldn't keep them open. "I want to get out of this bed and get you in bed for a whole month."

"I guess the meds *are* working, because you're talking nonsense." She stretched her neck to reach his mouth and kissed him gently. "Sleep tight, baby. I'm not going anywhere."

He didn't answer her, but his hands held her close to him when she tried to get out of bed—he didn't need her to go to be more comfortable. She lay her head down on his chest again, and closed her eyes. Before long, the two of them fell asleep.

True to her word, Keira stuck by Declan's side, both during the ride in the ambulance back to Cork and later at the hospital there. As soon as he was settled in his new hospital room, and while the Ashe family checked in at a nearby hotel, Declan patted a spot on the mattress beside him.

"Come sit here, love, I want to talk to you."

When Keira sat down on the bed, he laced his fingers through hers and looked into her gorgeous eyes. He would gladly drown in those deep blue pools.

"The painkillers did a number on me yesterday, but I clearly remember a conversation we were having before they kicked in." He lifted her chin when she tried to look down. "Please, Keira, don't avoid it. No matter how hard an issue might seem to be, it's better to deal with it than run away from it. Don't you trust me?"

She looked full of guilt. "Of course I trust you. That's not an issue. That would never be an issue for me. I—I …" She took a deep breath. "Maybe I'm overreacting a bit, but I did something way out of character for me. I loathed myself for having to do it—you've got to believe me—I truly didn't see a viable alternative."

"Keira, the more you dodge the issue, the more worried I get. What *did* you do? I'm freaking out, here."

Another deep breath and Keira searched his eyes. At length, she stopped avoiding the topic, "We already knew O'Hallon was a dangerous psychopath, but over these last few days, I found out he was completely delusional. While I had the amnesia, he fabricated a complex, detailed story about me and him, as a married couple, and fed it to me. I could tell he believed his tale. On my part, I had some flashes of memories that seemed to confirm his story to some extent. Deep down, I felt something was wrong, though. Also, I felt sick and weak and slept most of the time. The good thing was that he didn't take advantage of my debilitation and make any advances. When I recovered my memories, I figured I would have a better chance of survival if he didn't know I knew his story was bogus."

"You're a smart woman. The detectives told us that your chances were connected to your ability to live out his fantasies. Thank God you did." Declan smiled and kissed the back of her hand to reassure her that he was fine with what she was telling him.

252

"I gave him a sedative, the same one he carried around and had given to me on the day he tried to rape me. I ran away as soon as he passed out on the dinner table. It was just my usual bad luck that the cottage was so isolated that I had no idea where I should run to. I didn't know where the nearest house was and I couldn't see a thing. It was late at night, dark, and very cold. I didn't have a car or proper clothes."

"You would have frozen if you'd tried to walk around looking for help. You didn't try that, did you?"

"My thoughts, exactly, sweetie." It was her turn to kiss his hand and smile. "I hatched a Plan B and went back to the house to execute it. That's when I was forced to do something I knew I would regret because it was going to hurt your feelings."

"Before you say another word, my love, let me just tell you something." He held her face in his hands, and caressed her full lower lip with his thumb. "Whatever you had to do there and then, I'm glad you did it, because it brought you back to me. That's all that matters. Do you hear me, Keira Faith Ashe?"

She closed her eyes and took a few deep breaths. "Why do you have to be so sweet, Declan?"

He covered her lips in a quick kiss, whispering, "Go on, love."

"Since O'Hallon thought we were a couple, I assumed I would get the information I needed from him if I played the loving wife. The tranquilizer knocked him out pretty deeply, so I was able to take him to the bedroom and strip him down to his underwear without as much as a peep out of him. I left him there until the beginning of the afternoon. When he regained consciousness, I lay beside him and pretended we had slept together the previous night."

She stopped again, but this time Declan didn't say anything. He knew she needed time to come to terms with it on her own. He ran his thumbs over her cheeks and waited. She swallowed hard and resumed talking, "I swear nothing happened between us. Thank God he spilled out what I needed to know right

253

away, and I managed to tie him down and hit him with the lamp before he even kissed me." She made another brief pause as she closed her eyes and steadied her nerves. When she opened them again, they reminded Declan of a stormy sea. "What's killing me is that I considered the possibility that O'Hallon might have overpowered me at some point, and I went through with the plan anyway. I felt sick to my stomach at the thought, but it didn't stop me. I hated it that he put his hands on me, that he touched me at all. I hated being so close to him, but I just couldn't think of anything else to do. I'm so sorry, Declan. Can you forgive me?"

He hugged her tight against his chest, and caressed her hair and back. "Hush now, love. I've got you. He can't harm you anymore. It's over. You'll be all right."

Declan's heart skipped several beats, and felt like he had lead inside him, but not because of Keira's words. He hated the fact that she had to go through such an ordeal alone and that she still worried about his feelings. When her breathing returned to normal, he pulled away so he could look into her eyes.

"I don't deserve you. ... Please, let me finish it." He gave her his one-million-watt smile when she opened her mouth to argue with him. "You've overcome the direst threat you ever had to face in your life. You did it all on your own, but still you worry about *my* feelings?" He kissed her open mouth until they were both out of breath and had to control himself not to deepen it. They would have plenty of time for that later. He only needed to make her understand that he supported her. "I'm sorry you had to go through that and I don't give a damn about the 'what-ifs'—you hear? The only thing that matters to me is that you're here, safe and sound, in my arms. And don't ask me to forgive you, because there's nothing for me to forgive. Do you understand that?"

She smiled back at him. "Aye, aye, captain."

"Good. Now that's out of the way, can I go back to kissing you senseless?'

254

Keira threw her arms around his neck and offered her mouth to him, which proved all the answer he needed. Their kiss was deep and sweet, passionate and blissful. Their mouths savored each other as their tongues caressed and teased. Their hands explored and rediscovered each other's sensitive spots, until they remembered they were in a hospital room.

Gently pushing Declan away, Keira cupped his cheek in her hand. "As much as I'd love to spend the rest of the day in bed with you, I don't think the nurses and doctors would approve of it. I want you to get back on your feet as fast as you can. We'd better not risk your recovery, huh?"

Declan leant back against the pillows and closed his eyes, but held her hand tightly when she tried to stand up.

"Where do you think you're going, missy? You're not leaving my bed that easily. I may not be able to have my way with you for now, but you're not going anywhere."

She sighed and rolled her eyes, pretending to be bored, and they laughed.

"It's so good to hear your laughter again, honey," Rick Ashe spoke behind them. He stood by the door with Keira's mother and sister.

"I didn't hear you come in," she said, blushing.

"You were too busy." Her father grinned. "Hmm, Mr. Slane, I have to ask you ... when do you plan on making an honest woman of my little girl?"

"Daddy!"

"It's okay, sis. He's only teasing. They became best buddies when Declan asked dad for your hand a couple of days ago. Mom's hooked by his charms as well. She's even started planning the wedding."

Keira looked at her family, and Declan, as if they had just fallen from another planet.

"Who are you people? What have you done to my family and my boyfriend? Or have you all gone insane?"

"Relax, dear. Megan's pulling your leg and you fell for it. You always do."

"Mom, Keira's got to lighten up a little."

Keira shook her head, chuckling, and shrugged, "You are a funny bunch. I don't know how I put up with you all. By the way, Mr. Slane, you've been talking to my mom quite a bit, haven't you?"

"Well, as a matter of fact, I have. She's taken good care of me. Why do you ask?"

"Because she's the only person who uses my middle name."

"Oops. I let it slip, Claire. I'm sorry." He winked at Mrs. Ashe, who blushed.

"That's fine, son. She doesn't like it, but I think it's a lovely name."

"Agreed."

Keira smiled and watched them all interact. A contented look settled on her face and brightened her eyes. Declan noticed, and felt warm inside. Despite her recent brush with death, she looked so happy and fulfilled just then.

* * * *

Soon, Colin and Brandon Slane arrived with their families, and Keira had the priceless chance to watch Declan with his brothers. An energy flowed around the three men that seemed totally different from the kind of connection she had with Megan. It felt more primitive and very male, as testosterone impregnated the room around them. Nevertheless, there was no mistaking what kind of bond linked the three brothers—love. Keira recognized it easily because it was the same glue that held her family together.

It felt comforting to know that Declan and his brothers shared so many positive emotions, in spite of their troubled past. She smiled to herself as she remembered his insecurities and worries about his ability to love and have a healthy, stable relationship. To judge by the way he behaved with his brothers and their families, he shouldn't worry about that at all.

The small group spent the rest of the day together like that—teasing, laughing, and telling stories. Keira learned about a lot of revealing episodes from Declan's childhood while Megan delighted Declan with many colorful stories about Keira's as well.

When the Slanes made ready to leave, Keira was surprised to see her family gathering their belongings too.

"Hey, guys, what are you doing? Are you going to the hotel already? It's not even seven o'clock. I thought you'd stay for a while longer."

"We're tired, honey. You and Declan must be exhausted, too. We'll be back tomorrow," her mother promised, then kissed Keira's cheek and blew a kiss to Declan.

"You didn't accept our offer to get a nap at the hotel room earlier today. So, I bought you this special pillow. Believe me, sis, these chairs are awful. You won't be able to get any sleep."

"Thanks, Megan. It was very thoughtful of you. I think." Keira had to laugh at the strange-looking thing her sister gave her. It looked like a crossover between a pyramid and a child seat. At least it looked cozy.

"Don't let this chatterbox keep you up all night, young lady."

"I won't, daddy. See you tomorrow?"

"You bet."

As her family left, a nurse showed up to check on Declan's medication chart and change one of the IV bags. Keira took that opportunity to go to the bathroom and refresh herself by splashing a little water on her face. Her mother was right—looking at her reflection in the mirror, it didn't surprise Keira to notice the dark circles under her eyes. She was exhausted and she knew it. It was too bad the night ahead of her promised to be a long and sleepless one.

Luck of the Irish

When Keira returned to the room, the nurse had already gone. "Is everything okay, baby? What did the nurse say?"

"She said I should try to walk around the room for a bit. You know, to exercise my legs. Can you give me a hand to get out of this bed?"

Once on his feet, Declan needed a moment to recover his balance.

"I think I laid down for too long. I feel dizzy."

Keira hugged his waist to help him stand up and he kissed her hair.

"I adore the smell of your hair, love." He pushed her away and held both of her hands. "You know, I had planned a completely different setting for this. I'd pictured a very romantic date with my beautiful girlfriend, but this room will have to do. I can't wait any longer."

She gave him a lopsided smile when he turned her palms up and kissed them tenderly.

"What the heck are you driving at, mister? This room is practically a public place with the hospital staff coming in and out all the time. Don't get any naughty ideas in that thick skull of yours."

She frowned when he didn't respond to her jesting with a wisecrack of his own. He looked too serious and she felt her heart leap inside her chest. Something wasn't right.

"Keira, I can't put in words what you mean to me, or how much I love you, but I'll give it a shot. You're more than my better half. You're the air that I need to breathe to survive. I know you *are* my soul and my heart because, these last days, I was nothing without you. And, most of all, you make me want to be a better man to deserve you and your love. I promise I'll strive to be that man for you every day, for the rest of our lives, if you let me."

She choked and lost her ability to breathe or think when Declan got down on one knee in front of her and held a blue, velvety box open. In it, an old and gorgeous Claddagh ring sparkled under the bright, cold lights of the hospital room. But so much warmth, so much love, shone in his eyes that they held her

258

captive, and Keira forgot where they were. Declan was all that mattered to her in that moment. He was all she could see or hear. There was nothing else in the world for her.

"Will you make me the happiest man on earth, Keira? Will you marry me?"

"Yes! Yes!"

She knelt in front of Declan, hugging and kissing him with the same passion he kissed her with. Equal measures of laughter and tears mixed together as their mouths sought each other. Her arms snaked around his neck, her hands pulled gently at his hair, and his hands circled her tiny waist and held her tightly against his solid chest. It seemed as if he wanted to meld their bodies together—while she wanted to lose herself in him forever.

A riotous little crowd soon interrupted their idyll when the Ashes and the Slanes returned to the room. They'd been waiting impatiently in the corridor while Declan proposed. Colin and her father helped Declan up as Brandon helped Keira. She realized they all knew about Declan's intentions.

"You were all in on his plan, weren't you?"

"Guilty as charged, sis."

Declan took the ring out of the box and placed it on Keira's left ring finger, with the point of the heart turned towards her fingertips. He kissed it and looked up at her.

"Now, everyone will know you're mine."

"That I am, sweetie."

"Can I see it, honey?" Her mother's eyes filled with tears when she held Keira's hand to better examine the beautiful ring.

"It's exquisite, Declan. And it has such an interesting design, too." She admired the gold ring, on which two hands held a minuscule emerald heart, surrounded by small diamonds, and surmounted by a sparkling little crown of gold and diamonds.

"What does it mean?" Mr. Ashe asked.

"It's a Claddagh ring," Keira told her dad. "It shows the three qualities necessary in a marriage—the heart represents love, the hands symbolize friendship, and the crown stands for loyalty. Granddad Padraic used to describe his mother's ring to me, as a child." She turned to Declan and grinned. "I always wanted to get a Claddagh of my own, but I'd never seen one as beautiful as this. How did you get it? When did you get it?"

"Well, a few days ago, I told your mother I regretted not having told you I loved you when I had the chance to say it. I promised her I wouldn't make the same mistake twice. I said to her that, when you returned to us, I would ask you to marry me."

"So, you weren't kidding earlier, Meg?"

Her sister smiled and shook her head in reply, but didn't say a word. For the first time in Keira's life, her sister was speechless. That was a sight to see. She held her tongue, though, when she realized Megan was on the verge of tears. Keira held out her hand to her sister and squeezed her hand, mouthing, "I love you."

"Did you ask somebody to buy it for you, then?" she asked Declan.

"No, I brought it for Declan today," Colin said. "I kept it in a safe at the bank until yesterday. Brandon and I didn't need it because my wife, Erin, and Brandon's wife, Kim, both had their own family rings that their mothers had given them."

A suspicion formed in Keira's mind but she dismissed it. It couldn't be true. Could it?

"Do you mean to say this was your mom's ring?" she asked Colin.

He nodded, but she didn't feel convinced. "Is that so, Declan?"

"Yes, love. Do you mind it? I mean, if you'd rather have a new one, I can get it for you."

Keira opened her mouth to soothe his obvious anxiety but the words refused to come out as her throat went dry. She felt so moved by Declan's gesture that she had difficulty finding what to say. She just shook her head, held her hand up, and admired the ring. Then she remembered the dreams she'd had when his mother had come to help her in the worst moments of her life. She felt Iris was there again, blessing them in the happiest moment of her life. It felt fitting.

"I don't know how to thank you." She nodded to Colin and Brandon. "It means so much to me that you've given me something that belonged to your mother. I'll treasure it always."

"Hey, hey, how come my brothers get all the credit? What about me?"

"You've got me, sweetie." He'd returned to the bed, so she had to lean down to kiss him, and ended up sitting on his lap, while their families cheered and whistled.

"I don't need anything else, love," he whispered into her ear, so quietly that only Keira heard.

* * * *

CHAPTER 11

On the following day, Inspectors Heller and Dwyer paid Declan a visit. When they arrived in the hospital room, they found Keira and Declan alone.

"Good afternoon, Miss Ashe. Slane, … how are you feeling today?"

"Much better. Thank you," Declan answered.

"You're still quite pale," Dwyer said.

"I guess it'll take a while for me to recover from the blood loss."

"Have a seat, detectives," Keira said, but they refused.

"We won't be long," Heller said. "We just wanted to check up on both of you."

Keira held the Inspector's gaze. "I haven't had a chance to tell you how sorry I am about Katherine Murphy's death. I liked her very much. She was a sweet girl."

"Thank you. Fortunately, Kerry and Morris are recovering well from their wounds. Not as fast as Slane, here, but they'll soon be out of ICU."

"Say, I've been meaning to ask you—how exactly did you find Keira?"

Inspector Heller answered, "We crossed information about O'Hallon with information from the earlier investigations into the rapes. His name never appeared in connection to the victims, except for the truck he drove to tow their rental cars. We knew he would have to be in the same cities, maybe in the same hotels as his victims, in order to commit those crimes. Still, we couldn't find any evidence of him being anywhere near."

Dwyer added, "In the beginning of our investigations, we arrested and interviewed a Mr. Kevin Riordan, a name which consistently appeared in the records of every hotel where the victims stayed. This led us to believe he was the rapist, back then. But, he had solid alibis for all the attacks. We had to let him go. What we didn't know, at the time, was that he had lost his wallet some

262

time before the attacks started. We know now that O'Hallon found it and used Riordan's ID when he stalked his victims, to cover his tracks."

Like a tag-team, Heller took up the narrative again, "But he used it only for registering at hotels, for example. He never left a trail that could lead to him. This time, he used the ID to get a credit card. When we found out a Mr. Kevin Riordan had rented a cottage in a remote area of Youghal, we looked into Riordan again. Even though we knew he wasn't responsible for O'Hallon's crimes, we thought he might shed some light on the matter and help us. We were running out of time and we started pursuing even the seemingly useless leads."

Dwyer picked up the tale again, "Mr. Riordan moved to Los Angeles a couple of years ago, but we called him there. He said he had seen the news about Miss Ashe's attack and kidnapping on TV. He told us that he was moved by her story and that, when he learned her case was connected to those crimes he had been accused of in the past, he racked his brain, trying to remember anything that might help with the investigation. But he had come up with nothing. Talking to us, he finally remembered having lost his wallet and ID."

"With that information, our suspicions that Paul O'Hallon might have used Riordan's name were confirmed. I went down to Youghal to assist the local gardai and got there around the time they found the ditched car. I had the address to the rented cottage. You know the rest," Heller concluded with a shrug.

"Why didn't you say anything about it to us? The Ashes were distraught. I was a wreck myself."

"For one, we didn't want to give you any false hopes, in case the information didn't amount to anything useful," Dwyer replied. "Besides, it was part of an ongoing investigation. We couldn't tell you everything."

"Fair enough. Still, you could have said something when we were going to Youghal."

"You mean, after you twisted my arm into taking you with me? I wasn't in a very chatty mood, remember?"

Declan laughed wholeheartedly and Dwyer was forced to relax his stern expression.

"I'm sorry about that, old chum. I just couldn't help it. I had to go with you."

"Yeah, about that, Slane. Why the heck did you insist on going with me like that? You were fresh out of surgery. You were in terrible pain. Still, you wanted to risk your recovery and go on something that might well have turned out to be a wild goose chase. You said you knew we would find Keira there. How could you have been so sure?"

Declan looked at her before answering, and spoke to the officer without letting his gaze stray from her blue eyes, "I don't know how to put it into words, detective. I woke up that afternoon, feeling a little strange. I still can't remember details of the dreams I had while they operated on me. I remember sensations and feelings only. And when I came to, my guts told me Keira was alive, but in danger. I had to go to her."

Eyes brimming with tears because she recognized Declan's feelings as similar to her own, Keira smiled tenderly at him and squeezed his hand.

"You know I would do anything for you, baby. Right? I had promised to protect you, but I failed you when I let O'Hallon take you away from me. Logically, I wanted to be the one to rescue you from him. Unfortunately, that psychopath had knocked me out of the way."

"I know you would risk your own safety for me because I'd do the same. You don't need to prove anything to me, or to yourself."

Keira kissed him gently and forgot the two officers standing near the bed. That happened every time Declan touched her—she was transported to another dimension, forgetting everything else around her. Apparently, Declan felt the same because he eagerly returned her caresses.

264

"Well, Dwyer, I guess we'd better get going and leave these two lovebirds alone."

Agreeing with Heller's assessment, the younger detective cleared his throat and smiled when Declan gave him a dirty look. "Sorry to interrupt you, Slane. We've got to go."

"See you later."

"Miss Ashe, may I remind you that we'd like you to stay in Ireland for a while because you'll testify at O'Hallon's trial in a couple of months?"

"That won't be a problem, Inspector." She grinned and showed him her ring. "I'll be around for a long while yet."

"Oh, congratulations, my dear. I hope you can keep this young man out of trouble."

"I can't promise I'll be successful, but I'll try, Inspector Heller."

"You lucky son of a gun, Slane. Take good care of Miss Ashe."

"I intend to, Dwyer."

A little while after the police officers had left, Keira remembered something she had been wanting to discuss with Declan.

"I'm curious about those dreams you said you had, sweetie. Don't you remember anything at all?"

"No, I don't. I've tried to, though. When I concentrate, I get bits and pieces of images and dialogs. Nothing makes much sense, really." He shook his head and gave her a weak smile. "Your family told me I said some pretty weird stuff while I was unconscious, but I can't remember a thing."

"You may call me crazy, you may not believe me, but I've got to tell you something."

Luck of the Irish

As she searched for the best words to describe her dreams to him, without sounding too much like a basket case, he grew worried, "Come on, Keira. It can't be that bad. Spill it, hon." He nudged her.

"Okay, here goes nothing. While I was unconscious, after O'Hallon hit me in the head, I had some pretty strange dreams, too. When I woke up, I didn't remember much, just like you. I thought it was related to the amnesia. I mean, if I couldn't remember my own name, it seemed fitting I couldn't remember my dreams, either. However, I will never forget the last dream I had. The one which helped me remember my name and recover my identity."

She eyed him while carefully weighing her next words. He didn't say anything, but his expression was a reassuring one. He didn't seem to be about to commit her to the booby hatch so she felt encouraged.

"I was in a strange room where I couldn't see well because of the bright light. I could see only a beautiful woman. She told me she was your mom and she brought you to me. She said you didn't want to live because you thought I had died, so she had taken you to see me … to see that I was alive. When I saw you, in the dream, everything came back to me."

Declan mulled over her words before saying, "I've never wondered much about what might happen after we die. I can't honestly say I believe in the afterlife. I also can't say I don't, simply because I've never given it much thought. I guess I've always had so many problems going on in *this* life that I didn't care much for the afterlife."

"I believe in it." She smiled, a little shy. "I'm not sure what to expect from it, but I'm convinced there's another dimension to our material world; another realm, if you like. One we can't ordinarily see. I like to believe it exists and is filled with beings similar to us—good and bad."

"Honestly, love, this dream you've described just now makes sense to me. Like I told you before, I remember only scattered scenes from my dreams, though I remember feeling desperate, desolate. I've got the impression I saw an

266

angel, who talked to me and soothed me. It could have been my mom; I don't know." He hesitated and Keira waited while he processed his feelings about that topic. "Who knows, honey? I do know I woke up feeling hopeful, in spite of everything that was going on with us, and your family thought it was the medication. I knew it in my heart that it was more complicated than that. When Dwyer said they had found the car, I just knew you were there. That certainty might have come from the dreams." He shrugged.

Keira held his hand and kissed him. "What I do know is that you, somehow, restored my memory. It was like your face and your voice were etched in my mind, even if you weren't with me."

A phone ringing interrupted their conversation and Keira picked it up without noticing it wasn't hers. It was Declan's phone.

"Hello?" Keira answered it.

"Oh, hello. Is Declan there?"

Keira frowned because she didn't recognize the female voice on the other end of the line.

"He is. Who's calling, please?"

"A friend. Jennifer Williams."

Keira smiled widely and it was Declan's turn to frown. He gestured for her to give him the phone but she just ignored him and moved away.

"Oh, hi, Jen. This is Keira. How are you? I've told Declan I'd love to chat with you sometime …" She laughed at something Jennifer said. "I'm sure you will."

Declan rolled his eyes. Keira sat more comfortably in her chair, blew him a kiss, and winked. Her husband-to-be looked as though he'd like to give them both an earful.

Luck of the Irish

Over the next week, Keira stayed beside Declan at the hospital. Her family and the Slane brothers visited often. They even celebrated Megan's thirty-third birthday there. Tender loving care sped up Declan's healing process and he was released earlier than the doctors had expected. Without any previous planning, both his brothers showed up, at the same time, to pick him up and take him home.

"You're staying with us. End of discussion." Colin glared at his stubborn youngest brother, while he helped Declan stand up from the bed and then sit down in the wheelchair.

"Brother, you've got two very active little girls," Brandon started, but added quickly when Colin scowled, "Whom I adore, by the way. I don't have children, so it's quieter in my house. Declan will be better off there. Right, Declan? Tell him you'll stay with me."

Declan looked at Keira for support. She held her hands up and shrugged, "Sorry. It's your family. I wouldn't dare say anything." She chuckled.

Watching the Slane brothers argue about even the smallest, most insignificant things over the previous days, had taught Keira to stay out of their way. They had given her the impression that quarreling was more like a sport for them—or a twisted way of bonding. Either way, she respected them, even though she didn't understand their behavior. Now, while they fought over where Declan should stay, she would rather keep her opinions to herself.

"Brandon, my house is bigger. Keira and her family will be more comfortable there."

Despite her misgivings, Keira spoke to Colin, "Thanks, but don't worry about my family. They'll stay at the hotel. It's going to be just Declan and me until we figure out what to do."

"See, she doesn't want to go to your house," Brandon said with a grin.

Keira blushed. "I never said that. I just said …"

268

"Brother, Declan and Keira will stay with *me*. I won't hear another word about it."

Colin started pushing the wheelchair out of the room and down the corridor, ignoring Keira's dumbfounded expression as well as Declan's attempts to stop him. Brandon shook his head, as he offered Keira an apologetic smile.

"Has he always been like this?"

"He's getting worse as he gets older."

Brandon and Keira, both laughing, got Declan's stuff from the room and followed the other two Slane men, who were arguing as they moved towards the exit door, and had almost reached the hospital reception by the time Keira and Brandon caught up with them.

Colin's house was indeed bigger than Brandon's. There was even a small guesthouse in the back, where he helped Keira and Declan settle. When he was about to leave, he winked at his little brother.

"You need your rest, so I'll tell Iris and Allyson to leave Uncle Declan and Aunt Keira in peace until you decide to show up in the house. Is that okay?"

"That's very thoughtful, thank you," Keira said.

"Don't thank me. I just don't want to scar my children for life if they walk in on you two having sex."

Declan kissed her red cheek, laughing. "Sorry, love, you should see your expression right now. Colin, you're lucky you're my brother. I guess you'd be a dead man otherwise."

"You bet he would!"

"Bye, now. Don't do anything I wouldn't do."

Colin's laughter echoed in the room even after he had closed the door behind him. Keira felt mortified.

"Don't be embarrassed, love. Sex is a natural thing between people who love each other, especially after everything we've been through. Plus, we've had to wait for too long to celebrate our reunion. Colin knows that's what we'll do, and that's why he was joking."

"I get that. It's just that it's a private matter. I was embarrassed to talk about it in front of him."

"I hear you. Well, you'll have to get accustomed to that kind of thing around my brothers and me, baby. We talk about sex, joke about it, tease one another about it, all the time."

"I'll try."

She shrieked when he scooped her up in his strong arms. "What are you doing? You shouldn't be lifting heavy stuff. You've just got out of the hospital."

"Precisely. I've stayed in bed for much too long, doing nothing. I need the exercise, love," he said, laughing, as he carried her to the bedroom and settled her gently on the bed, then knelt beside her. "I have a couple of ideas for some very invigorating cardio workouts. Care to join me, milady?"

She laughed at his self-mocking expression as he impersonated Valentino, or some other leading man from a silent movie. Her carefree laughter died away when he covered her body with his and kissed her. He parted his lips, then grazed her bottom lip lightly, and when he heard her involuntary intake of air, as a reaction to the feelings that little gesture brought to her sensitive nerves, Declan grabbed the soft flesh of her lower lip between his teeth and tugged. She moaned and pressed her hip up against his. Her hands raked through his hair. Their kiss got deep and hot as fast as always.

Declan deliberately and slowly took off each piece of clothing that Keira wore. However, she felt impatient at his sluggish pace, and tried to yank his shirt off, but Declan stopped her hands, taking them to his lips and kissing each fingertip, without saying a word, just smiling at her.

270

"Declan, I've missed you so much. I want you badly right now. I'm about to explode. Please, don't torture me."

"I'm not torturing you or me. I'm making love to my fiancée, my future wife, for the first time today. I want her to feel loved—worshipped—cherished."

He emphasized each word with an open-mouthed kiss on a different sensitive spot on her neck, shoulders, and chest, until Keira forgot about anything other than her fiancé, her future husband, and his expert hands and mouth, trusting him to set the best rhythm for their passion.

When he had stripped her to her thin bra and panties, he let Keira take care of his clothes. She loved the feel of his hard muscles and soft skin undulating under her hands while she undressed him, kissing his exposed flesh as she went. He stopped her when her fingers grabbed the waistband of his briefs.

"Not so fast, love."

He pecked the corner of her mouth when she pouted, and rolled her over onto her stomach. Declan took his time roaming his hands up and down her body, causing goose-bumps on her skin, rediscovering the shape of her soft curves with his warm palms, the satiny feel of her skin under his fingertips. Things he had never forgotten, but was delighted to remember. She grew impatient. She wanted to feel his body filling up the void inside her.

"Declan, please, I need you. Don't toy with me."

"I'm not toying with you, baby. I'm worshiping you like you deserve. I want to savor each moment with you, because they are precious."

He rolled Keira onto her left side and snuggled behind her, then unhooked her bra and slid the thin material down her arms, then he held her breasts in his palms. His hands felt hot against her hardened nipples and she moaned softly when he squeezed them together as his tongue licked her ear. Her body throbbed when he bit her earlobe and she covered his hands with hers.

Declan kneaded her soft breasts, nibbled her neck and shoulders, and licked her ear until Keira felt feverish, on fire.

"Declan, I can't take it any longer. Please, I need you inside me."

"Your wish is my command, love."

With a gentle nudge of his leg, he lifted Keira's knee a little, but she was too lost in the sensations he had created in her to notice that one of his hands had left her breast and moved slowly downwards until he cupped her mound. Her blood pressure skyrocketed when his naughty fingers found and played with her curls. She threw her head back over his shoulder, and couldn't hold back a soft whimper when the sensual movements of his fingertips invaded her more intimately. He knew exactly where to press, where to tap, and where to touch in order to make her lose control. When he increased the rhythm of his fingers going in and out of her, she felt like she was about to burst into flames under his hot hands.

"I can't hold back for long, baby."

"Then let it go. I've got you."

Declan pressed her back tightly against his broad, solid chest as she rode the first waves of pleasure when they hit her. He sought her mouth and kissed her deeply, drinking in her moans and cries. Their tongues slid against each other, their lips devoured each other, as he increased the speed of his fingers and her slippery body squeezed him in response.

When her heart rate slowed down, Declan turned her over onto her back, nestled his hard body between her soft, still trembling thighs, and pushed inside her in one swift but gentle movement. She locked her feet behind his back when his lips captured hers in another passionate kiss. He settled a slow, steady rhythm to his movements, bracing himself on his arms, hovering over her, and stared into her eyes as he went in as deeply as he could before coming out almost entirely, until he stiffened with his climax approaching.

272

Declan knelt on the bed and pulled Keira up with him, then crossed his arms behind her back, as she rocked her body in time with his. They moved up and down, and slid against each other, and their bodies built up their own release. Keira grabbed his gorgeous face between her hands, locked her gaze with his, and gave him a knowing smile when she felt the first signs of Declan's pleasure deep inside her and her body contracted then expanded around him.

Her soul spiraled and spun upwards, and her heart swelled with the amazing emotions he awoke in her. Still, her eyes never left his, marveling at the expression on his face when his climax finally came. His abandon, his surrender, matched her own at that sweet moment. A moment filled with passion and deep feelings, in equal measures. Keira basked in the mesmerizing light that shone in the depths of his green eyes, recognizing it as the undying love he felt for her. She leaned in and stole a quick kiss before whispering against his lips, "I love you, too, Declan Slane. Now and forever."

****

When he heard those words, felt her total surrender to him, and watched her give herself so completely to him, it took Declan's breath away. Their lovemaking had always been passionate and steamy, but knowing that her feelings for him ran as deep as his for her made all the difference in the world. His heart threatened to explode in his chest just as his body exploded inside hers. Their cries of joy mingled in the air as their mouths merged in a kiss that was equally tender and deep, passionate and sweet.

Slowly coming back down to earth from the heights of ecstasy they had reached, Declan and Keira tumbled together onto the bed, laughing and crying, touching and soothing each other's quivering flesh, both feeling fulfilled and happy as they had never felt before. Sleep came over them fast, but their bodies remained tangled in a comfortable embrace while they slept.

Luck of the Irish

Keira and Declan spent the next couple of days in much the same way—cherishing and caressing each other at every chance they had, either in private or in public. Keira was gradually learning to find a balance between her shyness and Declan's family's teasing.

"Thank goodness you two make a cute couple. Still, I can't stand this constant cuddling any longer," Colin told them as he entered his living room. "You were supposed to watch over your nieces, mister! Not fool around with your hot girlfriend."

"His teasing is starting to sound a little like envy, don't you think, Declan?"

"Ouch! The kitten has sharp claws." Colin laughed—totally not offended.

"You have no idea, brother!"

"Come, my little princesses. Daddy's going to give you a bath and then mom will fix us dinner."

Allyson and Iris ran to their father, who picked each one up in one arm, and went to their bedroom, bouncing them along the way. Keira could hear the girls' shrieks and pearly laughter as well as Colin's muffled voice.

A few days later, her father offered Declan a partnership in the family business. He wanted his future son-in-law to run an Irish branch of the Ashes' restaurant. She had laughed at Declan's reaction, when her father asked him to do that. Rick Ashe had needed to use his natural charm combined with a lot of persuasion to talk Declan into accepting his offer.

"Don't get me wrong, Rick, I'm honored." Declan had tried to explain his concerns. "It's just that it's a huge responsibility. I mean, we'll have to make a big investment and Keira has told me that lately you've been facing some money problems in your restaurant. Do you think this is a good time for that kind of expense?"

"Declan, my son, it's not spending when one is investing. We'll get the money back. And then some. You'll see."

Once Declan had been convinced, they spent the rest of their time together planning the details of the project. Location would be a key element for the new restaurant. Her father told Declan he should decide that one on his own, arguing he didn't know Ireland enough to make a call either way. Declan asked for some time to think about it.

Torn between staying in Dublin or moving back to Cork, he had turned to Keira for help on the previous day, while they cuddled in bed, after another hot session of cardio exercises.

Declan ran his fingers through her soft curls and said, "These last weeks with my family have made it quite plain to me that I've missed them more than I'd realized before I returned to Cork. My brothers are nutcases, and I know they can be royal pains in the posterior, but I love them." His voice broke off and Keira kissed his knuckles as if to encourage him to continue. "I missed them. I missed being around them."

"That's very clear, baby."

"On the other hand, I guess it would be better for business if we opened the restaurant in Dublin instead of here. I mean, it's a new restaurant so the odds will be in our favor if we have a larger number of potential clients."

Keira lifted her head from his shoulder to read his eyes, but didn't say anything.

"Should I follow my heart or my head, honey?"

"I don't see why you can't do both. Dublin isn't that far from here. We can live there and come visit them as often as we want." She tested his resolve with her words—she'd given him the practical option—not what he wanted to do.

"You've got a good point there, love. However, a restaurant demands a lot of time and work. We might not be able to leave it and come visit them for months. Years, even."

He paused, as many different emotions warred inside him.

With a soft laugh, she put an end to his misery, "I think you've already made up your mind. Let me guess. We'll stay here."

Declan smiled and kissed the tip of her nose. "You do know me well."

"It was a safe bet. I mean, you've done a pretty good job of following your heart so far. I didn't think you'd change that now."

"You're right. Maybe I should go back to Dublin for a day or two. You know, go by the hotel, thank my boss and quit my job officially. Would you go with me? It's a good chance for you to meet Jen."

"Absolutely!"

On the following day, right after lunch, Colin asked Keira, "What time is your family leaving?"

"In the early evening."

"Would you like me to give you a lift to the airport?"

"Thanks. I'd appreciate it."

Declan spoke up, "If Colin is taking us to the airport to see your family off, we can take a late evening flight to Dublin tonight."

"Sounds great."

"It's set, then; I'll buy our tickets."

"I'll pack."

****

As she finished packing and locking the suitcase, Keira reflected about the past few days and smiled. Her future with Declan looked bright and full of possibilities. When she rejoined Declan and Colin in the living room, her expression remained dreamy. She was surprised to see Brandon sitting on the couch.

"Oh, hey there. Did you come to say goodbye?"

"Why? Are you going back to America, too?" He pointed at her suitcase before turning to his younger brother, feigning annoyance. "Congratulations, punk. This must have been the shortest engagement ever in the Slane family."

"We've got to go to Dublin for a couple of days, dumb ass. Not that this is any of your business, mind you," Declan replied before turning to Keira, who had sat beside him. "Heller called while you were packing. He said he needed to talk to my brothers and me. That's why the freak came."

She frowned, but didn't have time to comment on that piece of information because the bell rang and Erin greeted Heller at the door, and showed him to the living room. Keira stood up to go, but Declan grabbed her hand and tugged it lightly. "Stay, hon."

After exchanging greetings, Heller took a deep breath and spoke, "Well, I don't want to waste more of your time than is strictly necessary, gentlemen. So, I'll go straight to the point."

"By all means, detective."

"Declan, I owe you an apology and an explanation. When I arrived in Keira's hotel room, after O'Hallon's vicious attack, I didn't know who you were, but when you stated your name I knew it and I didn't say anything. I figured it wasn't the time or the place to do that." He raised his hand at Declan's puzzled expression, as if asking for a little patience. "I'll get there, my son, so please bear with me. As we got to know each other better, and after some digging on my part, I found out how much your life, and your brother's lives,

277

had been affected by your mother's death. Then, I felt worse than I had felt in the past."

He took a brief pause to sip the tea Erin had served before sitting by Colin's side. The older man looked uncomfortable under the scrutiny of those five pairs of eyes; however, he summoned his courage and continued, "You see, I was the first responding officer to arrive in your house that night. I came in even before the paramedics arrived. I did everything I could to stop her bleeding, but the wounds were too extensive and deep. I'm sure nobody would have been able to save Mrs. Slane, even if they had arrived before me. Still, the frustration I felt was overwhelming. Guilt followed in my footsteps for a long time afterwards, as well."

"It wasn't your fault, detective," Keira said.

"I knew it … nevertheless, on some unconscious level, guilt tormented me. I was a green officer at the time. Hers was the first death I had to investigate and she had practically died in my arms. I wasn't able to sleep for days and finding the guilty party in her death became my only goal."

"I'm sorry to say it, but you did a bloody lousy job at that," Declan burst out.

"I get your bitterness at losing your mom, before your own eyes at six. But you shouldn't say that. The Garda in general, and me in particular, conducted a thorough investigation. That has always been very clear to me. I felt guilty I didn't arrive in time to save her."

"Oh, so you think accidental death covered all the bases, do you? In your thorough investigation, you must have overlooked that little part my father played in her death. You know, the murderer part."

"Come on, Declan, that has never been proved," Brandon said.

"My point exactly. Heller here didn't prove it."

"Guys, I know this was a theory back then, but—"

"A theory?" Declan interrupted the detective, shouting in frustration. "The bastard made a habit of beating mom up every chance he had—for no reason at all. I know my mother never pressed charges against him, but you should have taken their past history into account in your precious investigation. How could you believe that his last attack was anything less than an attempt on her life? Can you honestly say my father's family's money had nothing to do with the investigation's conclusion?"

"Most certainly. I'd be insulted if you thought that could be true. I had personally responded to a couple of domestic disturbance calls made by your neighbors. I was aware of that nasty habit your father had. However, I had my hands tied. Without a formal complaint from your mom, no police officer could do anything about that. So, yes, your father was the Garda's first suspect. On the other hand, I had seen the crime scene and your father's first reactions to Mrs. Slane's death. He was a brute, but he wasn't an actor. He wouldn't be able to put on such utter devastation. He was sincere. He didn't want to kill your mother. He loved her deeply."

"He had a very twisted way of showing that."

The inspector nodded to Declan. "I can't argue with that. He was a disturbed man, who should have sought proper treatment for his issues, before they caused other people so much harm. Unfortunately he didn't, and ended up destroying five lives in the process. Still, he couldn't be trialed for that."

"What do you mean by 'he destroyed five lives'?" Keira asked.

"I followed what happened to the Slane family for a while after Mrs. Slane's death. I watched Mr. Slane's self-destructive behavior. He was clearly in pain, didn't know how to deal with it, and his family thought money was the answer. It was a recipe for disaster. To speak candidly, I was surprised he didn't take his life or destroy his sons' lives further. All things considered, you three turned out fine, wouldn't you agree?"

Luck of the Irish

Declan's scowl spoke volumes and Brandon looked pensive, so Colin became the Slane brothers' spokesperson, "You've got a point there. Each one of us had to learn to deal with our own demons. We've probably had more stumbles and falls along the way than victories, but I guess the final balance was positive. For all of us."

"I'm glad to hear that," Heller said before turning to Declan and looking him in the eyes. "I'm sorry I wasn't able to save your mom. I'm sorry she had a rough life, and a tragic death. Even though I blamed myself for a long time, I came to understand it was humanly impossible to have saved her that night. I've accepted that and I dare say you should, too. I know you witnessed part of the scene, but you were too young to understand what you saw then or before that night. Your mother and father loved each other, regardless of how their relationship might have looked like on the outside. Mr. Slane was a despicable husband and a horrible father. However, while no man has the right to beat up a woman, your father wasn't a murderer, Declan."

Keira knew Declan well enough to read his eyes at that moment. She was certain that Heller's words were gradually sinking in as well as answering most of his life-long questions. But he was too stubborn to admit it, even to himself. He'd need a lot of time to admit it to others. He just stared back at the detective in silence.

It was no surprise Heller was a good detective, because he read people very well and he understood Declan wasn't ready to respond to the new information he had just heard. The older man respected that. He stood up and offered his hand in goodbye. First Colin, then Brandon, shook it. Reluctant, Declan shook it last.

"I'll be in touch, Keira, about the trial."

He looked surprised when she hugged him tightly instead of shaking his hand. The young American had always had the ability to surprise him, turning him into a pitiful emotional old man every time she reacted so spontaneously.

280

She stood on her tiptoes to kiss his cheek and whisper a throaty "thank you" in his ear. The bright smile she gave him, when she let go, made Heller shake his head and chuckle.

Once he'd gone, Keira figured the brothers could use some privacy to discuss what they'd just heard, but Declan wouldn't let her go when she tried to say she was going to go to their bedroom. The three brothers sat there for a long time, quietly staring into space. Erin had taken the girls out on some errand and Keira was the only witness to the Slane brothers' peculiar way of dealing with the information they had received—utter silence. Just when she couldn't bear it any longer, Brandon stood up. "I've got to go. Kim will be home soon and we've got a lot of stuff to do."

"That's okay, Bran. Catch you later," Colin replied, and as his brother left, he turned to Declan. "It's almost time to leave for the airport. Are you guys ready?"

Declan nodded and stood up to get a hold of Keira's bag. He caught his on the way to the front door and took both to the car parked on the street in front of the house, placing them in the trunk.

As she followed the two brothers to the car, Keira wondered if their behavior could cause them emotional problems in the future and decided she wasn't a shrink and so couldn't evaluate that. She was but a worried fiancée whose only option seemed to be standing by her man and hoping for the best. She laced her fingers through Declan's as they settled in the back seat.

"I guess I'm the designated private driver, right? Is there any way I can convince you to sit here with me, Declan?" Colin gazed at his baby brother through the rearview mirror. "I guess not." He had to laugh when the only answer Declan gave him was turning to Keira to kiss her.

Luck of the Irish

After an intense and emotional goodbye to her family, filled with tears and promises of future phone calls, Keira felt drained. Declan, noticing her mood, didn't insist on maintaining a conversation during most of their trip back to Dublin. They sat on the plane, holding hands, as each one reflected on their issues.

She was astounded to realize it had been little over forty days since she had left the capital of Ireland. It felt more like forty years to her. Obviously, she wasn't the same young woman who had set out to face her insecurities and test herself in the biggest adventure of her life. Although she had gotten so much more than she had planned for out of the trip, she didn't regret any of her choices, because they had led her to Declan. While she looked out the window, she realized that most of her newfound self-confidence was a direct result of having seen herself through Declan's eyes. He had told her, time and again, that she was stronger than she had thought. He had done that so many times that she ended-up believing it might be true, and then the day had come when she had to prove his theory and the outcome had convinced even her. Declan *was* right.

* * * *

Declan fought his inner demons as Heller's words took root in his mind. He had hated his father for so long that now it was hard letting go of the feeling, even though that sounded nuts. However, he felt an unsettling void inside his chest, where that hatred used to be, and it would take him a while to substitute it for any positive feelings towards his old man. At least Declan's fundamental fear that he might have inherited his father's murderous nature seemed to gradually vanish into thin air.

For the first time, he actually allowed himself to think there might be a bright future ahead of him. He looked at Keira's profile as she gazed out of the airplane window and his heart skipped a couple of beats. She had always believed in him. She had seen goodness in him from the start. Relieved, Declan realized he now believed in himself enough so that he could be the kind of man

282

she had always told him he was—a stable and confident man—just like she deserved.

Keira turned to face him with such a depth of feeling in her eyes that it took his breath away. Again. She leaned in and pecked him on his lips. "I love you, too, sweetie."

The next day was a busy one for them. Declan quit his job, then paid a visit to the owner of the apartment he rented to tell her about their wedding and his moving back to Cork.

"Oh, congratulations, my dear," said old Mrs. Dunphy. "It's about time you settled down. And you've chosen such a beautiful girl. I'm sure you'll be very happy together."

"We are, Mrs. Dunphy. Keira has worked a couple of miracles and turned me into a decent man."

"That's exactly how it works, my child." The sweet elderly lady winked at Keira, and patted her hand with her thin, wrinkled one, and laughed. "We women must stay strong and in control so that our men can thrive. The stronger we are, the more they prosper, inadvertently thinking they are the masters in the relationship. It seems Declan here is a smart one, Keira—he's figured it out."

They laughed at her good-humored remark and she refused to take the key ring Declan offered to give her.

"Stay in the apartment as long as you need to settle everything up, kids. When you're done, stop by and give me the keys. If you don't have time for that, just lock the door and leave them in the mailbox. I've got a spare set."

"Will do, Mrs. Dunphy. Thank you."

Luck of the Irish

Later, they met Jen and her boyfriend, Adam, for lunch. A potentially awkward meeting turned out to be a very pleasant one. Keira and Jen hit it off straight away while Adam and Declan talked for hours as if they had known each other forever. They promised to keep in touch when they went their separate ways.

* * * *

When they got to the apartment's street and entered the building, Declan had a mischievous smile playing on his lips. Keira raised an eyebrow. "What?"

"You'll see."

Her jaw dropped when she opened the door. A trail of red petals led from the entrance door to the dining room table, where an amazing dinner set was arranged, and a candle blazed. The trail continued towards the bedroom door.

"How? Why? When?"

The questions came out of her mouth all at once before she took a deep breath to calm herself down and repeated one question, "Why?"

"Because when you left Dublin, I promised myself to treat you to a romantic evening you would never forget. I knew I had to win you over and romancing seemed the best strategy, at the time."

She laced her hands behind his neck and leant into his wide chest, then smiled and looked up, "You've already won me over."

"I always keep my promises, love. Even the ones I make to myself." He returned her smile with a devastating one of his own as he nestled her soft body against his hard one, holding her by her waist. "Besides, one should never take a chance of losing love … losing romance. I must keep reminding you that you've made the right choice."

"Well, look around! I'd say you might be on the right track, sir. What else have you planned for tonight?"

284

"Oh, the possibilities are endless. But we should eat first. Màire would never forgive me if we didn't taste her dinner."

"So, that's how you managed to pull this off? How very ingenious of you."

"Well, you know what they say—you don't need to know everything as long as you know the phone number of whoever does know stuff."

All through dinner, Keira couldn't wait to get Declan into the bedroom and he noticed it. It was obvious in the smiles he gave her. And in the way he flirted with her. And in the warmth of his hand covering hers on the table. She was in a hurry to end the meal but he seemed to drag it on endlessly.

When they finally stood up, she held the collar of Declan's shirt and pulled him down to kiss him deeply. His hope of taking things slowly went up in smoke the minute their mouths connected. They yanked off each other's clothes as they moved to the bedroom leaving a trail behind them, mixed with the rose petals.

The same red petals covered the bedspread and framed Keira's white skin when they tumbled together on the bed, without breaking their kiss. Their hands caressed and explored, aroused and soothed each other. Her long nails scratched his back when he nibbled the underside of her breasts. His muscular thighs tangled with her soft ones when she flipped him onto his back and straddled him. Squeezing his hips between her legs, she teased him with her fevered body. He threw his head back on the pillow and closed his eyes as she leaned down and captured his lips between her teeth. But he stole her breath away when his hot palms cupped her breasts and his fingers played with her flesh. Her fingers moved between their bodies until they found his hardness and guided it inside her warmth.

Luck of the Irish

As she moved her hips in slow circles, Declan moved his up and down. His hands moved down to her waist to guide her as she planted her palms firmly on his chest for purchase. She tweaked his nipples when the first waves of pleasure hit. He winced, but the quick stab of pain soon became searing hot pleasure and he lost himself in her sweetness. He opened his eyes when he heard her gasps but his voice had deserted him. He wouldn't be able to utter a sound even if his mind weren't deliciously spiraling up through the vortex of passion they had created around themselves. Keira was also riding another mind numbing climax and barely noticed Declan's arms encircling her and locking behind her back when she collapsed onto his chest.

Most of the times Keira and Declan made love, words weren't necessary. The way their bodies completed each other, the way their skin felt against each other, and the way their hearts beat together, made up for all the words they didn't say to each other because those feelings were much stronger and meant much more than mere words.

Next day, they went back to Cork and told Colin and Brandon that they would move to town and open the restaurant there.

"That's excellent news, brother," Colin said with a big grin.

Brandon nodded. "Yeah, Colin's right. We couldn't be happier for you two."

"Keira and I have already started looking for a little apartment."

"Nonsense," Colin said. "You can stay here for as long as you need. You'll have a lot of expenses with the restaurant and the wedding. When is it going to be, by the way?"

"In six months," Declan answered. "Thanks for the offer, but I've got some money in the bank to cover the expenses. It will be enough. No worries about that."

286

"Besides, we could use a little more privacy. We're eager to try new positions in different rooms of the house, but we're afraid someone could walk in on us. We don't want to scar your daughters for life, Colin," Keira said with a laugh.

"Touché." Colin bowed his head slightly.

"Bravo, hon." Declan kissed her cheek and hugged her tight against his body.

Brandon laughed out loud before stating, "I guess we can say she's a Slane woman, now, brothers. Mission accomplished. Welcome to the clan, Keira."

* * * *

EPILOGUE

Six months later

Claire had started planning the wedding before the Ashes left Ireland, and she continued to do so from the other side of the Atlantic. The ceremony and the reception had begun to seem more Claire's dream than Keira's.

One evening, after one of her mother's endless phone calls, Keira plopped herself on the sofa beside Declan, closed her eyes, and covered her face with her right arm.

"I swear I'd rather elope. Please, let's do it. There's still time."

"You're just saying it because your mother made you angry, now. You'll feel better tomorrow."

"I don't know about that." She opened one eye to look at her fiancé. "I've never wanted a big wedding. Come to think of it, I've never imagined how my wedding would be—period. Now she wants me to have this fairy tale wedding and she's trying to convince *me*, that's what I've always wanted. I can't take this insanity much longer."

"You don't have to do that. Tell her that you want a small wedding."

"You obviously haven't met my mother."

He looked puzzled and she explained her meaning, "You've met her, of course, but didn't have time then to get to know her. My mom can be really overbearing."

"I won't argue with you on that."

"You're a smart man."

On the night before the wedding, Keira and Declan had the same dream. They dreamed they met his mother in the same luminous room they had met in their previous dreams. She hugged both of them at the same time before stepping back and looking at them.

"I'm so happy for you, my darlings. For a long time, I prayed you would find each other. I knew it was all it would take for your hearts to recognize the fact that they beat to the same rhythm."

"What do you mean?" Keira asked.

"You are soul mates. You were born to be together. Nobody else would do."

"Mom, if we were soul mates, why were we born on different sides of the ocean? We could have never met."

"That wasn't going to happen, son. You would eventually find a way because you wouldn't be happy otherwise."

Declan looked at Keira then turned to his mother, "Now that Keira's here with me, I know I would have done anything to find her if she hadn't come to me. Still, this is a dream, and I know that when I wake up I won't remember any of this. How would I have been able to know that my soul mate was somewhere else, away from me? That I needed to find her?"

"When the soul wants, the soul finds a way. Your soul would have known it. But things worked out fine and tomorrow you'll get married." She held Keira's hands in hers and smiled when the Claddagh sparkled under the intense white light. "I'm glad Declan accepted my suggestion. It looks great on your finger, honey."

Keira was so overwhelmed that her only answer was to hug Iris tightly. When she finally let her mother-in-law go, it was Declan's turn to hold his mother in his arms for as long as he could. She faded away, but they heard her voice clearly inside their heads, "I'll be with you always."

Luck of the Irish

In the end, their wedding was a big, beautiful, and romantic occasion, with their families and friends gathered at the hotel overlooking the bay. It was a warm day and the sun shone brightly in the sky behind Keira and Declan, while they exchanged their heartfelt vows. Keira had agreed with her mother in almost every aspect of the ceremony, except the vows and the hand fasting ritual. She had put her foot down on both.

"Declan, your love has given me a better understanding of myself. Through your eyes I have seen a different side of me—stronger, more self-confident, and more independent. You have made me a better person, not only because you believed in me, but because you helped me believe in myself. Today, before our families and friends, I promise to love you and cherish you for the rest of our lives together—which means forever."

"Keira, before I met you, I had never believed in eternal love. I had never believed soul mates existed. Now I know that my heart knew your heart before we were born because mine leapt inside my chest the moment you walked into my bar. I knew you were the one for me although I didn't know you were already mine. And not knowing it drove me into being the man you deserved, a man capable of winning your admiration and your love. Today, as you give me the honor of becoming my wife, I promise you I will devote myself to proving my worth to you, for all eternity, because that's how long I will love you."

"Clasp your hands together," the justice of the peace instructed them before he wound a white ribbon around their hands. "This ribbon symbolizes spiritual purity, truth, peace, and devotion—all things Declan and Keira want to bring into their marriage. As I wind it around their clasped hands, so do all the wishes, dreams, prayers, and love that their families and friends have brought here and offered them today. Finally, this knot I've tied around their hands means that Keira and Declan are eternally bound and they will never wish to be parted from one another."

290

Very few dry eyes remained in the audience when the groom kissed the bride.

A year later

After O'Hallon had been sent to prison for life, Keira's life returned to normal. Even though they hadn't noticed it before, it seemed as if they had been holding their breaths, waiting for the final act of that drama to unfold. When it did, both Declan and Keira were relieved because the defense attorney had tried to get a verdict of not guilty by reason of insanity. Justice prevailed, though, when the jury saw the clear premeditation behind O'Hallon's acts, which contradicted any attempt on his lawyer's part to establish insanity.

With a feeling of safety once more, Keira decided to go back to school and get a degree in Architecture. Declan agreed, and encouraged her.

"Are you sure you're okay with that? I can postpone it until next year to stay in the restaurant with you a little longer. It's a lot of work."

"I know it is, hon, but I'll hire a manager to help me."

"Can we do it already?'

"Oh, yeah! The restaurant is doing much better than I'd anticipated. We'll be fine."

She hugged and kissed him, then giggled.

"I can't believe you giggled like a little girl, Keira Faith Ashe Slane."

"I can't help myself, baby. You make me so happy I feel like laughing all the time. What can I do? In you, Declan Patrick Slane, I've found what I'd been looking for—everlasting love."

* * * *

Luck of the Irish

Other books by Liz Gavin

Upside Down

Carol Anne Sullivan is a tough New York stock broker. She's suffered enough in order to learn a hard lesson - never let love spoil her relationships. Her boyfriends know that rule from the start. She's domineering and assertive but also faithful and fair while the relationship lasts.

Mark Aikens is Carol's boyfriend. He's been in love with her for a while but his submissive side hasn't allowed him to rebel against her golden rule and to tell her how he feels. Fear of losing her forever might spur him into action.

Cindy O'Rourke has admired Carol from afar. So, she jumps at the opportunity to work for her idol. Little does she know, things will never be the same for her after that job interview.

Carol has been going through a rough patch: world economical crisis, dysfunctional parents, demanding clients, faulty equipment. Without much time for herself, her love life is suffering. So what is the big deal if she fantasizes about a new employee when her boyfriend, Mark, can't give her what she needs? The big deal is - the new receptionist, Cindy, is a woman who threatens to turn her world upside down.

This is the steamy tale of an unconventional love triangle which should be read with an open mind and an open heart. Sometimes, love comes to our lives in unexpected ways but with such overwhelming power that the best course of action might be to surrender to it.

* * * *

292

Flying High

Kay Montanaro is a successful professional who has focused all her efforts on building her career for the last ten years. She had to sacrifice much to achieve her goals including her personal life. She put on weight, lost touch with old friends, and never found the time to date or keep her love life going. Until her best friend couldn't take it any longer and convinced Kay to rethink her priorities.

On a flight to London, she finds exactly what she needs to rekindle her passion – a gorgeous man from her past who is willing to reconnect. But, can David give Kay everything she needs? Is he enough? Does she dare ask for more?

WARNING – This 6,800-word short-story portraits two hot alpha males who would do anything to entertain a gorgeous BWW passenger during a long otherwise dull transatlantic flight. Their encounter gets pretty steamy and naughty therefore it's not recommended for the faint of heart or for those who object to three people finding pleasure together also known as threesomes.

* * * *

Craving Her

***WARNING ***

This short story is intended for adults only due to its explicit language and steamy scenes. Moreover, if you don't like adult stories involving multiple partners, 'Craving Her' is not for you!

The Cast:

Sophia - a bright young woman who goes to an Ivy League college on a scholarship.

Bernie - her millionaire boyfriend who fools around behind her back.

Jim – Bernie's roommate and Ron, his boyfriend - both are billionaires turned celebrities.

The Plot:

Luck of the Irish

Gorgeous gay couple - deeply in love - decides to have an adventurous encounter with a woman to satisfy Ron's growing curiosity.

Jim thinks he might have found their ideal partner in Bernie's girlfriend.

Will nice and shy Sophia be up to something as naughty as their proposal? Should they ask her and risk Bernie's friendship? Or will Fate intervene in Ron and Jim's favor?

Sexy novels

> **Luck of the Irish**
>
> **Upside Down**
>
> **Maureen**

Steamy short stories & Collections

> **At the club**
>
> **BDSM & Paranormal BOX SET**
>
> **Between the Ghost and the Dom**
>
> **Club Desire Collection**
>
> **Craving Her**
>
> **Fallen Angel – Chapter 1**
>
> **Flying High**
>
> **Girls have fun**
>
> **Halloween at Club Desire**
>
> **Halloween Collection**
>
> **Halloween no Clube Desire (Portuguese Edition)**
>
> **Her favorite Ghost**
>
> **In the Lounge**
>
> **No Clube Desire (Portuguese Edition)**
>
> **Maureen's Tale (The Dark Side Series Book 1)**

Maureen's Lesson (The Dark Side Series Book 2)

Maureen's Reward (The Dark Side Series Book 3)

Powerless

Sem Força (Portuguese Edition)

Take me to the Domme

Too hot to handle

* * * *

ELESSAR BOOKS

THANK YOU for supporting indie authors.

FOR FREE EBOOKS visit our website and subscribe to the newsletter. New subscribers receive a link to a free ebook. The newsletter will also keep you up-to-date with all your favorite authors and their releases, plus a chance to get access to special offers, discounts, giveaways and fun competitions. Visit our webpage elessarpublishing.blogspot.com.br

If you liked this story, please rate it and review it on Amazon website. We at Elessar Books take our readers' opinions very seriously because what you say will definitely influence our future releases.

ABOUT THE AUTHOR

When Liz Gavin was in Second Grade - just a couple of years ago, really - her teacher told her mother the little girl should start a diary because she needed an outlet for her active and vivid imagination. She was a talkative child who would disrupt the class by engaging her colleagues in endless conversations. She loved telling them the stories her grandfather used to tell her.

Apparently, the teacher wasn't a big fan of those stories, and Liz's mother bought her a diary. She happily wrote on it for a couple of months. Unable to see the appeal of writing for her own enjoyment only, she gave up on it. She missed the audience her friends provided her in class. She went back to disturbing her dear teacher's class.

Since then, she has become a hungry reader. She will read anything and everything she can get her hands on – from the classics to erotica. That's how she has become a writer of erotica and romance, as well.

As a young adult, she participated in a student exchange program and lived in New Orleans for six months. She fell in love with the city and its wonderful inhabitants. NOLA will always hold a special spot in Liz Gavin's heart. Nowadays, living in Brazil, Liz's creativity has improved many times because it's such a vibrant, gorgeous and sexy country.

Welcome to her world of hot Alpha males and naughty, independent women. Add a touch of the paranormal in the presence of some wicked souls and you'll get the picture.

* * * *

Contact me via email lizgavin@elessarbooks.com.

COVER DESIGN – Created by Elessar Erotica Books by editing an image from Big Stock Photo with PicMonkey.

Made in the USA
Charleston, SC
18 January 2017